Weird Girl and
What's His Name

Weird Girl and What's His Name

A NOVEL

Meagan Brothers

THREE ROOMS PRESS

New York, NY

This is not a spoiler-free book.

Weird Girl and What's His Name
A NOVEL BY
Meagan Brothers

ISBN 978-1-941110-27-0 (print)
ISBN 978-1-941110-28-7 (ebook)
Library of Congress Control Number: 2015935226

COVER DESIGN:
Victoria Bellavia
www.victoriabellavia.com

INTERIOR DESIGN:
KG Design International
www.katgeorges.com

DISTRIBUTED BY:
PGW/Perseus
www.pgw.com

Three Rooms Press
New York, NY
www.threeroomspress.com
info@threeroomspress.com

for JWB,
who believed

and

for Liz Eslami,
il miglior fabbro

Weird Girl and
What's His Name

Spring 2008

———

Spooky Kid

one

"RORY," LULA SAID, QUITE GRAVELY, "I'VE just about had it up to here with all this horseshit alcoholic mumbo-jumbo nonsense." Then, like punctuation, she threw her copy of *The Sound and the Fury* across the courtyard lawn. I laughed. We kept walking to class. I don't know how she did on Mrs. Lidell's William Faulkner test, but afterward I went back to the courtyard and plucked her book from the spot where it landed, fanned out in the low branches of a hedge. I kept thinking about what Lula said, wishing I had the nerve to say something like that whenever I would come home from school and see my mother had rearranged the furniture again. She did that when she drank. Put shit in the weirdest places. I wished I had the balls to say it to her just once. *Patty*, I'd say, quite gravely. *I've just about had it up to here with all this horseshit alcoholic mumbo-jumbo nonsense.* Then I'd take my sixth-grade soccer trophy out of the refrigerator and put it back on the shelf where it belonged.

NOT THAT LULA WAS THE TYPE to go around throwing books. She was actually really smart, and she read all the time. Just not books about decaying old Southern families. Lula was more likely re-reading one of the Hitchhiker's Guide or Lord of the Rings books for the third or fourth time. This was part of why other kids at school called Lula "Weird Girl." Or, sometimes just to change it up, "Queen Weird." The other part was that she wasn't from some old Southern family—in fact, she was born in *LA*, of all the crazy places. And she wasn't even from LA. It was where her crazy mother *just happened to be living at the time.* (I can't even say it without imagining a room full of Junior League ladies looking stricken.) In our tiny North Carolina town, and even at our school, people actually cared about stuff like this, once they got wind of it. Some kids' families had been here since before the Civil War, even, and it was like all those families got together way back then and synchronized their secret decoder rings or something. No entry allowed into the Fortress of Southitude if you were from—*heaven forbid!*— California. (Me, personally? I occupied the weird limbo of a Hawthorne Lifer whose mom had the audacity to go off up north to a fancy college and marry a damn Yankee. She had the good sense to come back home, thank goodness, but she came home divorced and with clueless child. Also, my grand- parents used to work in the mills that some of my classmates' grandparents used to supervise or manage or even own. So they allowed me a strange sort of acceptance. They weren't actively mean to me or anything, despite the fact that I was a big fat guy and therefore easily make-fun-of-able. For the most part, my classmates politely ignored the inconvenient fact that I kind of, you know. Existed.)

Lula didn't seem to care about any of it, though. Which is one of the many things I liked about her. I mean, everybody

cares what other people think about them, right? Especially
in high school. But Lula didn't care if other kids thought it
was weird that she spent weekends golfing or playing tennis
with her grandparents, or watching Clint Eastwood movies
and DVDs of old comedy shows from the '60s with her
granddad, or if the girls in our class whispered behind her
back when she decided to show up for most of tenth grade
wearing her grandmother's cast-off dresses from the 1960s
and '70s, all way out of style, all polyester in unbelievable
shades. Because of her grandparents, Lula responded to our
teachers with lines from *Laugh-In* like "You bet your bippy"
and "Sock it to me," and when other kids made fun of her,
she always had a comeback, and it was usually pretty vulgar.
You know that expression, "cusses like a sailor"? It might be
relevant to note that Lula's granddad spent most of his life in
the Navy. Lula liked to drop the f-bomb, and she made no
secret of being, as my own grandmother used to say, contrary.
But, at our school, a lot of kids were pretty cavalier with the
colorful expletives, so, even paired with the excessive
reading, it wasn't enough to get a person labeled "Queen
Weird." My personal theory as to why the other kids called
Lula "Weird Girl" was that Lula didn't seem to mind not
having any other friends besides me.

The rest of the school may have known us as Weird Girl
and What's His Name, but we had already taken the liberty of
renaming ourselves. When we first met in Mr. Boyd's history
class back in junior high, we were Teddy and Tallulah, which
Lula said sounded like a bad lounge act or a couple of professional jugglers. She'd always hated her full name, hated all
the variations we thought up—Lu, Lula, Tally—until we saw
an old episode of *The X-Files* with this lady bank robber

named Lula, and then all of a sudden she thought it was the coolest name ever. My mom was the one who always called me Teddy, for pretty much my entire life. Theodore was my dad's grandfather's name, apparently. But Lula said I didn't look like a Theodore or a Teddy and rechristened me Rory.

That was back in seventh grade. The first time Lula called me on the phone—she called to ask me about our in-class presentation for Mr. Boyd—we ended up talking and laughing for something like two hours, until her phone died and she couldn't find the charger. It was hard to believe we hadn't been best friends our entire lives. And it all started because we got paired up for some stupid library research project way back when. It's weird to think how random that kind of stuff is—like how if Mr. Boyd had just paired me up with Stephanie Widdis or Mike Landy, Lula and I would've never become friends. Lula said we would have found each other, anyway. She said we have too much weird shit in common.

THIS YEAR, ELEVENTH GRADE, WE HAD two classes together. Advanced English in the mornings and Chemistry during seventh period. We both hated Chemistry and loved English, even when we had to read "alcoholic mumbo-jumbo nonsense." We were obsessed with Mrs. Lidell, our English teacher, who was brilliant and sarcastic, just like we wanted to be. Using a mixture of diligent Internet research and personal-life recon during after-class tutorials, Lula and I found out that Mrs. Lidell had gone to college in France and lived in Paris after she graduated. She wrote movie reviews for a French magazine under her maiden name, Samantha Glassman. We of course looked up the articles online and tried to read them—even with only a year and a half of high school French between us, we could tell that Mrs. Lidell was not impressed by *Charlie's Angels: Full Throttle*. Mrs. Lidell drove a hybrid car—a Prius with an Obama bumper sticker— which might be okay for Raleigh or Asheville, but around here, you may as well have walked down Main Street with a six-inch-tall purple Mohawk. She also had a decal on her back window that said MOJO NIXON, and she smoked exotic cigarettes that her Parisian friends sent her in care packages. Lula told me they were called Gitanes. I asked her how she knew, and Lula told me that one day, when she had to stay after to do a makeup Chem lab, she'd run into Mrs. Lidell leaving late and asked her if she could bum a smoke. Mrs. Lidell just gave her one of those classic Mrs. Lidell raised-eyebrow looks, then told her that they came all the way from Paris. As if she would've actually given Lula a cigarette if they were just Marlboros from the Li'l Cricket store. Lula and I often speculated on what a wonderful guy Mr. Lidell must be, that she'd come all the way back from Paris to our charmingly podunk North Carolina town of Hawthorne just to end up teaching English to a bunch of ungrateful slobs like us. Lula thought Mr. Lidell must have, as she put it, "a gigantic dick." But I liked to think it was something more romantic than that.

"YOU FORGOT THIS," I HANDED LULA her book as we crossed the parking lot after school. She tossed it up into the air and caught it again, clapping it between her hands.

"Gee, thanks. Hey, are you coming over tonight?" Lula asked, walking me to my car. I drove this completely mortifying old Buick station wagon that had belonged to my grandmother before she died. Lula named it the Beast. She rode a Schwinn ten-speed. "It's Tango Night at the Y." Her grandparents were taking tango lessons, which meant we'd have the house to ourselves.

"Can't. I have to work." I had a part-time job at Andy's Books & Coffee, the little bookstore/coffee shop on our refurbished Main Street. Part of the *Revitalize West Side!* project.

"Working, or working out?" Lula grinned, touching her tongue to her tooth. She was wearing her customary dark blue jeans, black T-shirt, and black Converse sneakers, which was this year's fashion statement, after the year of vintage dresses.

"Working," I said. "And don't make fun of my gym membership. I'm fighting off childhood obesity."

"You're seventeen; that's not childhood. And I don't care if you're a lardass."

"Nobody asked you," I said, trying out a withering glare à la Mrs. Lidell. "To comment on the state of my ass." Lula busted out laughing.

"I'll take a rain check until tomorrow," she said.

Lula and I told each other almost everything. The main thing we both had in common was our messed-up parent situation. My dad split so long ago, I can't even remember him, and, like I mentioned, my mom's kind of a boozehound. Lula never knew her dad, either, and her mom bailed on her, too. Lula lived with her grandparents in their condo at the retirement villa, right on the ninth hole of the golf course. They were the craziest old people I'd ever met. Her granddad flew helicopters in Vietnam and was now a retired Naval engineer. So, unlike most old people, he was a total tech head. Lula's grandparents were the first people I ever knew with flat-screen TVs or Wi-Fi. And Lula's grandmother was a former model, except that she only modeled certain body parts—mostly her legs and feet. She had a contract with the Nair people before she met Leo, she told me once. She still wore white lipstick and dressed like Nancy Sinatra, with puffed-up hair like Jane Fonda in *Barbarella*, and kept the whole house decorated in white, like the inside of a space capsule or something. White carpet, white furniture. They even drove a white Cadillac. I told Lula that she was probably lucky her mom ran off and left her with Janet and Leo (her grandparents), but Lula was more obsessed with her mom than she was with Mrs. Lidell, and that's really saying something. She'd probably Googled her about ten thousand times.

When Lula's mom split, the only thing she left behind was a little multicolored hippie backpack. Lula was about three when her mother took off. When Lula got older, right around the time we met, Janet sat her down and gave her the backpack. Lula said it was like this top-secret operation, because Leo refused to talk about Lula's mom. According to Janet, Lula's mom, Christine, and Leo had been on bad terms since she was a rebellious teenager and Leo's temper was worse. But after Christine dumped Lula at their house and left, there was some big falling out between her and Leo that nobody in the family talked about. Leo made Janet take down all of Christine's pictures—everything. Janet wasn't even sure where Christine was anymore. She'd stopped writing and calling a few years back. So, one weekend when Leo was away with his Navy buddies at a reunion in Annapolis or wherever, Janet gave Lula the backpack and swore her to secrecy. Inside, there was a Polaroid of Lula's mother in a black T-shirt and jeans in front of a marked wall, like somebody was measuring her height. Her eyes peered out of the blurry photograph with the same intensity as Lula's. I thought it looked like a mug shot, but Lula said it was from a theater tryout. That was what her mother ran off to do, according to Janet. She went to LA, then to New York to be an actress. There was a blue-and-gold scarf in the knapsack, and a postcard from California with nothing written on it. There was also a cassette tape by a woman singer named Laura Nyro that Lula played endlessly, until her Walkman ate it. Now it stayed in the backpack, the broken tape-ends flittering out of the cassette box.

Then there were the three books. One was *An Actor Prepares*, written by this Russian guy, Stanislavski. Lula read it and told me it was just a story about actors putting on a play, but when we looked it up online, it turned out it was like this major acting manual that all the heavy gangster-movie guys like Brando and De Niro swore by. I read it and didn't get it; but then, my only acting experience was playing a green bean in the fourth grade Health play, so what did I know? The other book was *Changing* by Liv Ullmann, an actress who, as we found out, was in all these boring Swedish movies. (Well, I thought they were boring, but I didn't tell Lula.) The third book was called *The Unseen Hand and Other Plays* by Sam Shepard. That was the one Lula used to make up her email address. BloomOrphan. At first I thought she just came up with that name because she was proud of getting ditched by her mom or something. But then she told me about the play. There's this one character in it, a drunk cowboy who lives in the back of a dead Chevy, but he's the only one who can save this race of people from the future who are all having their thoughts controlled by the

Unseen Hand. The only reason the cowboy can save them is because he's still got his emotions, but everybody else has been taken over by technology. The cowboy's name is Blue Morphan. The way Lula rearranged it, the play on words, I thought was pretty clever. Mine was just TKCallahan91. Except when I went on to the *X-Files* message boards, and then I went incognito. There, I was SpookyKid. Which probably fit me better than Rory or Teddy or anything else.

OVER AT ANDY'S BOOKS & COFFEE, I was left to work both the register and the coffee bar (which was basically just an espresso machine and two coffee pots in the nook where the graphic novels used to be) while Andy hooked up his new XM Satellite radio. Andy was ecstatic about it. They had entire channels devoted to the music he loved, which was old 1960s pop—not just the main bands everybody's heard of like the Beatles and the Rolling Stones, but stuff like Herman's Hermits, Dusty Springfield, Paul Revere & the Raiders, the Troggs, the Box Tops, the Dave Clark Five. Ever since the local oldies station changed to a hard-rock format, he'd been bummed out, because he only had that stuff on collector's-item vinyl, and he didn't want to have to keep flipping records in the store. I was happy to be manning the register—I preferred ringing up books to making coffee, which I never drank. I didn't understand the allure—it didn't make me feel more awake, just more unnerved. The coffee bar was a recent addition, anyway—something Andy thought would bring in more customers and make the store a cool nighttime hangout destination. But I'm not sure that my sloppy lattes and flat cappuccinos were much of an attraction.

Sometimes Lula came in to browse the Used Paperbacks shelves, or just to bug me by ordering the most complicated coffee she could think of, but she usually had to work. She had a job as a caddy at the golf course. Aside from her infrequent appearances, there weren't that many customers in the afternoons. Most people got their books online and their coffee from the drive-thru Starbucks over by the mall. I sat there beneath the faded framed picture of Kurt Vonnegut and the yellowed *Bloom County* comics pinned to the wall and watched Andy's thin, tanned arms installing the speakers. He was pretty handy with repairs around the shop, but he was really an outdoors guy. Always hiking and biking and kayaking. We'd been camping a couple of times together already that spring. I thought if we were characters in Tolkien, Andy would definitely be a ranger. Or maybe an elf. He would be totally happy just living in the woods, sleeping under the stars every night. Around town, Andy drove a Prius, like Mrs. Lidell. Unlike Mrs. Lidell, though, Andy's gay, which would probably come as a surprise to most people. Considering that most people think that all gay men ever listen to is Judy Garland or disco or show tunes. With Andy, forget it. He'd been going on for days about how, with the satellite radio, he could finally listen to Bob Dylan's radio show. Andy was probably a letdown if you were looking for some kind of stereotypical example of a gay guy. Like, he never cared about going to nightclubs or dissing everybody's gowns during the Golden Globes pre-show. Andy was more like the kind of guy who would take you on a nature walk and teach you the scientific name for crawdads.

Not to get all detailed about it, but . . . well, remember how I said that Lula and I told each other almost everything? Andy was my almost. And it was killing me that I couldn't tell her. But it could've gotten us both in a lot of trouble. I mean, aside from being my boss, he was way older than me. Technically, he could've gone to jail. We both knew this, so we had to be really careful. We weren't sure what we were going to do when I was legal. Andy kept saying I should go off to college and meet guys my own age, that he was only a steppingstone in my life, and he didn't want me becoming attached. But I wanted to stay with him. I wanted us to live together and run the bookstore together, and have a family together, once a few years had passed and there wouldn't be any question about it. Andy was a little touchy about the whole our-future-together subject, so I usually kept all that stuff to myself. It had taken him a long time to realize he was gay, so he already had a family. Two girls, eight and fourteen. Just three years younger than me, the oldest. Still living with their mom in Winston-Salem. So, that was the deal with Andy.

Also, Andy was the one who got me started going to the gym, and he paid for the membership. He didn't expect me to be one of those six-pack-ab guys, but he was concerned for my health. Last summer, when I went with him to an estate auction, I got seriously out of breath loading all the books he bought into the Beast. But it was, like, ninety-five degrees in the shade. Still, Andy got worried and told me I had to stop eating so much junk food and start working out. He wasn't totally wrong. I was five feet, ten inches back then, and clocked in at 317 pounds. I used to eat fast food every night, because my mom hardly ever cooked. Andy gave me a natural-foods cookbook, so I started buying my own groceries and cooking my own meals. (Of course, I didn't stop going over to Lula's whenever Janet made her insanely overboard Polish feasts, which was fairly often.) That spring, after my growth spurt, I was six foot two, and down to 280 pounds, with some actual muscle underneath all the fat. I told Andy I could bench press a car; he laughed and joked that I'd probably beat him at arm wrestling now. The first time Lula caught me at home post-workout, in my dumb baggy shorts and sweat-drenched T-shirt, I lied and told her that my mom was the one who suggested I start going to the gym. Lula said she thought I was fine the way I was and that the whole thing was ridiculous.

two

LULA AND I WATCHED ALL THE same movies and TV shows, usually together in Lula's bedroom on the weekends. Most of the TV shows we liked were old, like the original *Twilight Zone* and *Buffy the Vampire Slayer*, so we watched them on DVD from the library. When a show we liked came on during a school night, like *Lost*, we watched together on the phone, mostly silent during the show, then muting the commercials so we could argue and exclaim and generally go nuts about what we'd just seen. But Friday nights were special. Friday nights were reserved for Our Show.

"Rory! Come in! You're just in time for *The Way We Were*." Janet closed the door behind me. In the living room, there were two identical white leatherette recliners, parked in front of a huge flat-screen TV. She and Leo had this obsession with Barbra Streisand. Janet must've been picking me up on her gaydar, because every time I came over, she was asking me if I wanted to watch a Streisand movie with them, or showing off her Streisand box set, or whatever. It'd become like a ritual—I always politely declined.

"Ahh, no thanks—I'm holding out for *Yentl*." I headed upstairs, to Lula's room, which was the only non-white room in the house. In fact, it was all black. But you couldn't really see that it was black, because the walls were covered with posters from her favorite movies. And by "favorite movies," I mean there were posters from *Blade Runner* and *Star Trek II: The Wrath of Khan* somewhere among a collage of posters of Aragorn from the Lord of the Rings trilogy. And, of course, she has an entire wall devoted to Our Favorite TV Show of All Time: *The X-Files*.

The X-Files, in case you've never seen it, is about these two FBI agents who investigate paranormal phenomena, like UFO sightings and telekinesis and Bigfoot. They also investigate the government conspiracies to cover up so-called alien abductions. One of the agents, Fox Mulder, is a guy whose sister was one of these alien abductees. She disappeared when they were kids and he was supposed to be looking out for her, so it's his obsession, this quest to find her. To find out the truth, whether she was taken by beings from another world or government scientists performing top-secret experiments. Lula and I were born two years before the show came on, so we didn't see it the first time around, back in the nineties. We both caught it in reruns a couple years back, during a marathon on FX or the Sci-Fi Channel, and we were hooked. In case you haven't noticed by now, yes, the rumors are true—we're sci-fi geeks. It's another one of the things Lula and I have in common. My mom's older sister, my Aunt Judith, is sort of a cranky hippie. Like, she knew I was into *Star Wars* as a kid, but she would send me books by Ursula K. LeGuin and Madeleine L'Engle for my birthday instead of Luke and Han action figures. Lula got most of hers from Leo's secret stash on the homemade bookshelves down in his workshop; Leo had apparently harbored a secret desire to work for NASA when he was a teenager, before he went to war and stopped believing in utopias on Mars. He still had all his old paperbacks—short story anthologies with titles like *Dangerous Visions* and *Weird Heroes*, plus all the major classic guys like Asimov, Heinlein, Frank Herbert, and Arthur C. Clarke, and he let Lula borrow whatever she wanted. We traded back and forth and argued passionately about our favorites—she didn't like my Anne Rice phase; I didn't get Philip K. Dick. I made her read Orson Scott Card; she turned me on to Neil Gaiman. We both loved Douglas Adams; the year we read *Hitchhiker's Guide to the Galaxy*, we gave each other towels for Christmas. On the last day of school in eighth grade, Lula gave me a stack of Xerox copies, organized with different-colored paper clips. They were all her favorite stories by her favorite author, Ray Bradbury, copied because she couldn't bear to part with her books, and, according to Lula, summertime was the best time to read Ray Bradbury. She said he was "swoony." Pretty quickly, our reading habits bled into our watching habits, and Lula and I spent many a wee hour engaged in passionate debates regarding the superiority of Captain Kirk versus Captain Picard, the evil mastermindery of the Cigarette-Smoking Man versus the evil geniusosity of Benjamin Linus, and whether *Serenity* was a worthy successor to *Firefly* or just kind of a letdown. But when it came to *The X-Files*, there was no argument at all.

We were both obsessed. We'd already watched the entire series on DVD. All nine seasons, plus the movie. For a while we were just re-watching our favorite episodes, but now we were watching the whole series again, in order, from the beginning. No skips allowed. We didn't even skip the whistly-sounding opening-credit theme song, which we tried to whistle along with and see who made it longest and loudest without breaking into giggles. I usually won, because Lula was terrible at whistling and also at not giggling. (I mentioned that we're geeks, right?)

We were up to season three, which was probably my favorite. It had my favorite non-mythology episode, which was "Clyde Bruckman's Final Repose." And my second favorite, tonight's episode, the seventeenth of the season, called "Pusher." It's about a guy who controls people with his mind, due to a temporal lobe brain tumor, and also due to his study of Japanese mind-control techniques. He ends up controlling Agent Mulder's mind—and trying to make him shoot Scully. Dana Scully, in case you've never seen the show, is Mulder's skeptical female partner. She's also a doctor and a forensic pathologist, so she's always debunking his out-there theories with actual science. But even though she was originally assigned to the X-Files to poke holes in Mulder's work and discredit him as an investigator, she ends up becoming his ally. Well, more than allies. Over the course of the show, they pretty much become soul mates. But they're too professional, too dedicated to their quest, to go off and have a wild fling in the copy room or something. Mulder and Scully have huge amounts of what we fans call UST: Unresolved Sexual Tension.

"'Cerulean is a gentle breeze.'" Lula and I both quoted the lines during the show. We were totally annoying to watch this with. Since we knew what was going to happen, we hardly ever stopped talking through the whole thing.

"'Please explain to me the scientific nature of the whammy,'" Lula recited. She said that Dana Scully was probably her favorite character in all of fiction. I think Lula identified with her because Scully's stern, Navy Captain father reminded her of Leo. And also because she was short.

"'Mango Kiwi Tropical Swirl. Now we know we're dealing with a madman,'" I echoed.

"Good gravy. Is it just me, or is Fox Mulder in a bullet-proof vest, like, really hot?" Lula asked. She was not, at that point, quoting any line of dialogue from the show.

"It's just you."

"Liar. You love it when he's all Action Mulder. Jumping on trains. Going into the line of fire."

"I'm sorry, I don't find body armor a turn-on. I prefer Informative Slideshow Mulder. Preferably with the glasses."

"Hah! You would."

"Wait, shh! Shh! . . . Here comes the hand!"

We grabbed each other's arms, paralyzed. There was a three-second shot of Scully holding Mulder's hand after the final, life-or-death confrontation with the Pusher. They have a "moment." Lula and I didn't breathe. At the end of it, Lula let out this sound, something between a sigh and a high-pitched squeal. She wasn't normally so girly, but *The X-Files* had this effect on her.

"God, that's so intense! I totally need a cold shower right now," she said.

"I'm making an executive decision. 'Kitsunegari.'"

"Kitsunegari" is the sequel to the "Pusher" episode, but

watching it meant jumping ahead, out of sequence, to the fifth season.

"No way. We have to wait until we get there. Besides, the sequels are never as good as the originals. Except for 'Tooms.'"

"Let's at least watch the hand again," I insisted, reaching for the remote. There's something about it that gets to me, too, though I'm not as much of a Shipper as Lula is. Back in the day, according to the older fans online, you were either a Shipper or a Noromo. Noromos were in total denial of any hint of romantic attraction between Mulder and Scully. But Shippers wanted more relationship; they weren't happy with Mulder and Scully just having a deep platonic bond. They lived for every little moment that might give it away—a lingering look, a little hand-holding after narrowly escaping their demise. As the show went on, the Noromos pretty much got left in the dust, but I got their point. I liked all that Shipper stuff, but I didn't want to see Mulder and Scully rolling around in the sack, or whatever. I liked that it was restrained, like something out of Jane Austen. But then, I'm a sucker for the old-fashioned stuff.

"Take it all the way back to where he gives Scully his gun," Lula said. "That part kills me, too."

"Okay. The hand-holding, take two." We're not sure why, exactly, the Mulder and Scully Hand-Holding is better than the Mulder and Scully Actual Kissing that happens a few times in the later seasons. It just is. I skipped chapters on the DVD player, and we watched the Russian roulette scene again, grabbing at each other in the dark when Scully reaches for Mulder's hand to comfort him at the end. The credits came up, and Lula fell back on her bed, sighing.

"Best. Show. Ever." She sat up. "And I don't believe you're not totally fantasizing about Fox Mulder in the bulletproof vest." Lula didn't know about Andy, but she knew I was gay. "Ooh, Agent Mulder, can I hold your gun?" she said in a low voice, giggling.

"Sorry," I shrugged. "He's just not my type. Body armor or no."

"Wait a minute, he's not your type? I thought that's the whole reason you got into this show. The Hotness of the Duchovny." She starts singing, "David Duchovny, why don't you love me?" Which was a novelty single from the nineties that some girl sang about David Duchovny, the actor who plays FBI Special Agent Fox Mulder. (We'd only watched the YouTube video about two hundred times.)

"No, that's not the only reason. I mean, don't get me wrong, I'm not in denial of the Hotness, but—"

"You're more of a Walter Skinner type? You like 'em tall, dark, and balding?" Now she was laughing. She sent me some slashfic way back when I first came out to her, a short story she found online about Mulder having a thing with his boss at the FBI, Assistant Director Skinner. But I wasn't into it. It's the old-fashioned thing again. I think Mulder and Scully have one of those once-in-a-lifetime connections, even if we never do see them get it on.

"Bald guys are hot," I wanted to change the subject. "But you know me. I like those sexy Lance Bass types." Lance Bass was a boy-band singer. He just came out a couple of years ago. Big shocker there. I broke into my famous falsetto version of "Backstreet's back, all right!" which sent Lula into hysterics.

"Lance Bass was in *NSync!" She swatted at me.

"Sorry, I forgot you were a fan."

We finished up the evening like we usually did, arguing over whether we should watch another episode or not, or whether we should keep to our strict schedule of one episode per week to draw it all out. We ended up sticking to the schedule, so I went home, dealt with my mother's latest rearrangements, and got online. Lula was already on our favorite website, the *XPhilePhorum*, so named because the fans back in the day called themselves "X-Philes." The *Phorum* is our favorite, because even though it's been seven years since *The X-Files* was actually on TV, they still have live chats on Friday and Sunday night. Sometimes only four or five of us show up, but usually there's a pretty reliable core group that logs on to discuss the finer points of the series. And now that there's another *X-Files* movie coming out this summer, there've been a few more new people around, getting back into the show, spinning all kinds of wild theories on what the movie's going to be about. Anyway, Friday Night Live Chat goes something like this:

> BloomOrphan: watched pusher again tonight.
>
> FoxyLady2: Oh, soo good
>
> PendrellLives: The gun sceene!!! the hand holdingg!!! :-o
>
> SpookyKid: Should only be watched back 2 back w/ Kitsunegari
>
> Iwant2Bleeve: Modell may be best returning villain ever.
>
> PendrellLives: better than Tooms??!! nooo!!!!!
>
> ReynardMuldrake: Which one is Kitsunegari?
>
> BloomOrphan: I have it on good authority that spookykid doesn't care for mulder in the bulletproof vest
>
> PendrellLives: Cerulean blue . . .
>
> MorleyMan: Cerulean blue is a gentle breeze

Iwant2Bleeve: Muldrake, "Kitsunegari" is sequel to Pusher. Season 5 Ep 8.

SpookyKid: Bloom has an unhealthy obsession with Kevlar.

ReynardMuldrake: Kevlar??

BloomOrphan: the stuff they make bulletproof vests out of, Rey

FoxyLady2: Mulders hot in anything

FoxyLady2: Mulders hot in nothing!!!!

BloomOrphan: I heard they get it on in the new movie this summer

MorleyMan: they already did bloom how do u think they had william?

BloomOrphan: alien implants, Morley

SpookyKid: Do you think they still call each other by their last names if they get it on?

MorleyMan: they allready got it on, spookykid! It's too late!

It goes on like that for a while.

What Lula doesn't know is that I secretly did have this fantasy about Agent Mulder. But it's not what you think. See, in the show, right before it went off the air—spoiler alert, by the way—there was this plotline where Scully had a baby. And they suggested that it was hers and Mulder's, from this one episode where they hinted pretty strongly that, yes, they actually slept together, even though all you saw was Scully walking out of Mulder's bedroom. Anyway, she had the baby, William, but he kept getting kidnapped and threatened and stuff, because it turned out that, instead of being their baby, hers and Mulder's, there was a good chance that William may have been an alien–human hybrid, or a supersoldier, or created to destroy supersoldiers. Or something like that.

Anyway, Scully decided to give him up. She sent him away to live on a secluded ranch in South Dakota, so at least he'd be safe, even if it meant that she couldn't be there to raise her own son. And it's so heartbreaking, because after everything she went through, with being abducted and then not being able to have kids, you knew it was a big deal for her to have the baby. You knew that it was the ultimate sacrifice for her to give him up.

So I have this fantasy, usually during second period Algebra II, but sometimes during third period European History. I have to be really bored out of my skull, because this fantasy's really stupid. Honestly, I can't believe I'm telling you about it. But here it is. In the fantasy, I'm sitting in class, and there's a knock on the classroom door. The principal wants to see me. So I collect my books and go. It turns out there's an FBI agent who wants to speak with me. I'm scared, but the guy tells me not to be alarmed; I'm not in trouble. He's Agent Mulder, he says, showing me his badge. He asks me if I'd mind if we took a ride. He says he has something important to tell me about my father.

So we go for a ride. We drive out to the cemetery—the really old one by the community college. It's a cold, gray day, and we both wear long, dark overcoats in the faintly misting rain. We walk among the tombstones, our hands in our pockets, side by side. And he proceeds to tell me this story. About a couple of agents who work for the FBI, in a division that deals with the unexplained. The paranormal. The X-Files, I tell him. I've heard of it. He's surprised. I tell him I've always been interested in that sort of thing. Science fiction. Magic. The mysteries of the unknown. He tells me that he can't go into detail, but that these two agents, a man and a woman, became very close in their years investigating these cases. They became so close that they had a baby, a child they both loved very much. But, because of the nature of their work, they were constantly in danger, and even the child was threatened by forces neither of them were strong enough to stop. So, the agents decided that they would give the child up for adoption. For the boy's safety, they knew they could never see him again, not without seriously endangering his life. Then, Agent Mulder looks at me, and I can tell by the look in his eyes. He doesn't have to say anything. But he does. He tells me that my mother wanted very much to see me, but that she didn't think she could take it. She couldn't take leaving me again. His eyes fill with tears. And I understand. Agent Mulder is my father. Agent Scully is my mother. I'm the kid, the one they had to send away to this place, where no one knew them or who I really was, and no one would try to harm me. I want to tell him that he doesn't have to explain anymore. But now I'm overcome, and I can't speak, either. So I just put my hand on his shoulder. To let him know that I understand.

three

THAT SUNDAY WAS ONE OF THE first really hot days. Andy closed the store at six, and I met him back at his place. We put our shorts on and took a pair of black inner tubes and a six-pack down to the river behind his house. I waded slowly into the cold, trailing the six-pack on a rope. Andy dove right in. He scared me, doing that.

"Aren't you afraid you'll hit your head on a rock?" I asked when he surfaced. He shook his head, flopping his wet hair back with his hand.

"Nah. It's deep right there. Here," he clapped his hands, and I threw him an inner tube. He fell back into it with a splash.

"This is the life," he sighed. I eased myself into the bigger of the tubes, sinking down heavily into the water. The sun was setting, filigreed behind the trees, and I slapped a mosquito on my arm. It would be summer soon. I imagined us down here every evening, swimming off the sweat. Swimming toward each other. Our legs touching beneath the water where no one could see.

"What happened to that beer?" Andy looked around.

"I've got it. You want one?" I pulled at the yellow rope tied around the plastic six-pack yolk, and the beer cans bobbed to the surface. "I don't think they're cold yet."

"Leave it, then. I'll have one later." Andy, thankfully, wasn't much of a drinker. He just liked a cold beer now and then on hot days. Which was good, because one drunk in my life was enough to deal with. Andy closed his eyes and leaned back until his hair dangled in the water. I watched him. Noticing the trim lines of his biceps. The white threads of his cutoffs trailing against the dark hair on his legs. Noticing the things I liked about him that maybe nobody else even noticed at all. His farmer's tan from being outside so long on his hikes. The little crinkly lines around his eyes when he smiled or squinted into the sun. The gray hairs starting to show up in his sideburns and in the hair on his chest. He hated those gray hairs. I guess I'm weird, but I found it kind of hot. Older guys with a little gray in their hair.

"I can feel you watching me," he said, his eyes still closed.

"Sorry," I mumbled, feeling myself blush.

"Why are you sorry?" He squinted up at me. When he smiled, his eye lines crinkled in the exact way that made me sort of lightheaded. Andy had pretty much the world's cutest smile. "There's nobody around," he assured me. "You don't have to be sorry here." I didn't say anything, but that wasn't what I was sorry about. I didn't care about other people. I was sorry I was just staring at him. Sorry to realize I was pretty shallow. That I liked just looking at his body; that there was a part of me that didn't care how smart he was, or how successful his bookstore was. I just wanted to watch him, see him, look at how beautiful he was. In my head I wanted old-fashioned romance, courting, love letters, poems, and flowers, but the rest of me was too impatient. I was sorry for wanting to be a gentleman and turning out to be just a boy-crazy boy.

Andy slipped off his tube and tossed it back up onto the bank. He swam over to where I was, gliding beneath the water like a smooth-skinned fish.

"You scared?" he asked, after he surfaced.

"Scared? Of what?" People seeing us? Probably not as much as he was.

"Scared of the water." His hands slipped against the rubber. I slid off and felt my feet against the silty river bottom. Felt my toes slip against mossy rocks. Andy put his arms around me, and we kissed.

"That's better, don't you think?" He pulled back, looking at me.

"Yeah, I reckon." It was better that my big fat gut was underwater, that's for sure. Andy hooked an arm over my inner tube so he wouldn't have to tread water. I half-floated, half-stood there, the water grazing the bottom of my chin.

"You're right. It's deep here," I said. The current wasn't strong. In some parts of town, the river was barely even a creek. Andy was lucky—here in his backyard, it was like a private pool.

"I told you. Watch this." Andy dove down into the water and came up with a slick, flat rock. He popped up and, in a quick, flicking motion, skipped the stone five times along the surface of the water before it sank.

"Hey!" I was impressed. "Five skips!"

"I can usually skip it seven or eight. It's harder to do when you're in the water." Andy paused, looking at me. "What is it?"

"What's what?"

"That look. You've been thinking about something all day long. What's going on in that head of yours?"

I looked at him. "I was just thinking. You must be a really great dad."

Andy frowned. I didn't usually bring up his family.

"I *am* a great dad," he said, his voice halting. A little angry sounding. He hooked his arms on the inner tube again.

"We could have kids," I murmured. "We could adopt, or use a surrogate. We could—" I stopped. Andy's jaw tightened. He didn't have to say anything. He had said it before. *You're only seventeen years old. You don't have any idea what you want.*

"Or," he said slowly, "we could just swim." He dove underwater again, but this time he shot toward me underwater, jerked my swim trunks down, and swam away. I kicked the trunks off and they floated up to the surface while I dove underneath, my eyes open, kicking again to catch up.

"WHAT'S ON YOUR BRAIN, THEODORE?" LULA peered at me. We sat at Janet and Leo's big Lucite-topped dining room table, making flash cards for the Chemistry midterm.

"I dunno." I reached for another three-by-five card and a different-colored marker from the one I had. Maroon. The thought of dropping one of these on the white carpet was making my palms clammy.

"Aren't you, like, totally overwhelmed at the uselessness of this entire operation?" Lula uncapped a green marker. "I mean, do I look like I'm ever going to become a chemist? The only people interested in this stuff are the kids who want to start meth labs. Do you think Mulder and Scully had to take Chemistry to get into the FBI?"

I didn't answer. I don't know why not, just lag time between my ears and my brain, I guess. The funny thing was, Lula was actually acing Chemistry. I was the one who needed flash cards. Lula was nice enough to call this a study session instead of a tutorial.

"I mean, obviously, Scully had to learn chemistry to become a doctor. But does balancing chemical equations have any practical application? Seriously. What's the point?" Lula sighed, resting her chin in her hand. "Speaking of Mulder and Scully," she continued. "I was thinking about the *Guide*. What if we did like a *Mystery Science Theater*-type thing? Remember, that show with the snarky robots? It could be us, talking back to the screen. We can try it and see what it looks like. Leo's got a video camera."

Oh yeah, the *Guide*. Short for *SpookyKid and BloomOrphan's Incomplete Guide to* The X-Files, our blog that was actually pretty popular among the denizens of the *XPhilePhorum*. What with school and work and everything, I'd almost forgotten about it. Lula was the brains behind the operation, anyway. But our goal was to write reviews of all nine seasons before we graduated. We were only doing it for fun, for ourselves and our friends on the *Phorum*, though I knew that Lula secretly fantasized that Chris Carter, the creator of *The X-Files*, would someday stumble across our frighteningly thorough *Guide* and hire us to become part of the *X-Files's* "inner sanctum."

"What happens when we get to the inner sanctum?" I asked her once.

"I don't know," she admitted. "But we could be in charge of, like, destroying script pages, or leaking false information about new movies to the press. The Obfuscation Committee. Something like that."

"You really think Chris Carter has an Obfuscation Committee?"

"You never know."

Some of the reviews—the ones we wrote together—were more like arguments between us, debating the finer points. Lula let me write the "Scully-in-Peril" episode reviews, but her reviews always got the most comments from the other fans on the *Phorum*. She came up with the "Best Mulderism" award and the "Scullyometer," which rated Scully's skepticism level on particularly out-there cases. She also rated "FBI Fashion" (you can imagine the Mulder-in-a-Speedo episode got high marks there), and "Lone Gunmenosity," which gave high praise to any episode featuring her favorite supporting characters, Byers, Langley, and Frohike, aka the Lone Gunmen. They're a trio of paranoid conspiracy theorists who publish a newsletter called—you guessed it—*The Lone Gunman*. Mulder goes to them for help on top-secret stuff that he can't get away with at the FBI—computer hacking, code breaking, surveillance. Lula had recently written a Lone Gunmenosity/FBI Fashion crossover essay about the delightfully bizarre wardrobe choices of Melvin Frohike; she wrote it as if she *were* Frohike, giving fashion criticism in a column of his own called "The Cranky Hacker." It was really funny and the Philes, needless to say, loved it. I think that if

The Lone Gunman were a real newspaper, Lula would be trying to get an internship.

"Earth to Rory?"

I looked up at Lula.

"Everything okay?" she asked.

"Yeah." I snapped the cap on a blue marker, looking at the chemical equations written out on the study sheet in front of me. I wished I could shift my molecules somehow. Be something else. A different element. Part of a different compound. Not some sad satellite electron, drifting through my mother's drunken fog. I wished I could be orbiting around Andy instead. That I could live with him in his house by the stream, that we could be a new family. Bonded together, complete. With new electrons orbiting around our nucleus.

"Hey, Lula? Can I ask you something?"

"Uh-oh. You've got that 'this isn't just about Chemistry' tone in your voice."

"It's no big deal. I was just wondering . . ." I flipped over a flash card, trying to seem nonchalant. "Do you ever think about being a parent?"

"Being apparent?" She laughed. "You mean you can't see me? I'm sitting right here."

"I mean . . . being a mother. A mom. Do you ever think about it?"

"You mean, like, teenage pregnancy?" Lula arched her eyebrow at me. "Seeing as how I'm perpetually boyfriend-free, it's not exactly an issue that's keeping me up nights. What are you getting at, Theodore?"

"Well, I was just wondering if you'd ever think about— not now, but maybe, like, in a few years, after college, when we're grown up and everything—if you'd consider being a surrogate for me."

"A surrogate?"

"A surrogate mother. We wouldn't actually sleep together. I looked it up. I just figured, you know, instead of going through a whole egg-donor thing, since you're my best friend—"

"We wouldn't actually . . . sleep together . . ." Lula repeated.

"No! It's totally scientific. We wouldn't even have to be in the same room."

"Gee, Rory, you really know what to say to a girl." She looked at me. I couldn't tell if she was amused or insulted. "Why are you even bringing this up?"

"It's been on my mind a lot lately. I guess because . . ." I actually almost bit my tongue, trying not to say anything about Andy, about how serious I felt about him. About us. "I dunno, I guess those pre-college-admissions meetings with Mr. Peeler have got me thinking about all that rest-of-my-life stuff. College, marriage, kids. I know, I haven't even decided which colleges I'm applying to yet. But I know I want to have a family. And I want you to be a part of it somehow."

"But you want me to . . . you're serious. You want to get me knocked up, but in a sterile laboratory setting." Lula laughed. "How sexy, Theodore. You want to have a test-tube baby with me."

"Actually, I'd have a baby with . . . with whoever my boyfriend is. Or, hopefully, my husband."

"Your husband?"

"Depending on what state we live in. But you'd be the

birth mother. You'd still be a part of the kid's life. Like an aunt or something."

"Wow. This is kind of weirding me out a little." Lula pushed her chair back from the table. "This is kind of a heavy life decision to have to make while I'm trying to study for the Chem midterm."

"I'm not talking about doing anything right now. I just mean, theoretically. Someday. In the future." I looked down at the bright letters of my flash cards against the white. ORGANIC COMPOUNDS. Lula stood up and walked over to the white couch, where her book bag sat slouched open, spilling notebooks and binders.

"Forget I said anything." I kept talking. "I just really want to be a dad, and it's going to be different for me, that's all."

"I know. I just think maybe . . ." Lula's muttering trailed off as she rummaged through her notebooks. She found what she was looking for and sat down again at the table. More Chemistry notes. This midterm was going to kill us.

"Listen, Rory." She opened the notebook matter-of-factly. "I think you'd make a great dad."

"You think so?"

"Yeah. I mean, at least you actually want to be a dad. You wouldn't just run out on him. Or her." Lula frowned, flipping notebook pages quickly. Then, very abruptly, she stopped flipping and looked up at me, a thoughtful expression on her face. "Okay."

"Okay?"

"Sure, I'll do it. I mean, why not? I'm flattered. They'll harvest my eggs, just like on *X-Files*. We'll start a race of supersoldiers. Alien-human hybrid clones. World domination will be ours. The possibilities are endless."

She gave a little laugh. But there was a strange silence in the room, and I felt like I shouldn't have asked. I felt like I'd given something away, like Lula could tell now. Tell what? I hadn't said anything about Andy. But I felt like there was something loud and irreversible sitting on the clear Lucite table now, something buzzing and humming that we were both trying to ignore.

"I only have one requirement," Lula announced abruptly. "If we're going to do this baby thing."

"You name it," I said, tentatively.

"If it's a boy, we're totally naming him Fox."

"Fox?" I asked. "But I had my heart set on naming him Melvin Frohike Callahan."

Lula snapped the cap back onto her highlighter and threw it at me, trying not to laugh.

four

I CAME HOME FROM OUR NEXT *X-Files* session to find Rick, my mother's client from Denver, slouched down on our couch with his shirttail half out. Mom was mixing cocktails on the hall table, which she'd set up at an angle in the living room, like her own little bar. She had changed out of her work clothes and into her familiar green bathrobe and black ballet-style slippers. Her Patty the Pickle costume, I called it. And that's Pickle as in pickled. Pickled as in drunk.

"Hey there, squirt!" Rick called out. *Damn . . .*

"Teddy Bear!" my mother exclaimed. I was trying to make it to my room without her seeing me, but it was too late. "Get in here!"

I slunk into the room. Even in her happy-drunk mode, my mother was embarrassing. Lurching around, waving her hands carelessly. I guess it's not really dangerous. It's not like she's going to beat me up or anything. But it's stupid. She's like a big, dumb, oversized baby or something. She can't even stand up straight. It's humiliating, if you want to know the truth. Humiliating for everybody but her.

"Teddy Bear, guess who made Regional Sales Manager of the Month?" She held up a shot glass full of something, like she was making a toast, but she didn't wait for anyone else. She downed it in one gulp.

I looked around. Rick thumped his hands against the coffee table in an off-beat drum roll.

"You did?" I ventured.

"Ta-da!" Rick hollered. "Squirt wins the prize!"

"Yes, I did!" She set her empty glass down on the bar. "And did they give me a bonus? Yes, they did!" My mother pinched her fingers together. "A tiny, teeny, tiny bonus. But a bonus," she held up her finger, making an important point, "is a bonus. Don't you agree, Ricky Rick?"

Rick burst out laughing. Rick was married, by the way. But he stayed overnight when he came to town on these little business trips. I guess it didn't matter, because my mom dated other guys, too, when Rick went back home to Denver. So it's not like it was true love. Rick called me squirt, shorty, or pee wee. Which he thought was hilarious, because he was about half a foot shorter than I was. I called him Rick the Dick, but never to his face.

"Ricky Rick!" My mother was laughing her head off, too. "That's your . . . that's your rap star name! You're a rapper!" She was gasping for air.

"Ricky RICK!" Rick bellowed, Flavor Flav-style.

"Congratulations," I said finally, when there was a lull in the hysterical cackling. "I've got some homework to do, so—"

"Homework? Homework on Friday? Oh, no no no, Teddy. We're celebrating! Stay here and celebrate with us! Have a drink. You wanna vodka tonic? Whiskey sour? Martini? Dirty martini? Cosmo? You name it, kiddo, I'm mixing."

"You don't have to drink that pink shit," Rick offered help-fully. "With cherries in it. You want a beer, son? There's a twelve-pack of Bud Light in the fridge."

Most kids would probably be psyched if their parents offered to let them drink anything they wanted. If their par-ents were always trying to be the life of the party. But, trust me, it's not as cool as it sounds.

"No thanks, guys. I'm pretty tired. I'm just gonna—"

"Dammit, Theodore!" That was it. Now my mom had gone from Big Baby Drunk to Mean Old Lady Drunk with her usual speed. It only got more fun from there.

"How'd I get stuck with such a buzzkill of a kid? Huh?" she asked Ricky Rick, pointing at me. "Lookit how he's always 'Ooh, no, I can't have a drink. I have to study.' He's all, 'Maybe you shouldn't drink so much, Mom. It's a weeknight, Mom.' Blah, blah, blah. Lissen, mister. I work hard for this family. I'm the goddamn Seasonal Sales Manager of the Month."

"I'm happy for you, Mom. I really am—"

"Oh, *you're* happy for *me*." Now she was more like an old bum, staggering toward me, a vodka bottle in her hand. I couldn't help but cringe. "One of these days . . ." she nodded her head knowingly. She got as close to my face as she could, being so much smaller. "One of these days, Teddy Bear. You're gonna understand. It's very stressful to be in my position. One of these days, you're gonna have a family to support. And then, my friend." She looked very seriously into my eyes, to make sure I got the point. "And then. Boy. Are you gonna be sorry."

Rick the Dick started laughing again. But my mother wasn't laughing. And neither was I.

I walked out. I wished I could call my Aunt Judith, but she was off studying yoga at this place in Nepal with no phones, no Internet, even. Aunt Judith, my mom's older sister, helped me do an intervention once a few years ago, after my grand- mother had died and Mom's drinking got really bad. It was a whole big weepy scene, and Mom stayed sober for a few months. But then she got her new job, and she started drinking again. First when she went out with clients. Then she started having a drink when she got home from work. Then several drinks, and so on. She said it was part of being in business, especially for women. You had to show that you could hang with the boys. I didn't get how selling communi- cation system setups to random companies required getting totally bombed every weekend, starting on Thursday nights, but maybe she had a point. I didn't understand the stress she was under. And maybe I should just be glad she was working and paying the bills. So what if a few of them were late from time to time?

At the top of the stairs, I heard my mother laugh again. She was already over it. I closed my bedroom door and sat there for a minute in silence, waiting for the music that would inevitably start. Aaaand . . . there it was. Hall & Oates, or whatever the fuck it is she listens to. *One on one, I wanna play that game tonight.* Like clockwork. God, it was revolting. I shut my eyes and opened them again. My room wasn't like Lula's, crowded with posters and action figures and stuff. I tried to make it my sanctuary, plain and calm. Last summer, Leo helped me build extra shelves for my books—my collec- tion was growing all the time. I kept them arranged just the way I liked them, in sections only I understood. There were

"All-Time Favorites," "Classics," "Poetry," "Gifts from Aunt
Judith," "Still Haven't Read Yet," and, on the shelf next to my
bed, "Andy." Those were the books Andy had given me,
books like *Ceremony* and *Desert Solitaire* and *Blue Highways*,
books he said I should read because they were important, or
just because they were the books he loved.

But I was too restless to read. I turned my computer on
and logged in to the *XPhilePhorum*. The regulars were particularly argumentative, and I wasn't in the mood. Sometimes
I didn't give a shit if nobody liked when Robert Patrick came
on the show or—sorry, spoiler alert again—if it's way beyond
the realm of possibility, even for *The X-Files*, for Mulder to
have come back from the dead in Season Eight, because no
amount of alien antivirals in the world can change the fact
that a man's been embalmed and buried for three months
and so on. Lula and I knew the show wasn't always perfect.
But we were watching this for fun. There was enough to fight
about in the world without dragging our favorite TV show
into it.

So I logged out and loaded a DVD instead. *Sense and
Sensibility*, with Emma Thompson and Kate Winslet. I put on my
headphones, plugged them into my computer, and turned the
monitor so I could watch it in bed. Maybe if I fell asleep
watching it, I could dream myself there. Dream of a world
where men tipped their hats and behaved like gentlemen. A
world where, okay, things weren't perfect, and being female
pretty much sucked, but at least there was chivalry and
manners. Maybe Lula was the lucky one. Maybe her mother
had ditched her, but maybe that was better than if she was
downstairs blasting "Maneater" on her shitty-sounding CD

player and trying to put the moves on Rick the Dick. I yawned. I wished I could wear a double-breasted tailcoat and knee-high riding boots and look suave like Alan Rickman. That guy was cool.

It was unusually early on Saturday morning when Lula called on the landline.

"You're out of minutes again," she announced without saying hello.

"I forgot to go by the place." I let Lula think that my cell phone minutes ran out because of my own laziness, not because I'd decided to spend the money on organic groceries instead. It wasn't that I was embarrassed. I didn't want Lula to worry about me. She already knew that I'd bought myself a crappy pay-as-you-go phone because my mom kept forgetting to pay the bill on my old one. My mom's cell phone was paid for by her company, so she didn't have to think about it. I didn't know what her excuse was for not buying groceries, though. I guess it was that she ate out so much with her coworkers, she kind of forgot to stock the fridge. But it's not like I was starving or anything. And I was trying to do this new high-protein diet plan Andy had suggested, anyway. So that was why I didn't have minutes on my cell phone that week. Because I'd rather eat than talk, even if it did interfere with Lula's and my ongoing game of answering our cell phones with Mulder and Scullyisms.

"Hey, what happened on the Chat last night? You logged out without saying good night." She sounded wide awake.

"I know. Sorry," I apologized. "I dozed off. Did I miss anything good?"

"Just a sudden groundswell of pro-Monica Reyes sentiment. PendrellLives was, like, militant. I kept waiting for you to chime in with your whole 'Doggett and Reyes Aren't So Bad' manifesto."

"Guess I'll have to follow up next week." I coughed. It was a quarter to eight. "What's going on?"

"Are you ready to hear something really weird?"

"This isn't that Mexican goatsucker thing, is it?" I sat up in bed, yawning.

"No, not that weird," Lula laughed. "But close. Leo wants to borrow your car."

"Do what now?"

"Leo wants to borrow the Beast. Remember Trey Greyson?"

"The Burnout?" I rubbed sleep junk out of my eyes. "What did he do now, drive the lawn mower into the Caddy?" Trey Greyson, aka John Harrell Greyson III, aka the Burnout, was once, literally, a poster child for excellence. His family owned Greyson Pork, and Trey was the cute blond kid who sang the Greyson Bacon song in those commercials with the dancing pig. (I know—now the jingle is going to be stuck in your head for days. Sorry.) In addition to being a bacon heir, Trey was a star basketball player and scored so high on his SATs that our school district used a picture of him in their ads for *Raise Those As!*, their county-wide incentive program to get us mere mortals to stay in school and "A-chieve!" But, in the end, Trey Greyson flunked out of Princeton during his sophomore year. He'd fried his brain on LSD, which, apparently, he'd been doing since his sophomore year of high school, along with a whole buffet of alcohol and drugs I'd never even heard of before. After all that "A-chievement," he ended up back in Hawthorne mowing lawns, including Janet and Leo's, for a living.

"He walked off the job last week," Lula explained. "He said Leo 'harshed his mellow.' Leo got so pissed he said he'd do the yard his own damn self, but he just got the Caddy detailed, so he doesn't want to get the trunk all dirty with manure or whatever."

"So he wants to put a bunch of manure in the trunk of my car?"

"He said he'll pay for you to get it washed afterward. Whadda ya say, Theodore? Up for an outing?"

"Sure. Let me throw on some clothes."

"Right on, man," Lula drawled in her best burnout voice.

The house was quiet. Mom and Rick the Dick were still sleeping it off, so I left a note and went over to Lula's. Janet insisted on feeding me pancakes first. And sausage.

"Janet wants us to go organic," Leo explained as I drove us to Walmart. "She just read some damn book about reducing our carbon footprint. We'll see what she has to say about our carbon footprint when the whole front yard turns brown and dies."

"We could have a Zen rock garden," Lula piped up from the backseat. "You can rake it every morning. It's very relaxing. Your blood pressure will go down."

"My blood pressure'd go down if that damn lawn hippie hadn't up and quit on me," Leo groused from behind his aviator shades. Lula and I caught each other's glance in the rear-view mirror. We were both holding in laughs. *Lawn hippie.* "How in the Sam Hill is having to rake the lawn every morning going to make my blood pressure go down?" Leo asked.

"Leo," Lula sighed, as if it were obvious. "That's the mystery of the Zen." Out of the corner of my eye, I could see Leo get this look on his face like he always did when Lula was goofing on him. Like he wanted to be pissed off but was also trying not to laugh. Not that Leo laughed. It was more like a "humph" noise and a slightly-less-pissed-off-than-usual look. It was strange to me how a guy like Leo can actually be really nice, beneath his gruff exterior, while my mom could seem like she's being nice and pleasant and even fun, but then she turns around and cuts you down with some comment about what a burden you are, or why don't you get your lazy fat ass in gear and clean up the kitchen after you cook dinner, or whatever. Sometimes I wished Leo and my mom could switch places for a day. But I wouldn't want Lula to have to deal with my mom.

I pulled into a spot close to the Garden Center and gave Leo the keys. He wanted to try on golf pants while we were there. We were also supposed to remind him to pick up some low-sodium chicken broth and Scotch Tape. Lula pulled me along with her to the Electronics section to scope out the Blu-ray player she had her sights on. She was convinced that the eventual Blu-ray release of *Lord of the Rings* was going to be the ultimate viewing experience of her life thus far, and she wanted to be prepared, but Leo wouldn't buy the player for her. Tech nerd that he was, Leo said something better was probably just around the corner, and he wasn't con-vinced yet that Blu-ray wasn't going to be this decade's answer to Betamax. Whatever that meant.

"So, that's about ten more golf games I have to caddy to be able to afford the mind-boggling high definition of Blu-ray," Lula sighed. Leo had gotten her the golf course job, driving carts for the old duffers and hauling golf bags that were almost as big as she was. He always used to take her along during his golf games, when she was a little kid and Janet had a day job. So Lula actually knew a ridiculous amount about the game. Still, I asked her why she didn't just work in the pro shop, where all you had to do was stand around in the air conditioning, handing out towels and baskets of balls for the driving range. Lula said she liked being out on the links.

"You wouldn't believe the dirty jokes these old guys tell," she confided giddily. "Filthy. Absolutely the worst. Also, they think it's adorable when a short girl carries their bags, so I get big tips."

None of the DVDs were catching my eye, so I wandered over to the CDs. I browsed the titles, looking for something Andy would like, but it seemed like it was all Country, Heavy Metal, and Top 40. There was a greatest hits of Buddy Holly CD—Buddy Holly was sixties, right?

"Hey, Ronnie. It's Ronnie, right?" I looked around. It took me a minute to realize that someone was speaking to me, and that the person was Sexy Seth Brock, our school's requisite hot quarterback. Not that I was interested. I wasn't really into jock types, and Seth had a girlfriend, besides. But I have to admit, he was pretty easy on the eyes.

"Me? Uh, it's Rory, actually." *Or just good ol' What's His Name. Whatever works.*

"Oh yeah. Rory. Weren't we in Mr. Tanner's Biology class together last year?"

"Um. Yeah. I believe we were." He borrowed test notes from me. Twice.

"I knew I remembered you. I just couldn't remember your name." Sexy Seth flipped his shaggy surfer-hair out of his eyes. "Things were kinda crazy last year. It was my first year on varsity."

"Oh." *Yeah, I bet being a gorgeous, popular football player made life really difficult for you, Seth.*

"Find anything good?"

"What?"

"CDs." He motioned to the ones in his hands. "I'm gonna try this new Foo Fighters. I was into the early stuff, but then it kinda got too metal-y for me. I was looking for the Pavement reissues, but then I remembered, hey, I'm at Walmart." Seth kind of laughed. "Schoolkids Records it ain't."

"Yeah," I said, not knowing what he was talking about. Rock music wasn't my thing. I jammed the Buddy Holly CD sloppily back in the racks. "Not much, um. Cool music. Hey, uh. I like your T-shirt."

"Pretty awesome, right?" Seth pulled at the hem. The T-shirt had a sketch of a human head, like something out of an anatomy book, and said I AM A SCIENTIST. "It was my brother's. You've heard this album? *Bee Thousand*? GBV?"

"Actually, no, but I was thinking, uh—I have a friend who would be really into a shirt like that."

"Tell him he can probably find one on eBay. It's from back in the day. I think it's a collector's item now."

"Seth, honey." An older, petite, blond woman clipped down the aisle in a jogging suit, pushing a shopping cart. "We better go meet Dad. Did you find what you were looking for?"

"Sort of."

"Honey, aren't you going to introduce me to your friend?" Seth's mom asked.

"Mom, this is Rory. Rory, my mom."

"Hi, Rory. And what position do you play?"

"Excuse me?"

"He's not on the team, Mom," Seth explained. "We were in Biology together last year."

"You're not on the team?" Mrs. Brock exclaimed. "But you're so big!"

"Yes, ma'am. I know." *And thank you for pointing that out, Mrs. Brock. Now, if you'll excuse me, I'll be over here in Home Electronics, dying a slow death of embarrassment.*

"Well, Seth, you should get him on that team."

"I'll work on him." Seth gave me a look that said: *Parents. What can you do?* "We better go rescue Dad from the tire department."

"Nice to meet you, Rory." Mrs. Brock gave me a beauty-pageant smile. I could see the family resemblance.

"See ya 'round, man." Seth gave me a little wave. I drifted back over to Lula, who was digging through the discount DVD box.

"All these old *Star Trek*s are only six bucks," she said. "Where did you get off to, anyway?"

"I just had a close encounter with two extraterrestrial biological entities," I reported. "Their teeth were unnaturally white."

"What?" Lula laughed.

"Have you ever heard of the Pavement Reissues?"

"No, but I've heard of a band called Pavement. Midnight Pete used to play them on his radio show before he bailed and we got stuck with Midnight Steve."

"How about a CD called . . . something Be. Be something . . . "

"*Let It Be?* It's by a little band from Britain you might have heard about, Theodore. They're called the Beatles."

"No, no . . . hang on, I'll remember it in a second." Okay, so maybe I was a little bit swayed by the jock type. Now I could kind of see how he got the nickname. A few minutes of talking to Sexy Seth, and, without even realizing it, he puts the whammy on you. "And Schoolkids—is that the place in Chapel Hill?"

"The cool record store? Yeah. What's with the sudden interest in music, Theodore? I thought that aside from your odd affinity for the oldies station, you were a 'whatever's on the radio' kind of guy."

"Just trying to stay open to new ideas."

five

IT WAS TUESDAY NIGHT AND THE gym was packed as usual. I was doing leg presses when this guy in a Fighting Eagles (our mascot) shirt came up to me.

"Hey, you go to Hawthorne High, right?"

"Uh-huh," I grunted, not paying much attention to the guy. I'd never seen him before. I didn't know if he was giving me hell or trying to pick me up, or what.

"What're you, six feet, six-two? You go 'bout two-sixty? Two sixty-five?"

"What?" Was all I managed to say. If I was cool and I had the nerve, I'd have told the guy to fuck off. But I wasn't, and I didn't.

"Your weight." The guy realized I was looking at him funny, because he sort of stopped, then smiled. "Sorry, I'm Morris. I'm the offensive coordinator for the varsity football team over at Hawthorne."

"Oh." I finished my last rep and let the machine chunk back into place. I swung my feet to the ground and wiped the sweat off my face with my towel. I wasn't sure what this guy wanted from me. Then I remembered Sexy Seth's mom telling him to get me on the team.

"I go about two-eighty," I told him finally.

"I thought so. I saw you running on the treadmill a little earlier. How long have you been working out here?"

"Since last fall, I guess."

"You gonna come out for the team?"

"The football team? Not planning on it, no."

"Why not? Tryouts are coming up."

"I thought you guys didn't play again till next fall." I knew I was a big guy, but playing football had never occurred to me. Partly because, unlike pretty much every other male in America, I didn't give a rat's ass about football. But also because being a big fat guy wasn't exactly something I wanted to draw everyone's attention to. I hadn't bothered to attempt playing any sport since sixth grade, when our neighbor convinced my mom to sign me up for community-league soccer. Because it would be good for me. I spent most of the time riding the pine, but I got a trophy because everyone got a trophy. For being such good sports.

"We start practicing in the summer. Whip you guys' butts into shape." Morris winked at me. I wondered if Morris was his first name or his last. I thought about the way he introduced himself. *Sorry, I'm Morris.* It was almost like one of those word tricks, where it reads the same backwards and forward. Like *Madam, I'm Adam.* What do they call those? Anagrams? Palindromes? Lula would know. I'd have to ask her later.

"You ever play football?" Morris eyed me up and down again. "Pop Warner? Mighty Mite?"

"I played soccer one year. Community league." I could tell he was nonplussed.

"You should try out anyway," Morris said. "Can't hurt. Come by my office sometime. We need some big fellas like you. Fresh blood on the offensive line."

Fresh blood.

"See you 'round." Morris winked at me again. Was he just messing with me? Was this a trick? I thought about Lula, doing her best Mrs. Lidell Withering Stare. I wanted to say something like *I bet you'd like to whip my butt into shape.* Or *I've got an offensive line for you.* And flip him the bird. But instead I threw the towel over my shoulder and headed over to the pull-up bar. The one I was always afraid I would rip out of the wall. Because I was still just a lardass, any way you look at it.

LULA COULDN'T STOP FUSSING WITH HER hair. I told her I'd help her with it, but she was driving me nuts. And making me late.

"Is it getting too dark? I don't want it to be too brunette."

"It won't be. It's Natural Reddish Blond." Clairol Nice 'n Easy, number 108. Lula was going from her usual dirty-blond color to Scully Red. Even though I thought her original color was really beautiful. And Gillian Anderson's hair isn't really red, anyway. Gillian Anderson being the actress who plays Special Agent Dana Scully on *The X-Files*, of course. I even emailed Lula a picture of Gillian Anderson outside of some premiere or something, and her natural color is almost exactly the same as Lula's. Maybe a shade lighter. But Lula said she probably dyed it that color so that she wouldn't get bothered on the street all the time by crazed Philes. Lula wanted Scully Red, so that's what she was getting.

"I think it's time." She kept poking at the cotton around her ears.

"Two more minutes." I checked my watch. *Tick, tick.* Come on. . . .

"Thanks for letting me do this over here, by the way," Lula said. "Janet would freak if I stained her white tiles."

"No sweat." My mother wouldn't notice if we painted the whole bathroom red. Lula managed to sit quietly on the folding stepstool for the next minute and a half. Finally, I took my watch off and helped her tilt her head back into the sink. I rinsed her hair until the water ran clear, added conditioner, rinsed that, finally squeezed the water out of the ends and blew it dry. I could tell right away she was happy. Her head was a bright cap of flame.

"Scully Red," I presented the mirror.

"Oh my gosh. It's perfect." She looked at the back with the hand mirror. "I'm so super hot now."

I laughed as I gathered the empty dye bottles and tossed them in the trash.

"Seriously. I'm really into myself with this hair. I'm the FBI's Most Wanted. What do you think? I'm the hotness, right?" She puckered and made a supermodel face at herself in the mirror.

"I think it's remotely plausible that someone might think you're hot," I said, quoting *The X-Files* in my best Mulder deadpan. But Lula didn't laugh. I tried John Keats. "Actually, you're dangerously hot. Try not to swoon to death while gazing upon your steadfast hotness." At this, Lula cracked a brief half-smile. She really was pretty, with or without the Scully hair. She had Janet's model cheekbones. Lula didn't think she was pretty, though. She thought she was too skinny, too flat-chested. And, worst of all, she had Leo's nose.

"Would you go straight for Scully?" Lula asked. She was still looking at herself in the mirror. "Like, what if, one boring afternoon at Andy's, you're restocking the *Harry Potters*, and in walks Gillian Anderson—"

"Why on earth would Gillian Anderson walk in to Andy's Books?"

"Because she's shooting a movie on location in Hawthorne. And she's super bored, because it's Hawthorne."

"Why wouldn't she just drive into Raleigh, where something interesting might actually happen?"

"Because . . . traffic is terrible! I-40 is backed up in both directions for miles. So, she's stuck in Hawthorne, and you charm her with your legendary no-foam cappuccino and your extensive knowledge of the Edith Wharton oeuvre."

"The Edith Wharton *oeuvre*?" I laughed.

"Yep. And next thing you know, Scully's all 'Ooh, Theodore. You're such a charming young man . . .'" Lula giggled.

"Wait, Gillian Anderson, or Scully?"

"Same difference," Lula waved her hand. "For the purposes of this argument. A hot redhead walks into a bookstore. Would you go straight for her? If you liked her and she was into you? Would you just say, what the hell, and go for it?"

"For starters," I asked, "why would some famous actress be interested in me? Never mind a fictional federal agent who clearly has a thing for her partner."

Lula sighed. "Don't be so literal, Rorysaurus. This is a theoretical discussion. Theoretically, some chick thinks you're the bee's knees. Would you do it?"

"I don't think—it doesn't really work that way," I told her. I don't see how anyone can just "go straight" for someone. You either are or you're not, in my opinion. And I don't really want to think those kinds of thoughts about Gillian Anderson. She's probably my favorite actress ever; she's in the movie version of my favorite non-sci-fi novel, *The House of Mirth*, by Edith Wharton, who is, next to Jane Austen, probably my favorite writer of all time. *The House of Mirth* is so tragic and beautiful, and the movie's great. I've made Andy watch it, like, twenty times. Gillian's so amazing in it. I cry every time I see it. But I can't picture myself going to bed with her. It's not like that for me.

"You mean even if some hot girl wanted to sleep with you, you think you'd be unable to, uh . . ."

"Lula, this is getting into kind of a weird area, here."

"Sorry, I know. TMI." Lula laughed. I turned on the faucet and began scrubbing the dye off my wrists. "I guess what I'm trying to ask you is, let's say somebody came into your life. Let's say this person was female. And you weren't looking for it, or expecting it, but you really hit it off with this person. You connected on a deep level. And even though you know that normally you wouldn't be attracted to this person, because, you know. She's female. Uh. You realize that it's a pretty small town and you haven't found anyone yet that you . . . that you would prefer. Who prefers you back. So maybe you start thinking that it wouldn't be such a bad idea. With this . . . with this girl."

I turned the faucet off. "Lula, are you trying to ask me to the prom?"

"You're totally not taking me seriously."

"This is serious? I thought it was theoretical." I scrubbed red dye off the faucet handles, ignoring the petulant look Lula was giving me. "Okay, my answer is, no, I probably would not sleep with your theoretical hot babe. Small town or no. Look, the way I see it, even if some hot girl was into me right now, we'll be in college soon, where I'm sure we'll both have four years of awkward encounters with drunken frat guys to look forward to. So, no, I don't need some awkward attempt at hetero sex just to temporarily satiate my . . . whatever."

"Gee, Rory, you really are a romantic." Lula rolled her eyes. I scrubbed at the red splotches in the sink. This whole conversation was making me nervous. I mean, why did Lula care if I'd sleep with some random woman? Was she suggesting that she and I should sleep together? Surely not—our whole friendship was the exact opposite of Mulder and Scully, in that respect. Not a single molecule of UST between us. Did she know about Andy, and she was taunting me or something? This whole relationship with him was getting way too stressful. Maybe it was time to come clean. Maybe tonight I'd ask Andy what he thought about just telling Lula. She wouldn't let it get around. She could even help, maybe. I could tell my mom I was staying at Lula's and spend weekends with Andy. Maybe even entire weeks.

"Anyway." She tucked her newly red hair behind her ears. "You wanna come over and see Janet and Leo make their shocked faces at me? We could work on the *Guide*. The Philes are getting antsy for Season Four. I had an idea for 'Small Potatoes.' Remember, the one with the tail babies? You know the end part where Eddie Van Blundht impersonates Mulder and goes over to Scully's house, and . . . hey, Rory?"

"What, yeah?" I looked up from my sink-scrubbing.

"Are you mad at me or something?" Her voice softened. "It's like you're totally zoning out."

"No, I heard you. You said you're quitting the FBI to become a spokesperson for the Ab Roller." Another *X-Files* quote. I was starting to feel bad. Distracting Lula with jokes.

"Ha ha," she said. "I'm serious. Am I, like, bugging you or something?"

"Bugging me? No," I told her. "I just have to do some . . . other stuff now. For my mom. So . . . maybe tomorrow." I strapped my watch back on, trying not to be too obvious, checking the time. I knew Andy was waiting for me. This was the hardest part of being with him. Making up stories. Lying to Lula. It was the only time I wished I was straight. Or at least dating someone my own age.

"Okay." Lula said, her mouth turned down. "Have fun doing other stuff."

Thankfully, my mother came home at that very moment, and Lula always got uncomfortable around her. She hated drinking. Lula, I mean. So she left without me having to make any more excuses. I waited until my mother retreated to her room with her tumbler full of Chardonnay, and I walked out into the cool spring afternoon, cutting through the woods until I got to Andy's back porch, hidden in the safety of the creeping dusk.

six

THIS WAS PROBABLY A MISTAKE. FOOTBALL tryouts. I mean, yeah, I was one of the biggest guys on the field. And I could run okay for a fat dude. I guess all that cardio at the gym paid off. But I didn't know any of the terminology the coaches kept barking out. I kept getting in the wrong group of people, going to the wrong side of the field, getting yelled at by the revered Coach Willard, whose legend loomed large in town but who turned out to be a rather peevish little man with a whistle and a fat gut that strained above his belted khaki Dockers. After a while, it became funny, and I wished I'd told Lula I was doing it, so she'd be there to watch. She'd be laughing her head off. The whole thing was so stupid macho, and probably the gayest thing I'd ever done in public. All the grunting, everybody's butt in the air. And all the drills had these super gay names like "The Man-Maker," "The Machine Gun," and "The Rodeo." But when it came time for the sled, where they had all us big guys put on pads and helmets and run like hell at this sort of foam dummy on wheels and slam into it as hard as we could, I actually did all right.

"Hey, you're getting the hang of it out there, man." Sexy Seth slapped me on the back as I attempted to simultaneously catch my breath and chug Gatorade.

"Thanks," I wheezed unsexily. "You work fast."

"Huh?"

"Telling Morris about me. He came up to me at the gym, like, right after I saw you."

"I didn't say anything to Coach Morris," Seth said, confused.

"Oh. I guess I thought . . ." *Hey, wanna see my new football move called The Backpedal?* Seth probably had no recollection of running into me at Walmart. And why would he? I felt myself blushing a million shades of red, and I hoped that if Seth noticed, he would just think I was dying of heatstroke.

"Oh yeah, 'cause of my mom." Seth smiled, or maybe he was just squinting in the sun. "I know, she kept bugging me to talk to you about trying out, after we saw you at the store. But I never did go to Morris, 'cause . . . I mean, it's not like I didn't think you could play. I didn't think you wanted to. I figured, you know. You're one of those . . . bookish guys."

"Bookish?" *Is that what the kids are calling it these days?*

"I just meant, like, you're Mr. Straight As. I always see you guys reading in the quad—you and your girlfriend . . . uh. Lois?"

"Lula." I didn't bother to correct him on the girlfriend part.

"Right. Lula. Sorry, man—I'm shit with names."

"Come on, ladies!" Coach Willard barked at us. "You gonna stand around and gossip like a buncha hens, or you gonna play some *got damn football*?!"

"I'm just saying," Seth shook his surfer hair out of his eyes and put his helmet on. "I know you take all those College

Prep classes and stuff. And being on the team kinda takes over your life. You gotta wake up early as hell, work out all the time, rain or shine. Practice before school and after. You think you got time for it?"

"Do you think I'm gonna make the cut?" We jogged out onto the field, side by side.

"Ain't up to me," Seth smiled. "But if it was, I'd say we could use a big guy like you if we're gonna make it to State next year."

Coach Morris blew his whistle and called me over for something called pass-blocking drills. The other guys groaned, but I had no idea what that meant, so I just put my sweaty helmet back on and got in the back of the line.

"Callahan, get over here," Morris commanded. "Briggs, you too. Ty, put that dummy up right on the line." A few yards behind us, another one of the assistant coaches, Tyver, set up this thing that looked like a stand-alone punching bag, or an inverted exclamation point. "Callahan, that dummy over there is Seth Brock, okay?"

"I can definitely see the resemblance."

Morris squinted up at me. "Now, remember that two-point stance I showed you earlier?" I nodded, dropping into a sort of lunge. "That's it. Just keep those shoulders back, elbows in. Yep, you got it. All right, now, Briggs here is gonna try to get at Brock, right there behind you. And you're not gonna let him. That's all you have to do. Briggs gets by you, hits that dummy, you lose."

I nodded. Speed Briggs—a large, gregarious black kid— was pretty much the only guy at Hawthorne who was bigger than me. He shook his head as he dropped into a crouch in front of me.

"Set!" Morris yelled.

"Nice knowin' ya, rookie," Briggs chuckled.

"Hut!"

Speed came at me. I stepped back, my heel sliding in the muddy turf. Speed bore down; I felt wet clay oozing into my left sneaker. I pictured the dummy behind me, pictured Seth shaking his hair out of his eyes. *Bookish.* Suddenly it was like some spring uncoiled in my legs. This weird roar came out of my throat and I lunged, shoving Briggs off me like he was an overeager puppy. It was like I couldn't see for a minute, and then I could, and Briggs was face down on the ground. Nobody said a word.

"Oh, shit, man," I knelt down. "Are you okay?"

Speed was laughing. He rolled over and held up his hand. I pulled him to his feet. He was still giggling, picking a clod of grassy mud out of his facemask.

"Hot *damn!*" Speed hollered, spitting dirt. "That boy's a *monster!*"

"Attaboy, Callahan!" Morris slapped me on the butt. "Back in line. Lytle, Torres, you're up next."

Lula would be having a total fit right now.

"YOU DID *WHAT?*" LULA WAS INCREDULOUS. We were out in the courtyard, eating lunch.

"I just tried out. It's no big deal."

"It's *Hawthorne Football*, Rory. It's the biggest deal in town."

"It's not that big a deal to me. One of the coaches goes to my gym. He asked me to come to the tryouts, so I did. I probably won't even make the team. I just did it as a joke."

"Then why didn't you tell me about it?"

"I'm telling you now." I couldn't believe she was so upset. "I thought you'd think it was funny."

"I think it goes against everything you stand for." Her mouth was turned down, and with the red hair, she did kind of look like Scully for a minute. "I don't see how you could participate, even as a joke, with those jock assholes."

"Lula, come on. I told you, it's no big deal."

"Those are the kind of guys who take guys like you out into the middle of nowhere and leave them tied to fence posts—"

"Nobody's tying me to anything, Lula, geez. I'm almost three hundred pounds."

"Whatever, Rory."

Now I knew she was upset. Lula hates it when people just say "whatever" and leave the rest of the conversation hanging.

"None of those guys has ever done anything to me. They don't even know I exist," I tried to assure her. Actually, that wasn't entirely true. A couple of those guys had told me to "Move it, lardass," in the hallway from time to time. And one guy last semester, a linebacker who was graduating, asked me to help him write history papers for Mr. Kinney's class, but that was because Mr. Kinney asked him to ask me.

We spent the rest of the lunch in relative silence. Except that I couldn't really eat, not when Lula was upset with me. So I tried to make amends. I told her that her hair looked really Scully-esque today. I told her that we should watch the entire Lord of the Rings trilogy again, since we hadn't done that in a while. I told her she could even fast-forward to all the Aragorn parts. That got a little smile out of her. The bell rang, and we got up, collecting our trash. She still didn't say a word.

Later, in Chemistry, she passed me a note.

> *Sorry I freaked out about the football thing. I just felt weird that you didn't tell me. And it seemed kind of out of character for you. But if you make the team, I'll be there to cheer you on. L.*

I passed her one back:

> *Thanks, but don't worry. I won't make the cut. I didn't do too well on the drill they call the "Man Maker." If only Sexy Seth & co knew . . .*

From the other end of the lab table, she unfolded the note and laughed. It got Mr. Miller's attention, so she turned the laugh into a cough and hooked her arm around the note, hiding it and making it look like she was studiously pondering the periodic table of elements, as if it was crucial information we were indeed going to use later, rather than just memorize for the test and promptly forget.

seven

"I WISH YOU WOULDN'T START AN argument with me right now."
Andy was practically in tears. I didn't know how the whole thing
got so out of hand so quickly. I'd come over for our usual after-
work movie. And he wanted to watch *Brokeback Mountain* again.
He had this total obsession about it, especially since Heath
Ledger, one of the actors in it, just died. But I didn't feel like
watching it, because I thought it was sad and kind of boring and
I didn't like westerns, anyway. So I said so. And now he was upset.

"I didn't mean to start an argument. I just feel like
watching something else, that's all."

"It's the way you said it."

"How did I say it?"

"You know how you said it."

"Andy." I sank down onto the sofa. "I said it like I always
say it. You're being way too sensitive."

"I'm being too sensitive? You know how I feel about this
movie. It's beautiful, and Heath's beautiful in it, and you
stand there and talk about it like I'm forcing you to watch a
marathon of *Judge Judy*."

"Good grief, Andy, put the movie in, let it roll. Forget I said anything!"

"No, not if you're going to be that way." He flipped the DVD down on the coffee table.

"I think you're the one who's trying to start an argument," I muttered.

"As many times as I've sat up watching those bodice-rippers you like—"

"*Bodice-rippers?*"

"And you have to act like a spoiled child. But then, why should that surprise me?" he sighed loudly. "Serves me right for dating an overgrown adolescent."

That was enough. I stood up.

"Andy, I don't sneak through the goddamn woods in the middle of the night to get the third degree over whether or not I'm in the mood to watch some fag cowboy movie."

I meant to just walk out and keep walking, but this strange thing happened. Andy was between me and the door, so I had to get around him to get out. As I came toward him, he flinched and took a step back.

"So, what, you're going to knock me around like they taught you at football tryouts?" Andy asked, sounding defiant and nervous all at once.

"Why would I—" I stopped, shaking my head. Andy honestly thought I was going to hit him or something? "Don't be ridiculous," I said, but it came out sounding meaner than I meant it. I wasn't that much taller than he was, but I was a lot heavier. A lot stronger, probably, since I'd been working out.

"So then why are you still here?" Andy asked, his voice a hard edge. "Why don't you run home to Mommy because you didn't get your way?"

I exhaled hard. My hands were trembling, sweating. Andy waited. I stared hard at him. I could see his muscles tense, the caution in his eyes.

"This is bullshit," I muttered finally. I walked past him, out the sliding glass door, back into the woods. I took a long time walking home. Thinking about what Speed had said. *That boy's a monster!* Sure, there were certain things that could get me really angry if I thought about them too long—my mom getting drunk all the time, the guys she brought home, my dad being totally AWOL, Aunt Judith always leaving on her trips, people being mean to Lula—but nothing Andy said or did ever made the list.

But there was all the insecure stuff that crept into my mind on all those nights just like this one, where I was sneaking back into my house after being with him, and the more I thought about it, the angrier I got. *An overgrown adolescent? Is that all he thinks I am? Is that why he won't commit to me? He's always pushing me away, pushing me to go to college, to meet other guys. Talking about how handsome other young guys are, trying to get me to agree. Would he rather have some other handsome young guy? Because I don't care about those guys. I don't want some young Heath Ledger-type. I want Andy. And he doesn't want me.*

When I got home, my heart was pounding. My hands were still shaking. I wanted to run or scream or something. I paced in the clearing, behind a stand of skinny pines. I drove my fist into one of them, landing the punch with a grunt. It

didn't make anything better. I stood at the edge of the woods
for a long time, flexing my bruised knuckles, looking across
the backyard at the soft yellow light coming through the
kitchen window. *I should stay out here*, I thought to myself. *In
the woods. In the shadows. This is where monsters live.*

JANET AND LEO WERE STILL UP, sitting in their matching
recliners in front of the flat-screen. *Guys and Dolls* on Turner
Classic Movies. I managed to get past them without having to
say much, and I made it up to Lula's room. The lights were
off. She was tucked in beneath her puffy white down comforter, watching a DVD of *X-Files* outtakes she'd downloaded
from the Internet.

"What's the matter with you?" she said before she even saw
that I'd been crying.

"I . . . had a fight. With my mom," I lied. I felt like my chest
was going to explode, I wanted to tell her so much. I wanted
to tell her what happened, I wanted her to help me figure it
out. How I let myself behave like a brute to the man I loved.

"Shit, kiddo. You're a mess. You wanna talk about it?"

"Yeah. But I can't." At least that much was true. I sniffled,
and she handed me a Kleenex from the box on her desk. I
sat down on the floor, honking my nose.

"Lula, do you think I'm a . . . like a bad guy, or something?"

"What'd you do, rob a bank?" She tsked at me. "Rory.
Don't be silly. You're the best guy," she said softly. "C'mon.
Wanna watch *X-Files* blooper reels?" I nodded. Lula cued up
the DVD. I looked up at her, her face illuminated by the TV.

"Can I get into bed with you?" I asked suddenly. I don't
know why I said it. I expected her to laugh at me, to brush

me off with one of her usual jokes. I was already backtracking in my mind. *I didn't mean it that way.* What way did I mean it, then? I just wanted to be close to somebody right then. Somebody who wasn't going to ask me not to feel how I felt. Sometimes I wished it could be as easy with Andy as it was with Lula. On the other hand, now Lula was looking at me with this look of . . . what, exactly? Was she totally weirded out that I asked to climb into bed with her? I couldn't exactly blame her. The list of people who wanted to get into bed with me, for sleeping purposes or otherwise, was pretty damn short, even when I wasn't crying like a big baby.

"Rory, I—" It was like she was about to say no, but then she stopped. "Yeah. Of course. Come here."

Lula pulled back the comforter, and I climbed into bed with her. She curled up in my arms, and I cried quietly into her hair. She brushed my cheeks dry with the backs of her hands. And the TV flickered blue as Gillian Anderson flubbed her lines, David Duchovny dropped his gun, and the slate clapped and clapped and clapped again against the laughter while somebody's wary voice off-screen ordered: *Everybody, back to one.*

I WAS LATE TO WORK THE next day, not because I dreaded seeing Andy, but because Coach Morris called me into in his office. They thought that, with my size and my speed, I was a natural-born football machine, and they wanted to train me to be an offensive lineman. They wanted to entrust me with the extremely important job of keeping Sexy Seth from being sacked, whatever that meant. Coach Morris said I'd need to really buckle down and make a commitment, but that if I did, I might get some actual time on the playing field, because most of the current offensive linemen were graduating this year. I could maybe even get a college scholarship for this. But I would really have to dig in and learn the game. Devote my life to two-a-days. Play catch-up to guys who'd been playing this game since they could walk. This whole discussion was so ridiculously super-serious, you'd think he was telling me that I was Kal-El, last surviving member of the planet Krypton, and now I had to use my superpowers to save Planet Earth. I told him I had a lot going on and I would have to think about it.

"Well, it's certainly something to think about," Coach Morris said, leveling his gaze at me. "For your future." *Sorry, I'm Morris*, I thought, trying not to laugh. As if this guy knew anything about my future.

"I was afraid you wouldn't come in today," Andy said when we were finally alone in the shop. There had actually been some business that afternoon, so we spent the first hour avoiding each other, him at the register and the coffee bar, me busying myself in the back, unpacking boxes.

"I had to stay after at school. I should've called," I said, popping open a fresh box of paperback *Harry Potters*. It was hard to make eye contact with him. I still felt a dull ache in my chest, still angry at myself and at him, and not sure if I wanted to let him back in yet or not.

"No, it's fine." Andy took off his glasses and rubbed the little divots that they left in his nose. "Look, I really need to apologize about last night. You were right, I was being too sensitive. I was upset, and I should've talked to you instead of taking it out on you. My wife just told me yesterday that she's marrying some ski instructor from Utah, of all places, and she's taking the girls out there with her. I should have been more forthcoming with you, and I'm sorry."

"That's okay," I said softly. "I was a jerk, too. I'm sorry I lost my temper. And I'm sorry about your kids."

"Yeah, it's—" But he didn't finish. He was getting choked up. I pulled him into an embrace. Felt him exhale against my chest.

"I just didn't realize how much I love them," he said, his voice muffled.

"They're your kids," I said. "Of course you love them. You're a good dad. Now you just have to fly to Utah a lot, I guess."

"I know. You're right. I guess I'm going to start racking up the frequent flyer miles, huh?"

I tried to laugh, but, honestly, it was kind of a bummer to think about. How often were we talking here? Monthly? Every two weeks? How long would he stay out there?

Andy took a deep breath. Separated himself from me and wiped his face on his shirttail.

"All right, enough. We can make this Utah thing work. Cindy and me. What's done is done." He waved it off and looked up at me with a coy smile. "In the meantime, why don't you come over tonight and let me make it up to you?"

"Um. Okay."

The cowbell on the front door clanked.

"That's a customer," Andy said, skittish as usual. He pushed the stockroom door open and was gone back out into the store before I could say anything else. I set the *Harry Potters* on the restock cart and just stood there, listening to Andy and the customer, the customer ordering an Americano, Andy ringing him up, the bell clanking again. I ambled out, pushing the cart in front of me.

"Can I ask you something?"

"Shoot," Andy said. He was counting bills in the register.

"What made you marry her in the first place?"

"Cindy?" He didn't look up from his counting.

"Yeah. I mean, did you do it just to cover up that you were gay? Or did you really have feelings for her?"

"I loved her. I thought I did, anyway."

"But it just . . . went away?"

"Not all of a sudden." Andy stopped counting. "It wasn't like I woke up one day and had this revelation. It was more like . . . all these little attractions I had to other men . . . finally I realized that I couldn't ignore it anymore, and if I really loved Cindy, and myself, for both our sakes, I'd leave her so that we could both . . . so we could both be more complete. So I could figure out who I was and let her be free to marry someone else." His face turned pained again. "I guess I didn't think she'd actually go and do it."

"What do we have in common?" I asked him.

"What?" Andy closed the register. "You and me?"

"No. Me and Cindy. I mean, how did you fall in love with both of us?"

He didn't answer. He smiled and touched my arm, the slightest touch as he walked past me, back to the stockroom to get more small bills, and I felt my heart warm toward him again.

"I CAN'T BELIEVE IT. RORY. I cannot believe you're actually *fucking* your *boss*."

"Shh, Lula, damn!" She was waiting on my porch, in the dark, when I got back from Andy's. Between us fighting last night and the Coach Morris thing this afternoon and Andy wanting to make it up to me, I'd completely forgotten that Lula and I were supposed to meet up at my house to study for Mrs. Lidell's midterm. I retraced my steps in my head. I'd come home after work to drop off my stuff and shower, and I went over to Andy's instead. Lula must have just gotten here, she must have seen me cutting through the woods and followed me. And now she was back here, waiting. I fumbled with my house keys, dropping them somewhere in the dark near my shoe.

"You don't know what you're talking about," I insisted. Hoping my mother was passed out in her room upstairs, or else still out with the guys from work, somewhere out of earshot of Lula, who was shouting loud enough to wake up the whole street.

"I'll tell you what I'm talking about! I'm talking about you and that creep Andy Barnett—"

"First of all, could you please lower your voice?" I was on my hands and knees now, feeling around for my keys. *Why didn't I leave the damn porch light on?* "Whatever you saw, it's not what you think—"

"Okay, then, if I didn't see what I'm pretty sure I saw, then what the hell *did* I see? Because it looked a lot like you and Andy taking each other's clothes off and—"

"Dammit, Lula, shut up! Just shut the hell up!" I stood up, keys in hand. "It's none of your business!" My heart was going about five thousand beats a second. I kind of thought that maybe I could still convince her that she hadn't seen what she probably saw. But part of me was so tired of lying, all I wanted was to stop. I looked down at her. Lula's eyes were dark and swollen. Like she'd been crying for hours. I'd never seen Lula cry before. Not once.

"How can you say that it's none of my business?" she asked quietly. "How can you possibly say that to *me*?"

"Well, how . . . how could you follow me?"

"Because I was worried about you! I saw you running into the woods like a bat out of hell and I thought—I don't know what I thought! I thought something was wrong, I thought you needed help! Your mom's for shit, Rory. Who else is gonna back you up?"

"I don't need you to back me up. Did it ever occur to you that I have a private life? That I don't want you . . . *watching* me? Quit playing Mulder and Scully for five minutes, okay? Fuck off and leave me alone!" I jammed my key into the lock. Even in the dark, without seeing Lula's face, I knew I'd gone too far.

"Your *private life*?" Lula's voice trembled. "What the hell is that supposed to mean? I thought we didn't keep secrets! I thought we—I thought I knew everything about you!"

"I couldn't tell you," I tried to explain. I took a deep breath, trying to steady myself. The front door crept open, just an inch. I wanted to run inside and close the door on her and pretend that none of this was happening. But I stayed on the porch. "I wanted to, I wanted to tell you so many times, but he's afraid he'll get in trouble. If somebody got the wrong idea, he could be arrested—"

"Maybe he should be! Isn't he, like, in his *forties*? His *late* forties? He's old enough to be your *dad*."

"Lula, swear to me, please, swear you won't say a word to anybody." I turned to her, fully begging now. My chest was a mad flutter, all panic. I was so much bigger than Lula, but now I felt like a little kid.

"Are you serious? I saw him. Rory, this guy's *molesting* you—" she hissed.

"He's not, Lula, please, I'm begging you, he's not hurting me. I don't know what you saw or what it looked like to you, but I love him. I love him more than I've ever loved anybody. Please, please, you have to understand."

"You actually . . . you *love* that guy?" Lula sounded incredulous.

"Yes. I love him. And he loves me, too."

"And he loves you, too," she echoed, her voice even quieter now. "So, football tryouts. Romancing the boss. What else you got up your sleeve, Theodore? While we're having this little heart-to-heart."

"You know everything now," I told her, feeling the blood drain from my face as I leaned against the doorjamb. "No more secrets."

"I knew something was up with you. But I had no idea . . . I mean, I actually thought . . ." Lula exhaled, blinking her eyes like she was trying not to cry. She tucked her red hair behind her ears. "I thought that if we couldn't be . . . I thought at least we were in this thing together, Rory."

"What thing?"

"This . . . being alone." Her voice was barely above a whisper.

"Lula—"

"But I get it now. Okay? So, forget it." She gave me a funny smile. Her eyes were full of tears. "Just forget I was ever here."

She turned and walked down the two porch steps to the mailbox where her bike was leaning. I watched her kick the kickstand up, but she didn't ride away. She walked the bike slowly down the street. I could've caught up with her if I'd wanted to. When she thought I was in trouble, she came running after me. I should have gone after her. But instead I just stood there, watching her pass beneath the wan streetlamp, watching until she turned the corner, out of sight.

eight

THE NEXT MORNING, FRIDAY, IT HAPPENED just like my fantasy. Second period Algebra II. Except it was the vice principal. She pulled Mrs. Havens, our teacher, out into the hall, and I could see them looking at me as they whispered.

"Rory," Mrs. Havens waved me over. "Get your books."

My heart had already started to pound. And then I saw the goateed guy with his sleeves rolled up and the gun at his hip.

"Theodore Callahan?" the vice principal asked.

"Yes?" I felt dizzy. I kept staring at the guy's gun.

"This is Detective Addison from the police department. He'd like to ask you some questions about your friend Tallulah Monroe."

That big slamming noise that made everybody in the class stand up was all 280 pounds of me hitting the hallway when I fainted.

"AM I A SUSPECT?"

"We're just trying to piece together a timeline," Detective Addison answered without answering. There was something about him I didn't like, and I realized that it was because he reminded me of Krycek, the double agent on *The X-Files*. I sat back. My chair squeaked. I was sitting at the table in the faculty conference room with an icepack on the side of my head where I had hit the ground. The principal and vice principal were there, along with my mom, sitting on one side of me, and, sitting on the other side, Mrs. Lidell. Addison held a gold pen in his hand, tapping it against his fingers.

"When was the last time you saw your friend Tallulah, son?"

"Last night. Around ten or so. Maybe ten thirty."

"Ten p.m.?"

"Yeah. She came over . . ." I hesitated. I didn't want to say anything about Andy. My head was killing me, and I felt nauseated. "We were supposed to study for midterms. But I forgot. I was—I stayed late at work. To help with inventory."

"Where do you work?"

"Andy's Books & Coffee."

"Can your boss corroborate your story?"

Corroborate my story? Jesus.

"Yes." I licked my lips. My mouth was dry. "Yes, sir."

"How long did she stay at your house that night?"

"Not long. Like five minutes, maybe ten. She was . . . upset that I forgot." My voice broke. Mrs. Lidell reached over and took my hand.

"You and Miss Monroe argued?" Addison asked.

"Yes, sir. But it didn't seem like . . . anything serious."

"Mrs. Callahan, were you at home when this fight was going on?"

"I was—ahm," my mother cleared her throat. "I was out with some colleagues from work."

"You're acquainted with Tallulah Monroe?"

"She's been over to the house before. She seemed like a sweet girl. And Teddy's not the type that would do anything—he wouldn't have done anything to hurt her. I know he's a big guy, but he's a sweetheart, he really is." She was bleary as usual, but at least she stood up for me. I looked at my mom for some sign of how she really felt. Was she angry with me? Did she think this whole thing was all a big joke? Impossible to tell. Her face was blank.

Addison looked at my mother, then back at me.

"Son, what was the exact nature of your relationship with Tallulah Monroe?"

"She's my best friend."

Addison clicked his pen.

"Theodore, was your relationship with Tallulah Monroe one of a sexual nature?"

"No, sir." My face was burning. Mrs. Lidell squeezed my hand.

"I know it might be embarrassing. There might have been things going on between you and Miss Monroe that you don't want to talk about in front of your mother. But we need you to tell us everything about the relationship you and Tallulah had. Because anything you remember, any little detail, no matter how small, might help us to bring her home safe."

"Yes, sir," I nodded.

"Now, she told her grandparents she was leaving to go to your house at around eight p.m. You say you didn't see her until between ten and ten thirty. Any idea where she might have gone in the interim?"

"No, sir."

"And did she say she was going somewhere else, after she left your house?"

"No, sir."

"Did you make plans to reschedule the study session you'd missed?"

"No, sir."

"Was there another boy she was close to, or someone she might have gone off with to make you mad? To get revenge for standing her up?"

Revenge.

"No, sir. Not that I know of."

"Did she have any other . . . any girlfriends? Anyone she might have gone to spend the night with?"

"She used to hang out with Jenny . . . um. Jenny Walsh. But she goes to boarding school now. I think it's in Vermont or someplace."

Addison nodded. He paced back and forth.

"So you can't think of any other place she might have gone, any other person in this whole town she could be with?"

"Her mother."

"What?"

"Her mother. She might have gone to find her mom."

nine

LEO PACED THE KITCHEN, CHAIN-SMOKING LUCKY Strikes.

"God*damn* it." The veins on his neck were popping out. "I flew a helicopter off the goddamn roof of the embassy in Saigon, and this pathetic excuse for a police force expects me to sit around on my ass and wait for a *goddamned telephone call.*"

"Leo, honey, remember what Dr. Patel said about your blood pressure."

"Janet—" he started, and stopped. It was the first time I'd witnessed one of Leo's nuclear moods, and it was a little scary. "At least her mother had the decency to write us a letter," he growled. "At least we knew she hadn't been kidnapped in the middle of the night by a bunch of goddamned Hell's Angels."

I sat there at the white-and-silver Formica kitchen table. I sat there staring at the backpack. The one that had belonged to Lula's mom. The one the police had just turned up at a truck stop four miles from the house. The thing that made Leo so pissed was that they weren't even looking for it. A lady cop had gone in to use the bathroom while they were searching the woods, and it was sitting there in one of the stalls. When she looked inside it for ID, she saw that one of the books was marked with a ripped-off piece of Lula's class schedule.

There was no sign of foul play. But Lula hadn't left a note. Her bike was still in the garage—if she'd left on her own, she left on foot. She left her cell phone, too. The police tried to search the Flying J security tapes, but there had been some mix-up, and the tape from the night that Lula had gone missing had already been taped over. Leo fumed endlessly about why their ass-backward security system wasn't updated to digital. The clerks at the Flying J couldn't remember seeing anyone who looked like Lula, even though the cops did a special computer rendering of her last school picture, to update her blond hair to red. Detective Addison took her computer, to search all her files and see if she was meeting some Internet creep. There was a duffel bag missing, and some clothes. The bedroom window was locked. They were assuming that she was a runaway, but they weren't completely ruling out the possibility of abduction.

Abduction. Jesus.

I SPENT ALL DAY SATURDAY AND Sunday with Janet and Leo, printing missing posters on Leo's computer and putting them up everywhere we could. Leo and I went on long, tense, quiet rides out to neighboring towns, while Janet stuck to Hawthorne, walking the subdivisions, papering every lamp-post. My mother even tried to help in her way. She got up early and went out to Bojangles' for bacon, egg, and cheese biscuits that I tried to eat but couldn't swallow. She called coworkers at her company's other branches in Denver, Indianapolis, and Houston, and asked them if she could email them some missing flyers to print out and pass around. I couldn't see Lula ending up in Indianapolis or Houston, but it was nice of my mom to try. On Saturday night, I went home and waited for Lula to email or call, but she never did. On Sunday night, after another day of driving, I went back to Janet and Leo's.

"I know you guys are probably tired of me. But Mrs. Lidell's midterm is tomorrow," I explained to Janet, standing on the doorstep. I hadn't cracked a book all weekend. "Would it be okay if I . . . stayed in Lula's room tonight to study?"

"Sweetheart, we could never get tired of you. Come on inside—you look famished."

After dinner, Janet and Leo sat in their recliners, the TV turned to a Hitchcock movie on TCM, the volume low, their phones in their laps. I went up to Lula's room. I sat on her bed and looked around. There was a faint, dustless outline on her desk from where the computer used to be. Above her desk, in a place of honor, was Lula's latest acquisition from her favorite movie memorabilia website: the teaser poster for the new *X-Files* movie. The poster showed Mulder and Scully walking away from each other, toward a bright light. But, even though they were walking away from each other, the light made their long shadows cross the page, forming an X. It was reassuring somehow to know that, whatever terrifying alien mysteries might conspire to tear our heroes apart in this upcoming chapter of their adventures, at least their shadows remained connected. I wondered how far away Lula was from me now. I wondered if she could feel any connection still, if she could feel how much I wanted her back here with me.

Janet had put Lula's mom's backpack in its usual place on the shelf. I took it down and emptied the contents. The Laura Nyro tape was missing, but the picture of Lula's mom was still there. So was the scarf, the postcard from California, and the books. Lula's sacred texts.

I felt the weight of the three books in my hands. I laid them out on the bed in a straight line, as if placing them there might somehow conjure her back. Faintly, from outside, I could hear crickets and tree frogs. It was too quiet in this room without Lula. I looked up at the row of DVDs on Lula's bookshelf. Some of the spines bore orange stickers with the word USED stamped in black; those were the ones she'd bought secondhand from the Suncoast Video at the mall. I remembered the day Lula asked Janet to drive us there so she could buy *X-Files* Season One. She wasn't working as a caddy back then, but Janet and Leo gave her a bigger allowance than my mom gave me. *Just because I'm buying these with my money,* she'd explained, *doesn't mean they're mine. They're ours. It's our show.* I opened the DVD player under Lula's TV. The last Season Three disc we'd been watching was still in there. I took it out and put it away. Season Four was too dark, too sad . . . I skipped ahead, took out a disc from Season Five and slid it into the DVD player. I turned the TV on and turned the volume down until it was just loud enough to drown out all this quiet.

I spread out my notes from Mrs. Lidell's class, my highlighted books. But I couldn't concentrate. I was reading the same sentence over and over again without seeing it. I closed my notebook and reached for Lula's books. *Okay, Lula, where do I start?* I waited for some Ouija board-like guidance. Nothing came. There could be clues in any or all three of these. Some passage, some perfect arrangement of words that would make this make sense. I started with the Stanislavski. *An Actor Prepares.* It was full of highlights and underlines, fuzzy pen lines bleeding into the text. These were probably Christine's underlines, not Lula's. But it didn't matter. I flipped to a random page. *When you cannot believe in the larger action you must reduce it to smaller and smaller proportions until you can believe in it.* Okay, this was useful. I couldn't—wouldn't—believe that Lula was gone, maybe forever. Forever did not compute. Forever washed over me like a giant wave, destroying my balance, my sense of direction, leaving me nowhere. Letting myself believe that something bad had happened, that I wouldn't see her again, felt like falling into a deep, dizzy black hole. *Lula isn't going to be in school tomorrow,* I told myself. That wasn't exactly a comforting thought, but at least it was easier to digest. Like maybe she was off visiting a sick relative and she'd be back by the end of the week. It was false hope, maybe, but it was better than thinking I might never see her again.

I opened up the Liv Ullmann book and saw an underlined passage. Again, I didn't know if Lula had underlined it, or her mom: *All the time I am trying to change myself. For I do know that there is much more than the things I have been near.* I read for a while, then I moved over to the book of Shepard plays. Found more underlining. From the character Lula stole her name from, Blue Morphan: *Gotta make plans. Figure out yer*

moves. Make sure they're yer own moves and not someone else's. I
closed the book. *Okay, Lula. Are you out there, anywhere? Trying
to change yourself, looking for more than what's here? Are you
making your own moves? Are you running away, running to your
mom? Or did somebody take you against your will? You'd never let
that happen, would you?* I sat quietly, listening, waiting for
some epiphany, some certainty, but there was nothing. The
low murmur of Mulder and Scully, preoccupied with their
own mysteries, looking for their own truth.

I wasn't a big fan of cowboy-and-Indian western stuff, and
all those Swedish movies we watched bored me out of my
skull. But now, as I climbed into Lula's bed with her books in
my hands, I felt almost feverish with the certainty that they
would give me the clues I needed. The clues to figure out the
moves Lula had made that had taken her away. By the blue
light of the TV, I opened the books and started to read.

I STAYED UP ALL NIGHT, READING Lula's books while our show
played in the background. I pretty much forgot about Mrs.
Lidell's midterm exam. Now I sat there in her classroom, my
eyes burning, the coffee I'd gulped before class doing
nothing besides making me feel like I was either going to fly
off into space or puke. I had Lula's *An Actor Prepares* tucked
into my inside jacket pocket, poking gently into my ribs. I
scribbled through the short-answer part of the test, faking
my way through the finer points of *The Sound and The Fury*,
Hamlet, and "A Good Man is Hard to Find." But all that was
going through my head was Liv Ullmann's Norwegian winter.
Cowboy mind-control and Cajun beasts. The unbroken line,
an actor presenting the truth on a stage. Mulder and Scully,

adrift with no one to trust but each other. And Lula was
going through my mind. Lula, laughing, throwing her book
across the lawn. Lula, dyeing her hair Scully red. Lula
holding me beneath her comforter.

I was failing this test. I turned to the last page. The essay
questions. Make that question, singular. There was only one
of them. *Great*, I thought. It'd probably count for half the
midterm grade.

> *Choose one character from the literature we've discussed in class
> or from the independent reading list. Discuss how that character's
> inability or refusal to act drives the narrative. How does this lack
> of action influence the other characters in the story or play? How
> does action inform what we know about the character? Keep in
> mind the themes and narrative devices we've discussed throughout
> the year—the hero's quest, deus ex machina, etc. Your essay
> should be at least five paragraphs in length. Beginning, middle,
> end—you know the drill.*

I opened the blue book and folded back the cover. And
then I put my head down on my desk. I was going to fail Mrs.
Lidell's midterm. I looked up. She looked back at me and
gave me a sympathetic smile. I didn't want to disappoint her.
I didn't want to disappoint Lula. I knew that sounded crazy.
Lula wasn't even there, let alone reading my stupid midterm
essay. But I knew this was it—my big chance to prove myself,
to prove that I was true to her, that I'd read her books and
that I understood.

Still, I felt like I was gasping for air. I put my head back
down. I knew I had to pull something coherent out of the
muddle in my mind. *This should be obvious. Write about Hamlet.
There's a guy who's paralyzed by self-doubt. Easy enough. Or how*

'bout Sound and the Fury? *The brother . . . or, um . . . the other brother.* But it had all evaporated right out of my brain. None of the books I'd stayed up all night reading were on the independent reading list. Could I get away with a five-paragraph essay about Blue Morphan, and his choice to free the people of Nogoland? Was Liv Ullmann on a hero's quest? All I could think was *Lula. Lula, damn you. Why did you leave? Why aren't you sitting here next to me right now? Kicking my chair, trying to make me laugh? Lula, I can't do this without you.*

All of a sudden this completely trivial thought popped into my head. *Lula, our Incomplete Guide to* The X-Files *is going to remain incomplete.* I could never finish it alone. Tears pricked my eyes—oh, no. I couldn't start crying, not during Mrs. Lidell's midterm. I squeezed my eyes shut. Was I hallucinating? Maybe it was the coffee, maybe the lack of sleep, but I could've sworn I heard Lula's voice right then. Like she was right next to me, whispering in my ear. *Good gravy, Theodore. Pull it together, kid.*

I sat up. I smoothed out the page. I clicked my pen, and I started to write.

Faith and a Sense of Truth

It just popped into my head. It was one of the chapter titles from the Stanislavski book. Pretty soon, the rest of the words came tumbling out of me, as fast as my shaky hand could write them.

"WE NEED TO TALK."

"Yeah," was all I could say. I was exhausted, and Andy had been acting skittish, avoiding me in front of the customers even more than usual. Now that we were alone, Andy lowered his voice, even though it was just the two of us behind the counter.

"Look, I'm sorry your friend ran away, but I can't have this."

"Can't have what?" I asked.

"The police were over here. Questioning me about you. About you working late on Thursday night."

"I didn't tell them anything. I mean, I didn't tell them about us. "

"Rory, I think—" He swallowed hard. "Rory, I think you should leave. I'll send you your paycheck."

"Wait a minute—"

"I just can't have this right now. This . . . attention. If they knew about you and me . . . you know they wouldn't understand. I could lose the shop, my kids—everything."

"Andy." This wasn't sinking in. Was he saying what I thought he was saying? "Are you firing me or breaking up with me?" He wouldn't meet my eye.

"You have to see where I'm coming from on this."

"But I thought—" I looked at him. His face was stern. Expressionless. "I thought you loved me."

"Rory." He sighed. "Look, you're a great guy, and you're a lot of fun in bed. And I do—I care about you, I really do, I like you a lot. But this is getting way too heavy for me. Look, we've talked about this before—you think you want a long-term, serious relationship, and you're still just a kid. I just got out of a marriage. I'm not ready to take on all this . . . baggage and drama. It's not where I am in my life right now. And now, with the police and everything, it's just too much for me. I'm sorry it didn't work out, and I hope your friend comes home, but right now I really need you to go."

"You need me to go," I echoed. I nodded slowly. "My best friend just disappeared, and you need me to go."

"Rory—"

"Huh. All this time, I thought you were the grown-up in this relationship." I felt a tight, rough-edged knot at the back of my throat, like a little rock made out of anger and sadness and fatigue. I swallowed, but it stayed stuck there. "Andy. You never did love me, did you?"

"I didn't say that. It's just bad timing. I'm not good for you right now, and you're not good for me. And I'm sorry, sweetie. I really am sorry about your friend—" Andy put his arm on my shoulder. I shrugged him away.

"I'm not your sweetie," I said. "I'm your employee. That's all. And I quit. Effective immediately." I grabbed my book bag and walked out, the bell clanking dully behind me. Exit What's His Name, stage left.

I LOOKED UP COACH MORRIS'S NUMBER in the phone book, and dialed him at home. A little kid answered. I asked her to put her dad on the phone.

"Coach Morris?"

"Yeah?"

"This is Ro—. This is Theodore Callahan."

"What can I do for you, son?" His voice was clipped. "It's late."

"I know. I just wanted to say that if you still want me on the team, I want to play. I'll do the summer practices and everything."

"All right. Come by my office tomorrow and we'll get you started."

"Yes, sir."

"Son, I'm sorry about your girlfriend."

I wanted to say: *She's not my girlfriend. I'm an unrepentant queer and a former nice guy who really wants to shove some guys' faces into the mud all of a sudden. But thanks for the sentiment.* Instead I just said, "So am I." And then I hung up. Wishing all these assholes would stop calling me *son*.

ten

Mrs. Lidell asked me to see her in her office the next afternoon. She came in from outside smelling like tobacco. I knew what this was about.

"Rory, you're an excellent writer." She sat down at her desk and started in right away. "But I don't know what to make of this." She held up the two blue books I'd ended up using to write my midterm essay. I nodded.

"I know." I was kind of expecting this.

"I'm sure there are some places where an in-depth analysis of the platonic bond between Mulder and Scully will go a long way. But this class is not an AOL message board from 1997. And your midterm exam isn't the place to wax rhapsodic about old episodes of *The X-Files*."

"I fulfilled the assignment, didn't I?"

"Rory." I thought she was going to give me one of those looks and keep lecturing me about how I was supposed to be writing about literature. But instead, she looked away, blinking. Was Mrs. Lidell starting to cry?

"I know you're upset about Lula. I'm upset, too. But I

don't know how to grade this. I'm going to give you another chance. If you can stay late tomorrow and rewrite this essay, I'm willing to throw this out. But if I start letting students get away with writing midterm essays on television shows . . . you see where I'm coming from, right?"

"Yes, ma'am."

"You can retake this tomorrow?"

"Yes, ma'am."

"Here." She handed me the blue books.

"What for?"

"Save those for when Lula comes home. I'm sure she'd like to read them."

I STAYED LATE THE NEXT DAY and wrote what I knew was a passing essay for Mrs. Lidell. Afterward, as I was walking across the parking lot, I heard someone call my name from far off, and for a weird second, I thought it was Lula. But it wasn't even a girl. It was Sexy Seth.

"Hey," I called back. He was walking toward the school from his pickup truck, big headphones hanging around his neck, a raggedy one-subject notebook in his hand. The notebook had the word STUDY! written on the bright yellow cover in heavy black marker. He had on a black T-shirt with another random saying. This one announced, in big white letters: BOSTON SPACESHIPS IS REAL!

"You in for this SAT Prep thing?"

"Me? No, I was just . . . rewriting a midterm essay. For Mrs. Lidell."

"Oh, shit, man. I'm supposed to have her next year. I heard she's impossible."

"Nah, she's possible. I just goofed it up, is all."

"Dude!" Seth slapped me on the arm with his notebook. "I heard you're on the team! Right *on*, man!"

"Yeah, I—" My voice hung up. It was the weirdest thing. The way Seth said "Right on, man," drawing out the "on." Lula used to say that all the time. Probably imitating Trey the Burnout Yard Guy, but I thought of it as a Lula Saying. It took me a second to remember what Seth was talking about. Oh yeah, football. "I guess I am. On the team."

"Coach Morris was freaking out. He says you're a football progeny. He couldn't believe you never played before."

Progeny? I started to ask, but there was a weird lump in my throat.

"Man, it's gonna be righteous," Seth went on. "Friday nights, five thousand people all going apeshit in the bleachers. Talk about a rush. We are gonna have a serious GT, I promise." Seth gave me his sexiest of Sexy Seth grins.

"A GT?"

"A *good time*," he drawled happily. "Hey, listen, though. Seriously, uh. I wanted to say sorry. About your girl Lula. I heard about her. Going missing and all. I know what that's like, man. I lost my brother. He passed on, a few years ago. I know it's tough."

"Lula didn't *pass on*," I said. "She's just missing. She'll be back."

"I hope she will, brother." Seth gave me one of his squinty, serious smiles. Like he's George Clooney or Sawyer from *Lost* or some shit. Like he's Mr. Charm and he feels so sorry for the rest of us because we aren't him. "I truly hope she will."

"Seth." I threw open the driver's side door to the Beast, which gave a horrific rusty metal squeal. "I'm not your brother. The word you're looking for is prodigy, not progeny. And your T-shirt is grammatically incorrect."

I got in the car, slammed the door, and drove away. In the rearview mirror, I could see Seth, just standing there in the parking lot with his stupid notebook that said STUDY! One hand in his pocket, his floppy hair in the breeze. I didn't have to be so mean. Seth was trying to be nice. At least he remembered Lula's name. But I didn't want to be nice. I wanted somebody to blame. I didn't care who. If this really was *The X-Files*, this would be the part where I turned into Action Mulder, and I put on my bulletproof vest and went after Duane Barry or Krycek or the Cigarette-Smoking Man. But I wasn't Mulder, and there was nobody I could beat up and threaten to bring Lula back. Putting a masking-tape X on my window wasn't going to lure any secret operatives to my house to give me clues in the middle of the night. I didn't have any Lone Gunmen to help me uncover any secrets. Maybe there weren't any secrets to uncover. Lula was gone. Just gone. And whoever had taken her was gone, too. Or she was gone by herself. Because she didn't want to be around anymore. And if that was the case, I was useless. I had been useless from the start. Or, worse than useless, I was the monster Speed Briggs said I was. The liar, the deceiver, the damage. I had this thing inside of me that she was right to run from. This black fear, this anger I couldn't keep down. I thought about the things I said to her that last night, and it made me sick inside. Lula was right. We were supposed to be in this together. I should have told her about Andy. I should have trusted her, above anyone and everyone else. But I failed. And now there was nothing I could do but sit around and wait for her to come home.

THOSE FIRST FEW DAYS HAD BEEN little marathons, dividing up the town with Janet and Leo, taping up MISSING flyers in every shop window that would let us. At home, it seemed like the phone was always ringing, or about to ring. Then it wasn't. Almost two weeks had passed since Lula disappeared, and there was still nothing I could do but wait. There was no job to go to after school. No Friday nights watching *X-Files* with Lula. I finished my homework early and studied football strategies. I stayed home and had uncomfortably quiet dinners with my mom. I stopped going to the gym—Andy had probably dropped my membership, anyway. The school gym was uncomfortable, the older guys on the team either making halfhearted attempts at hazing me or acting all sympathetic about Lula when we both knew that, two weeks ago, they would've been calling her Weird Girl just like everybody else. I built homemade weights and worked out in the garage. Whenever I left the house, I saw the flyers Janet had posted on telephone poles, Lula's picture getting faded and tattered from the rain. I went for long runs, looping past the woods that the police had combed again and again when Lula first went missing. I kept thinking how stupid that was. Lula hated the woods. She hated camping. Then I realized they weren't expecting to find her *living* in the woods.

I knew Lula wasn't dead, though. I didn't have any proof, but I was becoming more and more convinced that if something bad had happened to her, I would've felt it in my bones, like a disturbance in the Force. I went to Janet and

Leo's almost every night, to check up on them. Leo smoked too much and studied maps and bus routes and talked about getting in touch with some of his buddies in army recon. Despite the endless stream of casseroles and Crock-Pot dishes brought over by friends and neighbors, Janet cooked massive amounts of Polish food and sent the leftovers home with me. Dark gray roots showed in her brassy blond hair. Her white lipstick was often smudged and she took up smoking again. She kept a box of Benson & Hedges in the back of the silverware drawer and taught me how to mix Manhattans. They would answer the door by saying, "No word yet," and I never knew if they were asking me or telling me.

I stayed up nights, thinking about Lula. Laughing at things she'd said months ago. Her impression of Mrs. Dalrymple, the librarian. The way she'd put down this smartass senior in the cafeteria one day. I became obsessed with the late-night radio show on the community college's station, the one Lula used to listen to, hosted by a guy named Midnight Steve. I called Midnight Steve every night to request Lula's favorite songs, the ones she'd burned for me once on a mix CD. I requested "Teenage FBI" by Guided by Voices and "This is Hell" by Elvis Costello. I requested "Walking After You" by the Foo Fighters. I requested "Man of Steel" and "The Marsist" by Frank Black. I requested "Love is Nothing" and "Fantasize" by Liz Phair. I requested "View of the Rain" by Urge Overkill and "Do You Love Me Now?" by the Breeders. I requested Laura Nyro. Midnight Steve never had any of the songs I wanted to hear, but he told me how 'bout if he played some Dashboard Confessional instead. I finally told Midnight Steve that he and Dashboard Confessional could go fuck themselves.

For a while, I kept up my visits to the *XPhilePhorum*. Mainly because I was looking for her. All the regulars on the message boards knew about Lula, I guess because the police investigated all her online comings and goings. But pretty soon I got tired of waiting and waiting for the next comment that popped up to be from BloomOrphan and getting some dumbass rant about supersoldiers or whatever from MrsSpooky82 or LordKinbote instead. I got tired of their crackpot theories. I finally blew up at everybody in the chat room one night and said it was total bullshit; Lula didn't get abducted by aliens, or members of a shadow government, or Bigfoot, or some run-of-the-mill psycho. She ran away. Plain and simple. She ran away to some better place. To be with her mother, to live some fun, bohemian life in New York. To find some new best friend who wouldn't keep secrets or run around with older men behind her back.

Lula was always talking about the places she wanted to live when she finished school. She wanted to live in Seattle, or Vancouver. The rainy, romantic Pacific Northwest. She wanted to go to Paris, like Mrs. Lidell. Have adventures and lovers and smoke Gitanes. Why wasn't anybody looking there? Why were they wasting their time combing the goddamn *woods*?

eleven

"Janet Monroe called you. Twice," my mother announced when I came in from running. She was sweating, but she was sober. Rearranging the furniture again. This time, though, it kind of made sense. At least, the coffee table was at a normal angle in front of the sofa.

"Did she say anything about Lula?"

"She said not to get excited. But they found something they hope is a clue, and they want you to look at it."

I didn't even shower or change clothes. I ran all the way over. When I got there, I saw a blue Chevy Cobalt with an Enterprise Rent-a-Car sticker on the back, parked in the driveway behind the white Cadillac. I knocked hard on the door.

"Rory, honey, come in. I guess you got the messages." Janet pulled me inside.

"My mom said you had something you wanted me to look at."

"Come here. My goodness, you've been out running in this heat?"

"Yes, ma'am." Immediately, I felt like I should've showered and changed. There was a woman sitting in the kitchen, perched on one of the barstools. She was tall and thin and had cheekbones like glaciers. Her hair was the same sandy blond as Lula's, the same sandy blond that Janet got out of a bottle. She wore silver bracelets, a silver ring on her long, tanned thumb. Dark blue jeans and a loose black T-shirt. Worn-out cowboy boots.

"Rory, this is Christine. Lula's mother."

I didn't know what to say. She didn't look like the bleached-out Polaroid that Lula kept. This woman was so beautiful, it made my chest hurt. She looked just like Lula. I wanted to put my arms around her. I wanted to believe that this was really Lula, somehow. Taller and transformed. Time-traveling Lula, returned from the future to tell me that everything was going to turn out okay.

"Hi, Rory. I've heard a lot about you." Christine put out her hand to shake mine.

"I've, uh—me, too. " I didn't know what to say. "It's nice to meet you. Finally."

"Rory, here," Janet put a glass of ice water in my hand. "Now, take a look at this and tell us what you think." Janet drew me away from the woman sitting at the kitchen bar, the one I had a hundred questions for. She put a piece of paper into my hand, a copy of a printout from a computer, stamped and numbered and signed off with looping initials.

"It turns out Lula had a diary she kept on the computer. This is the last entry—she didn't date it, but according to the computer, she wrote it the night she left."

I don't know how Rory deals with it all. Even with Patty the Pickle at home and no dad, it's like none of that bothers him. He totally just accepts who he is and he's fine with all of it— with being gay, with not knowing his dad, with some coach wanting him to play fucking football. He just takes it all in stride. That's what I love about him, and what's so infuriating. I'm fucking drowning over here, and he's leading a charmed life. But he's so good about it. I don't know how he puts up with me. I don't deserve him. And I wish I didn't love him so much.

Wait a second, I do know. I know exactly how Rory deals with it all. I understand now. He's got somebody. Somebody he loves, somebody who loves him back. Somebody who isn't me. Is it really just because I'm a girl? Or maybe I just didn't love him enough.

I wish I could be like him. I wish I knew what I wanted. I've tried to get him to explain it to me. Like when we were doing my hair and talking about GA. But he says it's not like that for him. As far as he's concerned, love only goes one way. No exceptions, no loose feelings flying around, no maybes allowed. So then how can I explain what happened tonight? Why I even went to Sam in the first place?

I don't know why I did it. I can't believe I did it. I guess I thought that if it worked for Rory, it could work for me. What was I thinking? I told Sam everything about Rory and me. About him sleeping in my bed the other night, about what I found out tonight. I thought Sam would get it but boy did I miss the target on that one. I'm so mortified. I guess I just wanted to be close to somebody, close like Rory was, but, as Janet and Leo have shown, it takes two to tango. I forgot the crucial element. That the other person has to love you back.

Fuck it. I'm sitting here in the dark, waiting on the sunrise. One thing is certain. I know I can never go back. I can't go back to pretending like everything is okay with me.

I realized that all the stamps and the writing in the margins were from the police. Marking it as evidence.

"Rory, honey." Janet touched my arm. I wasn't even embarrassed that she knew I was gay. I was almost lightheaded with relief that Lula didn't mention Andy. But I couldn't believe this. Lula, in love with me? This had to be one of her jokes. I must've been reading it wrong.

"I didn't know. I didn't know how she felt. I didn't know she—I thought everything was okay."

"We all did, honey."

"Everybody thinks their kids are fine," Christine chimed in. "They all say they never saw it coming."

"That's enough, Chris. You want to get your digs in at me, fine, but we've been raising your child for the past fourteen years," Janet said.

"And doing a bang-up job, Mom."

"Hey, knock it off!" Uh-oh, I said that out loud. I looked at Lula's mom, who looked surprised.

"Hey, yourself," she said. "Who do you think you are, anyway?"

"Who do you think *you* are?" I felt the printout of Lula's diary entry crumple a little in my grip. "I've been Lula's best friend since seventh grade. You left her without even a goodbye. Do you have any idea how much time she's spent thinking about you? Reading your stupid actor books? Looking you up on the computer, trying to figure out where you were?"

"Rory." Janet patted my arm.

"And now you show up—why? You think it's going to help anything now? You don't even know her."

"I'm her mother," Christine said, her face flat.

"So what?"

"Rory, that's enough." Janet put her hand on her hip. "Can you please look at this letter and tell us something helpful?"

I looked the letter over again. Christine clipped off into the dining room, her boots tapping on the parquet.

"I don't know, Janet." My hands were shaking. I'd just totally gone off on Lula's mom. What had gotten into me? I had to stop losing my shit like this. "We fought because she was upset that I was seeing someone else. But she knew that I, uh—"

"You don't like girls. That's fine, Rory. But—what's this about sleeping in her bed?" Janet opened the silverware drawer. Looking for her cigarettes.

"I stayed over. One night before she left. She let me sleep in her bed. Instead of on the floor. That was all."

"You don't think she could be pregnant?" *Now there's a theory.*

"It wasn't like that. I promise."

"Oh, Rory." She lit her cigarette. "Honey, I'm sorry. I'm asking you all these embarrassing questions. I feel like a fool. But I'm grasping at straws, here. We just want to bring Lula back home, and the police are losing interest. They figured out what she looked up on the Internet the night she left: Amtrak and Greyhound schedules. But the people working at the bus station and the train station that night can't remember seeing her there. The police are still looking, but now they're saying she's just a runaway." Janet shook her head. "*Just* a runaway. Can you believe that? They

won't even put out an Amber Alert, because she's too old
and there isn't enough evidence to prove that she isn't just
. . . off partying or something, I don't know. It's ridiculous.
Missing is missing, I don't care how it happened." Her voice
was bitter, exhaling smoke. "But where else could she go?
We checked out the boarding school where her friend Jenny
goes now. Jenny hasn't heard from her in years. We're trying
to remember the name of that girl she was pen pals with a
few years ago—Stacy or something—one of the girls she
went to drama camp with. But there's nothing on the computer and we can't find the letters. Did Lula ever mention
anything to you?"

"Not about any pen pals, no." Lula had told me about
going to Drama Camp for Teens at the community college.
Something she'd done over the summer to try and get closer
to her mom. I remembered that Lula said it was lame, having
to visualize yourself as a tree or whatever, but she'd met a
cool older girl there. They hung out a few times before the
girl moved away, but I never met her, and Lula never told me
about writing any letters. As for Jenny, she and Lula stopped
hanging out back in junior high, back when Jenny started
trying out for cheerleading and Lula started spending her
weekends watching *Star Trek: The Next Generation* reruns with
me. Janet studied the letter again.

"What about this GA? What does that mean? Leo's on the
phone with someone he knows in Atlanta right now—do you
know why she would've gone down there?"

I hated to let her down. "No. GA—we were talking about
Gillian Anderson. The actress. From *The X-Files.*"

"Oh, for Christ's sake." Janet sighed and sat down.

Deflated. She put her hand to her eyes, shaking her head, muttering softly to herself. "Her favorite show. I should've known that. I should've known."

Janet already knew who Sam was. And I did, too. Sam was Samantha. Mrs. Samantha Lidell.

twelve

THERE WAS A FRAMED, BLACK-AND-WHITE PICTURE in the foyer of the Lidells in their wedding garb, both of them wearing wide-mouthed smiles, like they'd just been caught laughing their heads off at a joke. Beneath it in the frame was a handwritten note on a cream-colored card. *To Sam and Mark, wishing you all the joy in the world.* And, beneath that, an illegible signature. In real time, right before my eyes, Mrs. Lidell looked exhausted. But I couldn't wait until school the next day.

"It's a little late for a tutorial, don't you think?"

"I know." I had gone home to shower and look up Mrs. Lidell's address. And to plan in my mind what I was going to say. "But I saw Lula's last diary entry. I know she came here that night and she told you about me."

Mrs. Lidell's shoulders dropped.

"What do you want from me, Rory?"

"You have to tell the police! If they know she was here, maybe it changes things. Maybe it changes how they investigate—"

"The police know." Her voice got quiet. "I told them every-thing I knew as soon as I heard she was missing. I let them search my house, my office, my hard drive. It didn't change anything. They still think that she left because of you, not because of me." She stopped, catching herself. "Of course, presuming she did indeed leave under her own power, you know she didn't leave because of either of us. She left for her own reasons, and whatever the outcome of this is, you have to know that it wasn't your fault."

"You don't have to—" I swallowed. "You don't have to say it like she's already dead."

"I'm sorry, Rory, I—" she shook her head. "Why don't you come in, have a seat?" I followed her into the living room. There were a bunch of guitars propped up on stands in the corners. Electric ones, acoustic ones. Somehow, I wasn't expecting Sam Lidell's living room to look like a music store.

"Your husband plays guitar?" I blurted out.

"No." She sat down on the couch. She didn't seem tired anymore. She had on her all-business face, the one she got when we had a lot of material to review for a test. She lit one of her cigarettes from a soft pack on the coffee table. They were just regular Winstons. "So, are we having it out, or what?"

"I guess we are."

"Lula came to me that night after she saw you with the bookseller. Rory, did you have any idea that Lula was in love with you?"

"I know." I said. "I mean, I know it now. But I didn't know it then."

"I suspected it. She alluded to having feelings for someone who didn't return them, and I assumed it was you. Lula and I talked a lot over the past semester."

"About me?"

"About everything. She kept signing up for tutorials—I didn't understand why, at first. Aside from a rather irrational intolerance for William Faulkner, she had no trouble grasping the material. I realized pretty quickly that she just needed someone to talk to. I probably should have advised her to see Mr. Peeler, but it wasn't . . . she wasn't *troubled*, she was just lonely." Mrs. Lidell exhaled smoke. Mr. Peeler was the guidance counselor at school, and he wouldn't have helped, anyway. He was, like, twenty-five and always tried to solve your issues using extreme sports metaphors. "Lula's grandparents were very supportive, and of course she had you, but I think the fact that her mother was out of the picture was a . . ." Mrs. Lidell stopped. "My mom left me, too. She divorced my dad when I was a teenager and went off on her own to pursue her art career. She made it clear that me coming with her . . . wasn't an option. It's not something I talk about much, but I told Lula, because I wanted her to know that I understood where she was coming from. She started coming around more after that, hanging out in my office, just wanting to talk. Maybe she saw me as a sort of maternal figure. Anyway, I thought it was okay, considering she didn't have very many female role models, or even female friends in her life. But then it seems she developed something of a—" She hesitated. "A crush on me, I guess you could say. When she came here that night she . . . confessed her feelings. And I had to let her down."

I nodded. Mrs. Lidell looked away, touched her finger to her tongue to retrieve a loose tobacco leaf. I had a moment of feeling almost out of my body. I never expected to be here.

To be sitting on a sofa in Mrs. Lidell's living room, talking about Lula, who was in love with one or both of us. Lula, who was suddenly gone.

"What did you say to her?" I asked. *What did you say to make her leave?*

"Well, I was in shock, at first." Mrs. Lidell frowned. "And then I was sort of weirdly flattered and horrified at the same time. Look, it's never easy to have to let someone down, but I think she understood that it wasn't personal. I liked Lula a lot, she was a bright kid, really sweet, great student. But that's as far as it goes. I'm heterosexual, I'm married, I'm her teacher, and she's only seventeen years old, for God's sake. Not all of us are as unscrupulous as Andy Barnett." She gave me a hard stare, and I blushed.

"Now is probably not the best time to give you a lecture on ethics," she said, ashing her cigarette into a small, red glass bowl. "And you're not the one who should hear it, anyway—"

"It doesn't matter," I said. "We already . . . he broke up with me."

"I could tell you I'm sorry to hear that, Rory, but it would be a lie." Mrs. Lidell said. "You're a little young to be involved with a married man—"

"He's divorced," I interrupted. "And why does everybody think I'm so young, like I'm some little kid who doesn't get it? We were in love—why is that so hard to believe? I mean, Lula thought he was molesting me. But I'm the one who came on to him in the first place." My whole face flushed hot, remembering it. Closing up the shop, asking him to help me with some boxes in the back. Palms sweating like crazy, scared to death. Scared he'd fire me right there, and

I'd never see him again. Scared he'd beat the hell out of me, because I was pretty sure he was gay, but I'd never worked up the nerve to just come right out and ask him, and what if he wasn't? Scared, just utterly scared shitless that he wouldn't want me, this sweaty repulsive fat kid. Rehearsing my speech in my head, this whole confession that I was all set to swear I would never mention again if he didn't feel the same way. And then as soon as we were behind the curtain, just going for broke, kissing him right on the mouth. He pulled back and looked at me all surprised, and for a second I thought I was going to die. Like time had stopped and I was already dead. And then he kissed me back. And everything that happened in my heart and my brain and my blood after that was unnamable but was the exact opposite of dying.

"It doesn't matter if you started it, Rory. It's still statutory rape, and he shouldn't have let it continue," Mrs. Lidell said angrily. I was beet-red and trying to wipe a tear out of the edge of my eye without her noticing. "I'm not saying what he did was your fault. I'm not saying that at all." Her voice softened. "Look, I know from experience that being involved with a divorcee with kids is difficult at any age. And that sometimes when you're involved with someone who's older than you, it's easy for them to forget that you might be a little more vulnerable than they are. That, for them, maybe it's just dating, but for you, it's your first real love."

Now I was crying. I didn't care if I cried in front of her. So she knows I'm a big baby. Big deal. She handed me a wad of Kleenex from the box on the end table and patted my back while I blew my nose and composed myself.

"Well, what did Lula care, anyway? Especially if she had some big crush on you. Why should she give a damn if I want to date somebody who's too old for me? Why should she care if Andy Barnett breaks my heart? It's my stupid heart, not hers."

"Rory." Mrs. Lidell sighed. "Whether she was attracted to you or me or the man in the moon, did you really think that Lula didn't care about your heart? She was your best friend, and she didn't want to see you get hurt."

"*Is* my best friend," I corrected, imitating Mrs. Lidell's classroom voice. "Tenses, tenses." She smiled faintly but didn't laugh.

"She's your best friend. And you're hers. Lula didn't have a big group of friends, Rory. She wasn't part of any teams. She had you. *Has* you. And, for better or for worse, you met someone and fell in love—and I know, Rory, believe me, what it does to you. Falling in love for the first time, for real. It rearranges your molecules, it turns you inside out. And you kept all of that from her. Never mind the fact that she had feelings for you, herself, even though she was too busy trying to be your friend to mention it. I think she knew, deep down inside, that you were never going to 'come around,' you were never going to fall in love with her like she hoped you would. But she didn't have anybody else. She was just a lonely kid, Rory, trying to find some little sliver of what you already had. Trying to find what we're all looking for, you know? Love. Real, serious love."

"So she came to you."

"Yeah. She came to me. And I couldn't help her. Not with that." Mrs. Lidell scratched absentmindedly at her thumb. "I don't think she was serious, though. About having feelings for me. Romantic feelings, anyway. It's easy to mistake affection for infatuation, at her age."

I thought about me and Andy. Did I mistake affection for infatuation? Did he?

"Do you think Lula had real feelings for me?" I asked her. "I mean, do you think it was really love?"

"Affection, infatuation—you tell me, kiddo. She's your best friend." She took a long drag on her cigarette.

"Why didn't you—why didn't anybody tell me she came to see you?"

"Probably for the same reason you didn't tell anyone about Andy." She exhaled smoke. "We're all trying to protect someone, aren't we?"

"Except Lula. Nobody tried to protect her."

"Lula's exactly who I was trying to protect. And I think I've done a pretty fair job of it up to this point. Right now, you and Detective Addison and I are the only ones who know the whole story. And her grandparents now, with this diary entry." Mrs. Lidell gave me the chilliest of her cool looks. "I don't think having the details of her clumsy teenage longings splayed out in the daily paper would make Lula feel very welcome back home, do you?"

"No, ma'am. I don't reckon it would."

So much for *no more secrets.*

thirteen

I sent Lula emails every day. I don't know whether she got them or not. Maybe the only person reading them was Detective Addison. Or maybe even he'd given up.

To: BloomOrphan
From: SpookyKid
Subject: Family Reunion

Tallulah dearest,
I think you should know about the startling plot twist from yester-
day's episode. A long lost visitor has made a surprise reappearance.
Your mother's back at Janet and Leo's. Not sure how long she's
staying. Would you at least give a call? So that we can make our
shocked faces at each other?

yrs,
Theodore

To: BloomOrphan
From: SpookyKid
Subject: I want to believe!

L,
just saw the preview for the 2nd XF movie! July 25th! You better
be here by then because I won't go see it without you!
R.

To: BloomOrphan
From: SpookyKid
Subject: Mulder, it's me

Lula,
I've had it up to here with this absentee bullshit. School sucks. I
can't watch XF without you. I don't even care about XF without
you. I just want to see you again. Lula, if you're reading this, just
know that I can understand why you don't want to come back
here. And know that I love you.
R.

To: BloomOrphan
From: SpookyKid
Subject: no subject

lula,
what makes you so sure I wasn't drowning, too?
r.

JANET CALLED THE FOLLOWING SATURDAY TO invite me to
dinner, and to tell me that Lula's mother was flying out
that night. I went over, even though I hadn't spoken to her
since that first day, when we got the diary entry. When I
got to Janet and Leo's, Janet was making pierogies. Leo
was on the back porch, smoking cigars with another old
guy I'd never seen before.

"Can I help out?" I asked. I'd always liked helping Janet in
the kitchen.

"Of course. Why don't you run upstairs first? See if Christine's bags are ready to come down."

I walked up the stairs, hoping that this was going to end up like a movie. Lula would be there, sitting on her bed. Her mom braiding her hair. No, not braiding her hair. They'd be watching *Lord of the Rings* together. They'd both be fast-forwarding to the Aragorn parts.

But it was just Christine, alone in Lula's room. Sitting on the bed, her boot heels crossed in front of her. Looking around at all the posters. The Mulder and Scully action figures, still in their plastic packaging. The books stacked against the peeling black paint.

"Janet wanted me to see if you needed any help," I said.

"Thanks," she looked up at me. "Rory, right?"

"Yeah."

"I'm Chris. We didn't really get off on the right foot the other day, did we?"

"No, ma'am."

"Oh, can the ma'am crap. I hate all that southern-manners bullshit." She looked around the room again. "I'm just sitting here trying to figure out who this kid turned out to be. I can't believe I gave birth to a sci-fi nerd."

"Lula's not a nerd."

Chris just smiled at me.

"Of course she's not." She raised her eyebrows. "So what is she, then? Just between you and me? Your lover? Friend with benefits? Or maybe you've got a boyfriend hidden away somewhere, and Lula's your loyal, long-suffering fag hag."

I took a sharp breath and didn't say anything. I was ready to walk out of Lula's room. I wanted to remember Lula and me there, alone. Just us two. Not Lula's mother. Not this mean interrogation.

"Or is she the one that's putting on the act? I still haven't figured the two of you out. What's all this business with the English teacher? Is my kid a dyke, or is she in love with you?"

"I don't know," I said. "I don't think she knows, either."

"But you did sleep together, right? I mean, I know you'd never tell Janet, 'cause she's a square from Delaware, but come on. The two of you, alone up here. Your hormones are raging. Why not, right?"

I jammed my hands in my pockets. Shrugged. "I don't kiss and tell."

"Oh, fine. What do I care, anyway?" Chris stood up and stretched. She reached behind Lula's desk to unplug her BlackBerry charger. "It's just funny, that's all. Well, maybe not *funny*. Lula's father was gay. She didn't know that, did she?"

"No," I said. "She didn't know anything about him." Wow. I wondered for a second if I heard Chris say what I actually thought she said. Did I just project myself weirdly into her speech somehow? I almost wanted to say, *No, you misunderstood, Lula's dad isn't gay, I am.* What did she mean? That Lula's father was really, actually, gay? Was that why her mom left her? Was that why he left? Would it have changed anything if Lula had known?

"Of course, her father didn't figure it out until it was too late." Christine stuffed the BlackBerry and its charger into her purse, a faraway look on her face. "Too late for him and me, anyway." She looked up at me. "I guess that's genetics for you, though. However you look at it. The kid's either just like me, falling for her gay best friend. Or she's just like him. Either way . . ." Lula's mother trailed off. She zipped her purse decisively. I thought about Andy and his girls. Maybe Lula's dad was like him. A guy from a small town, a conservative family. Maybe it took a little bit longer for him to figure himself out. Maybe he loved Lula, like Andy loved his daughters, but he couldn't lead a fake life. I felt a weird pang of sympathy for Lula's absentee dad.

"Hey, is Janet still making pierogies?" Christine asked, changing the subject.

"Yeah."

"She's still literally trying to feed an army. You know who that guy downstairs is, right? With Leo?"

"Um. No."

"Leo never told you about his legendary black-ops buddy Harry Kemp? It'd be right up your alley, all this *X-Files* government conspiracy stuff." She picked up her duffel bag, stood it on its end, and latched it closed with expert speed. The bag was her only piece of luggage, and it was exactly like the one Lula had. Standard Navy issue. Leo must give them out at Christmas.

"Anyway, they'll find her. Harry's the one who found me, all those years ago. She'll probably be home before the week's out. I wouldn't worry anymore about Lula."

"So you're leaving? Before she gets here?"

"I have to get back. I've got a theater to run. Besides, Leo and I have just about maxed out our temporary peace treaty. I should leave before we end up in an unintentional reenactment of the infamous You're-Wasting-Your-Life-With-This-Acting-Bullshit Battle of 1985."

"But, wait. What about—I mean, where do you even live? What if—" I stood there at Lula's desk, bare without the computer. I felt my face go hot, angry. I wanted to shake this woman. I wanted her to unlock some mystery, to explain the pieces she'd left behind for Lula and me to decipher. I wanted her to show me how everything was supposed to fit. How could she expect to just show up here and throw out all these pieces, like telling me Lula's dad was gay, drop these bombs and leave?

"She's been looking for you for so long. She . . . she Googles your name."

"Which name did she Google?"

"Christine. Christine Monroe."

"Well, there you go. I'm easily found, if that's what Tallulah wants. I'm in the Santa Fe phone book, just tell her to look under MacKelvey, not Monroe. And before that, I had to use a stage name, because there was already a Christine Monroe in the Screen Actors Guild. Why didn't Janet and Leo tell her? I haven't been Christine Monroe since high school." She shook her head. "Google. Christ."

I couldn't believe she didn't understand. That Leo didn't talk about her. Wouldn't talk about her. That Lula's room was the only place in this house where she existed anymore. Lula was the only one here who was keeping her alive.

"What if she's there right now? Waiting for you?"

"My husband's at home. He knows she might show up there. I'm not taking this as lightly as you think I am."

"I didn't . . . I just wanted to know . . . I think Lula would want to know why you left her. She still keeps that bag of yours." I nodded at the backpack on the shelf. "She's read your books a hundred times. She practically worships you."

"I left her because I realized that I didn't want to be a mother." Chris shrugged. "Simple as that. Couldn't and didn't want to. Nothing against Lula—I was just too selfish. I knew I couldn't get where I wanted to be and stand around being a mom, too. And then her father left, so, a single mom, forget it." Chris leveled her gaze at me. "I think it's better I gave her to someone who wanted to be there all the time, don't you? Instead of dragging her around all over creation, like I was dragged all over creation when Leo was in active duty? That's hard on a kid. I would've been too hard on a kid."

"You're still her mother. You could at least call her or send her an email every once in a while."

"Rory, forgive my cliché, but when you get older, you'll understand." She reached over to Lula's shelf for the backpack that Janet had put in its usual place. "My God, why did she keep this ratty old thing?"

"Because it was yours."

"Ugh. This is a terrible picture." Chris went through the bag, tossing everything out on the bed like it was nothing. Like these weren't serious relics that had been pored over and contemplated and studied.

"So that's where my copy of *Unseen Hand* went. Liv Ullmann—did she actually read this? This is what she's been worshipping all these years? A cheap Liv Ullmann memoir from the Strand? Good grief." She laughed. "Be careful what you leave in the back of your closet. You never know when it might end up on a pedestal."

"She just wanted to know more about you."

"Well, when she comes home, maybe we can talk on the phone. I'm pretty busy, but maybe we could arrange a visit. Sometime next summer, if I'm not working in LA. Maybe the fall."

"*Maybe* you should just—" I wanted to say something sarcastic and awful, to make this woman feel as awful as I felt right now. I wanted to know what Lula would say. But my mind didn't work that fast. Instead, I was gripped by the thought that I wanted that little knapsack and the books. They weren't Christine's anymore. She'd given them up. They were Lula's, and I had to keep them safe for her until she came back.

"Anyway, why is this all on me?" Christine went on. "Maybe she went to find her father. He's over in Nashville—that's, what, a couple hours' drive from here? Maybe she Googled him. I told Leo, but he's obsessed with this idea that she went to New York. Why wouldn't a girl want to find her father?"

I didn't have an answer. If Lula had ever looked for her father, she never told me about it. Maybe she never mentioned it because she knew I didn't like talking about my own dad leaving.

"Maybe girls just need their mothers more," I theorized.

"She's got a perfectly good grandmother downstairs," Christine said, warily. "I mean, does Lula really need me, specifically, to explain the joys of the menstrual cycle?"

"Then why did you bother coming here at all?" I said finally. "You don't even care."

"I care," she shrugged again. "I just don't think it's the dire situation you all make it out to be. She packed a bag.

She's off having adventures; let her have them. Anyway, Leo thought it would help if I came back." She shrugged. "But, obviously, he was wrong."

"Obviously."

fourteen

BACK IN MY ROOM AT HOME, I opened my notebook. Lula's backpack sat on my desk; I told Janet I wanted to keep it for a little while, just until Lula came back. I took out Lula's books, and began copying the underlined sections down in my own handwriting, in between pages of notes on end-arounds and wildcat plays. I never got to ask Christine if she was the one who underlined them, or if Lula did it herself. It didn't matter. Either way, Lula knew these lines by heart, either way. There's one section of *An Actor Prepares* that I kept coming back to. Where the director tells his acting students that they have to light a spark within themselves, that every person who's really an artist desires to create a more interesting life than the one they have. Maybe that's all Lula wanted. To create a more interesting life for herself, just like her mom did. Maybe we just weren't enough to light her spark. I wasn't, Sam Lidell wasn't, Janet and Leo weren't. Maybe Lula was on her way to Santa Fe, to finally meet her mom. Or maybe she was making a whole new exciting life for herself in

New York or Seattle, someplace where they didn't call her Weird Girl in the halls.

The passage I copied down after that is from the Liv Ullmann book. The part where Liv and her daughter go back to the Swedish island where her ex-husband, the movie director Ingmar Bergman, lives in their old house with his new wife. She talks about how nothing in the house has changed, that even the furniture is all in the same place. She says: *The circle is closed. Nothing ever comes to an end. Wherever one has sunk roots that emanate from one's best or truest self, one will always find a home.*

It kind of reminded me of me and my mom. But it was also the passage that reminded me most of Lula. It made me hopeful that, someday, she'd find her way back home.

LATELY I'VE BEEN FIGHTING OFF NIGHTMARES in my sleep. In the nightmares, I have to get home, because I know that I have to save someone—sometimes it's Andy, sometimes it's my mom. Once it was Janet and Leo. In the nightmare, I'm running through the woods, trying to get to wherever they are. But the woods turn into a football field. Suddenly there are giants everywhere, guys a hundred times bigger than me, impossibly huge, tackling me from all sides, dragging me down into the mud. The more I try to struggle, the harder they are to fight off. Just when I think I'm winning, I realize I'm sinking down into the turf, the mud slurping me under until I can barely breathe. I've been waking up drenched in sweat, exhausted, my sheets twisted in damp, sloppy ropes. Once, after one of these nightmares, I even called Andy. He didn't pick up the phone.

Sometimes I have this other dream, too. It started as a fantasy, something for my mind to idle on during the boring parts of Algebra II. But now I'm actually dreaming it at night. In the dream, I'm sitting in class, and there's a knock on the door. It's a man with a badge and a gun on his hip, and he tells me not to be afraid. He's Agent Mulder, from the FBI, and he'd like to ask me some questions about my friend, Tallulah Monroe. I nod and tell him I have some ideas. We drive out past the community college. Past the cemetery. Past the woods. Out to Janet and Leo's, where there's a redheaded agent in Lula's bedroom, already looking for clues. This is Agent Scully, Agent Mulder introduces. We shake hands. I tell her my friend Lula is a redhead, too. And Agent Scully starts to tear up. She has to look away. Agent Mulder pulls me aside and tells me that this case is personal to Agent Scully. He explains that Agent Scully is Lula's mom. That she loves Lula and cares about her very much. But that she had to leave her here, with Janet and Leo, to keep her out of harm's way. Because of the nature of her work. *Their* work. Agent Mulder puts his hand on my shoulder, and I tell him I understand. I tell him that I'll do anything I can to help. I tell the agents to come with me, that I know a few places where the police haven't looked. I take them back to my house. My mother isn't home. The place is full of furniture, all askew. We make our way up to my room through a narrow path between end tables and easy chairs. And I find Lula there, sleeping in my bed. But, in the dream, the bed is like a lake. A deep pool of water where she sleeps beneath the surface. I lift her out of it, and her body is still. I kiss her, kiss her forehead and her red hair and her mouth until she coughs and spits and breathes again. I hold her close to me and I promise the agents that I'll take care of her from now on. I tell the agents that their case is closed.

Summer–Fall 2008

———

Bloom Orphan

one

HAVE YOU EVER WATCHED SO MUCH TV that you feel like your eyeballs are burned out of their sockets? You're sick in bed or something, and at first it's fun, no excuses, no place else to go, you just lie there in your feverish daze watching the pictures swim. Or it's raining out and you decide to stay in and watch movies all afternoon. But after a few hours, your body gets stiff and you start to lose your perception somehow. Like, the trees outside are a little too distant, and your own limbs don't seem to move the way you want them to. You're surprised to find that you're real, that you're moving around in some completely different world from the one you were just watching so closely. You're real and your voice is too loud and your movements are all over the place. You look in the mirror, expecting to see someone else—this character you thought you were—but it's just boring old you, same as ever.

That was how I felt after I'd spent almost the entire weekend on an *X-Files* bender. Just lying in bed, going from one episode to the next, only getting up to pee and eat and change DVDs. When Rory and I used to watch it, we rationed it out. One episode every Friday night, exactly at 9 p.m.—just like when it was first on the air. With other shows we watched, we didn't care—we'd throw in a *Buffy* or *Star Trek: The Next Generation* DVD on a Saturday night or a Sunday afternoon, whenever. But with *X-Files*, we wanted it to be as real as possible. We wanted to feel what it felt to be older, to have been watching the show when it was originally on. But more importantly, we wanted a sense of ceremony. The *X-Files* wasn't just any TV show we were watching. It was *our* show. It was our escape hatch. It was our secret world. It spoke to our solitude, to that inescapable feeling we had that we were the only two people on this whole miserable planet who understood each other. And, in our minds, we were just as cool as they were—at least, we wanted to be.

The other FBI agents on the show might have thought Mulder and Scully were losers, banished to their basement office, chasing after UFOs. But we knew better. Mulder and Scully had to deal with a lot of weird-ass situations, and they suffered their share of damages on their quest to find the truth, but they never lost their shit. They were the coolest of the cool. And, more than that, they had each other, even when it seemed like the rest of the world was out to get them. They were connected. It didn't matter if Mulder and Scully weren't officially boyfriend and girlfriend. They were beyond those kinds of labels. The connection they had was deeper than kissy-faces or pet names or making out in the back row of the auditorium during Special Assembly. It was the same kind of connection that we had. Rory and I. He was my Mulder and I was his Scully, or at least, I wanted to be. If I couldn't be his girlfriend, then I wanted to be his soul mate, that one person that he confided in, that he trusted with his deepest, darkest dreams. But Mulder never went and got it on with his gay boss. Not unless you read Internet slashfic, anyway. And would he have told Scully about it if he did?

But that was the Rory and me of four months ago, back before I left. Now I was back at Janet and Leo's, and Rory wasn't speaking to me and there was nothing else to do all weekend long, even if I had been allowed to leave the house. It was the sticky end of a rainy summer, steam coming off the pavement in thick waves, too hot to go outside. I'd read all the books I checked out from the library, and now I needed something to quell the air-conditioned boredom. I figured I'd work on the *Guide*, with or without Rory. Before I left, we were in the process of creating a comprehensive guide to every *X-Files* episode that ever aired. Rory was the best at it—the kid literally wrote epic poetry about Agent Scully. But now he was too busy doing the deed with his creepy boss to care about some TV show. Not to mention the whole not-speaking-to-me thing. Fine, then—I was no slouch. Who's to say I couldn't finish it by myself? The only problem was, I hadn't seen an episode of The *X-Files* in months. I had to get back in the loop.

So I picked up where we left off, Rory and I. I watched the entire end of Season Three on Friday night. Spent Saturday watching Season Four and part of Season Five. Sunday was the rest of Season Five, then the first movie, and now it was time for Season Six. At this point, it was dark out again and I was hitting the fast-forward button from time to time, skipping a few episodes here and there. Truthfully, I was so fuzzed out on TV overload, I was starting to feel like I didn't care if I never saw Mulder and Scully again. *Guide* or no *Guide*. But I had to keep going. I'm not sure why, but in the back of my mind, it had something to do with Rory, with proving some kind of point.

I knelt down to put the Season Five DVDs away and start on Season Six. My ears buzzed in the artificial-feeling silence of my room. I could hear Janet and Leo downstairs. Leo was practicing his short game on his indoor putting green. I heard the tap of his putter against the ball, the faint *pok!* sound it made when the ball landed in the shallow plastic cup at the end of the narrow green felt.

"She's eighteen in a week. You can't keep her under house arrest," Janet said. I stayed very still, listening.

"As long as she lives under this roof, she'll go where I tell her to go and do what I tell her to do." *Pok!* Leo hit another ball.

"You're not in the Navy anymore," Janet said, pausing. I could almost see her, swirling her glass, taking a drink. "And I've already lost a daughter. I'm not going to lose my grand-daughter, too."

"Now you're being melodramatic." *Pok!* "And it's two different things. Chris abandoned her child. I'm supposed to condone that behavior? That's not the way we raised her. That's her own rebellion. I won't have it."

"Yes, Leonard, you've made that abundantly clear. And I know you wanted to protect Lula from Christine's irresponsibility, but you made it impossible for Chris to even try—"

"*I* made it impossible? You think this situation is my fault?"

"Not entirely, no. But you never could understand—" Janet said something else, speaking so quietly I couldn't hear.

. . . *Pok!*

"At any rate, you're right that this is different." I heard the ice in Janet's glass again. "But I think we have to give Lula some freedom. She's been up there alone all weekend. You want some vegetable for a granddaughter, just lying around watching TV?"

"Of course not. Why don't you take her down to the Tennis Club or something?"

"She hates tennis."

"Jan, when school starts, she'll have plenty to do. I'll take her and drop her off. And if she can behave herself, then maybe she can have her extracurriculars. But I don't want her running all over creation, doing God knows what with God knows who."

Pok!

"I think this requires a more delicate touch," Janet said, so quietly I almost didn't hear.

"Delicate." Leo grunted. He tapped the ball again. This time, silence. I guess he missed.

WHEN YOU'RE A KID, HAVING A birthday in August sucks. You try to have a party, and everybody's gone on their last-ditch vacation before school. Twice my birthday actually fell on the first day of school—that was the worst. And when you're not all that popular anyway, birthday parties are kind of a joke. They'd been getting better in the last few years, small events, just me and Rory going on a movie bender at the Regal 7, or Leo driving us over to the roller rink in High Point. But of all the crappy birthdays I'd had, this one, number eighteen, took the proverbial cake.

Janet and Leo thought their little surprise would be good for us. Rory actually wore a necktie. He looked miserable. This was the first time we'd seen each other since the night I left. Things had been weird between us ever since I first got back in touch with him. I called him from Santa Fe, and we had this strained conversation where I told him I was all right and he kept saying how he knew all along that I was going to be okay, and he was glad nothing bad had happened, but he kept almost-crying and then he hung up really fast. I emailed him a couple of times, but he didn't respond. His phone always went to voicemail when I called. When I got back to Hawthorne, I went by his house three times, and there was never anybody at home. And now, finally, here we were at my favorite Chinese restaurant, Empire Garden, with the Pu Pu platter flaming away in the middle of the table, and Rory still wasn't speaking to me. Leo wasn't really speaking to me, either. So. Wow. Happy birthday to me.

"So, Rory," Janet patted his arm. "You must be excited. It's finally senior year."

"Yes, ma'am." Rory smiled politely, tight-lipped. He didn't say anything else.

"Did I hear right, you're on the football team this year?" Leo chimed in.

"Yes, sir. I made the team. I don't know if I'll play any games, though."

"That's big news, son. Good for you."

"Thanks."

"Unbelievable," I muttered.

"What?" Rory said. I cleared my throat.

"I said it's unbelievable. You. Playing football."

"What's so unbelievable about it?" Rory looked squarely at me. "Unbelievable that I could play, or unbelievable that I didn't ask your permission?"

"No, it's unbelievable that—" I couldn't believe what I was about to say. Something really mean. I couldn't believe it would even come into my mind.

"Unbelievable that they'd have a fag like me on the team?" Rory said.

"Hey, now," Leo said, grimacing.

"Rory!" Janet gasped.

Wow, what I was going to say wasn't *that* bad. I was going to say: *Unbelievable that they'd let you on the team knowing that you'd rather read Jane Austen than* Sports Illustrated. But whatever.

"It's nothing you all don't know," Rory shrugged.

"They know?" I asked him. "You told them?"

"You'd be surprised what all gets talked about when you're not around." Rory looked at me, his mouth a steady line.

"Oh, is that the deal? You talk to everybody but me? Did my grandparents know about Andy before I did? That's awesome. You three just hanging out together, *sharing*."

"Who's Andy?" Janet asked.

"Well, you haven't exactly been available since last spring. Sorry I didn't fit into your busy travel schedule," Rory muttered.

"Hey, you're the one who told me to fuck off," I replied. "So don't be upset that you got what you wanted."

"Lula, that language!" Janet shushed me. Leo gritted his teeth. He never did have any tolerance for my severe potty mouth, even though I learned all my best swear words from him. Rory laced his fingers and pressed his fists against the table edge, like he was getting ready to pray. He looked at me. Then he looked at Janet and Leo. He cleared his throat.

"Mr. and Mrs. Monroe, thank you for inviting me. I think I should go." He stood up very quickly. "Happy birthday, Lula."

He laid his napkin neatly on the table, pushed his chair in, and walked out. A gentleman to the end.

OF COURSE, THE FIRST THING JANET did when she heard I was coming home was head over to Hawthorne High to tell them I was coming back to school and make sure everything was copacetic. She figured all I'd have to do was pass all my finals from eleventh grade, and then I'd be all set for senior year. But it was more complicated than that. I'd amassed triple the absences allowed by the district, the Summer School session had already closed, yada yada. There was no way around it: I was going to have to repeat eleventh grade.

"Repeat, my foot," Janet told me she told them, and marched straight down to the guidance counselor's office, which was empty, because it was summer. Once located, the guidance counselor, Mr. Peeler, suggested that I take the GED and spend a year at the local community college, making awesome grades and doing some awesome community service or working some awesome part-time job, maybe at an awesome non-profit, and then applying, with the rest of my appropriate age group, for some totally super awesome college, as if nothing un-awesome had ever happened. (No, my language skills haven't suddenly devolved—Mr. Peeler literally used the word "awesome" more than a fourteen-year-old skateboarder. He thought it helped us relate to him. Or something.)

So I took the GED. And suddenly I went from high school washout to—ta da!—college student. Even if it was *just* community college, Janet and Leo were pretty pleased. I only had three classes to deal with: Concepts in Earth Science, Intro to English Lit, and Intro to American History, despite the fact that English Lit, American History, and I had been introduced already, and we'd really hit it off. But mostly I was happy that I wouldn't have to deal with the humiliation triple-header of getting the cold shoulder from Rory every day, having to retake Sam Lidell's class, and having all my former classmates lord their senior status over me. As a newly minted college student, I was allowed to ride my bike again. And to hang out with my new friend, Jay.

Jay was actually named Julia. Julia Fillmore. But everybody called her Jay. I met her in the school library on Orientation Day—she was a student, too, but she worked at the library as part of the work-exchange. She caught me staring at her tattoo when I came back to check out a book. Jay had two interlocking female symbols, in rainbow colors, on the inside of her right forearm. She told me I looked like that girl from the Missing posters, and I told her I was. "Cool," she said. "I found you." We talked for a while, and then she asked me if I wanted to come over and hang out sometime. She lived right off campus, and we could just watch a movie and drink some beer or whatever. I went over one afternoon, and next thing I knew, I was telling her the whole story. About Rory and Sam and how I ran away and all. I felt like I was reeling off this epic tale, but Jay seemed pretty unimpressed by the whole thing. She just cocked an eyebrow and said, "Interesting" or "I can see your point there." Anyway, it was nice to finally have someone to talk to.

Jay was biding her time, just like I was. She'd been right in the middle of getting her master's degree in Art History from Smith College when she dropped out. She'd gotten into a messed-up relationship with one of her professors, a woman named Carol who had a kid. It left her so wrecked, she moved back home to Hawthorne, where she rented a crummy little factory house from her elderly aunt. Jay was trying to leave art behind completely and start over with a degree in psychology. According to Jay, my crush on Rory and my Incident with Sam was no big deal, and I shouldn't even worry about whether I was gay or straight because my whole thing was less about sexual identity than it was acting out a whole psychological somethingorother, which Jay described using terms like *Kinsey scale* and *gestalt* that I only pretended to understand. At any rate, I figured Jay should know, since she was twenty-six and she'd had a whole, serious, life-altering *relationship* with this woman at Smith. This woman who had a kid.

"Kids make it complicated," Jay told me, exhaling smoke and looking sad. No, not sad. Jay had a great way of looking like she was too cool to care but like it was the heaviest thing and she couldn't carry it anymore. She looked both ways at once.

"How old was the kid?"

"Seven. She was great, too. I thought I never wanted kids, you know? But then . . . ughhh." Jay groaned and waved her hand. Conversation over. Jay could do that, just wave her hand and change the subject. It seemed like Jay was always in charge, even though she insisted that her life was a mess and she couldn't believe she was back in this shithole town. Jay dressed like she couldn't decide if she was a hippie or a punk. Like, she'd wear bellbottom jeans and Doc Martens with a ripped-up T-shirt that had some band name on it: The Slits or The Breeders or X-Ray Spex. Jay was tall and dark-haired and really pretty, but she never wore makeup because she said she hated all that beauty regime bullshit the media forces down our throats.

Well, sometimes she wore eyeliner. And mascara.

two

So I GUESS YOU MIGHT BE curious about my aforementioned epic tale of running away and generally behaving like a mixed-up doofus. All right, you asked for it. So here goes.

Okay, so, basically, without going into the gory details, the Humiliating Incident of last spring was that I witnessed my best friend Rory, who I was kind of secretly in love with, bumping uglies with his gross boss, and I retaliated by going over to my badass English teacher's house and making a pass at her, because I was also kind of secretly in love with her, too, but all she did was laugh at me and tell me to go write down all my mixed-up feelings in my *journal*, for crying out loud. And when I confronted Rory about the whole boss thing, he told me in no uncertain terms to butt out, even though we're supposed to be best friends. Hm, come to think of it, maybe that's Humiliating Incidents, plural.

Anyway, since Rory and Mrs. Lidell were the only two people in Hawthorne besides my grandparents who gave me the time of day, I decided it was high time to get the hell out. I quickly formulated a plan. I would go live with my mom for a while. Simple as that. Except for the fact that I had no idea where she lived. Or if she would have me if I found her. I'd been trying to find out about my mom for a long time, and yeah, I could have just asked Janet and Leo, but the thing about Leo was he basically lived his life as if my mom no longer existed. He seriously wouldn't even talk about her. No pictures in the house, nothing. So, trying to get any information out of him was going to be like trying to walk up to the CIA headquarters to politely ask what was really going on down at Area 51. It would only result in Pissing Leo Off, and no one wanted that. I had long ago made up my mind that, once I saved up enough caddy money, I would hire a private investigator to find my mom, and I would keep her whereabouts to myself. But, after the one-two punch of seeing Rory with Super Creep and the Humiliating Incident with Sam, I figured it was time to pack my bags and go. I was going to reunite with my mom, wherever she was. Because that's where I was really meant to be.

This is where Tracy came in. She always said I could come up and visit any time. We'd become friends at Drama Camp a few years back. She was really funny, always bursting into song from some musical. She turned me on to all these weird cult movies like *Rocky Horror* and *Clue.* When her parents split up, Tracy's mom moved to Ohio, and her dad moved to Washington, DC—only a few short hours from New York City, where, I felt pretty sure, I'd find my mom. Tracy still lived with her dad while she studied theater at George Washington University. I didn't realize it then, but the fact that her dad was kind of nutty was part of why everything got so crazy, with Janet and Leo thinking I'd been abducted and all. Tracy's dad was phobic about computers and cell phones—he said they gave off beta waves that could fry your brain or something. So Tracy and I mostly kept in touch through postcards and letters via snail mail. When I packed my bag that night, I was moving fast. I could've copied down the return address and all that, but instead I just grabbed the whole stack of letters from my desk drawer, figuring I'd read back through them for her telephone number on the way.

I'd planned to take the bus up to DC—it was cheapest—but before I got to the station I stopped off at the Flying J Truck Stop. In the dark arcade, by the light of the claw machine, I took out Tracy's letters and looked for the one where she'd written her new cell phone number; last year, her dad had finally allowed her to have a phone for emergencies. I'd left my own phone behind, because, well, I was feeling kind of screw-you-guys when I left, and I didn't foresee myself being in much of a mood to chat with anyone. Rory in particular. So I changed a few dollar bills for quarters at the change machine and headed down a smoky hallway toward the pay phones. Tracy's voice was groggy, but she picked up.

"Hi, Trace, it's Lula Monroe." My voice came out all high-pitched and squeaky. I was nervous as hell. "Sorry to call you so late."

"It's all good. I'm up. What's going on?"

"This is kind of crazy, but . . . you know how you always said I could come up and stay with you if I was ever in DC?"

". . . Uh-huh."

"Well, ah. Long story short, uh . . ." Where did I even start? With a lie. *Forgive me, Tracy—all will be explained soon.* "Actually,

George Washington is one of the schools I'm applying to, so I'm coming up for a tour. And Janet and Leo said I could go by myself if I was staying with a friend, so . . . I know this is short notice, but I was wondering if I could stay with you?" I was literally holding my breath.

"Hell yeah you can stay with me. You've got my address, right?"

"Yeah." I exhaled. This was going to work.

"Call me when you get here. Are you driving in, or flying or what?"

"I'm uh . . . taking the bus."

"All right. Call me when you get here. You're coming up this weekend?"

"Actually, my bus gets in . . . tomorrow night." There was a slight pause on the other end of the line. "I know, it's totally last minute, it's totally fine if you can't—"

"No, it's fine! I'm psyched to see you. Just call me when you get to town."

"Okay. Thanks. Wow. Thanks. I'll see you tomorrow!" I hung up the phone. The plan was underway. Now I just had to get to th—

"Tallulah's in tr-oouu-ble." I jumped a mile. Around the corner from the pay phones, with his elongated, basketball player's frame bent at crooked angles over a video poker machine, sat Trey Greyson. Professional Acid Casualty, and Janet and Leo's former landscaper. So much for my covert operations.

"Sorry, Lulu. Didn't mean to startle ya, there." He turned from the glowing jingle of the video poker machine and smiled at me, his eyes heavy-lidded, his white-guy dreadlocks tied back in a rubber band. "Where you catchin' a bus to in the middle of the night?"

"It's Lu*la*," I corrected him. "And it's none of your business where I'm going."

"Hey, you don't look so hot," he said. "What happened? Did that fat kid get you knocked up?" A laugh gurgled in the back of Trey's throat.

"I'm not pregnant. I'm leaving on a . . . college visit." Like Trey Greyson needed to know the truth.

"Leo the Enforcer's letting you catch a bus by yourself in the middle of the night? And did he finally let you drive the Caddy, too?"

"Fuck off, Trey," I muttered, hurrying off down the hall. I had a bus to catch.

"Hey, seriously. Wait up." Trey was following me. Great. "Are you taking a cab? Because I know you don't have a car. And the bus station's way up on Northside—aka Crystal Methville. It's not too safe, walking up there alone this time of night."

"Thanks for the safety tip, Officer Greyson. I think I'll manage," I said over my shoulder.

"Dude, hey. Lula. For real." Trey grabbed my arm. "You shouldn't—"

"Miss, is he botherin' you?" The cranky old lady behind the counter put down her issue of *People* magazine. Trey held up his hands. "'Cause I can call the cops," she said, giving Trey the death-glare from behind her thick glasses.

"It's okay," I told her. "He's . . . my granddad's yard guy." The old lady gave us both the hawk-eye as I walked outside, Trey following at a respectful distance. She finally gave up and went back to her *People*.

"Why don't you let me give you a ride?" Trey lurched up alongside me. "I've got my car. I can take you to the station. Or, what the hell, I can take you wherever you want to go."

"I'm going further than you're driving. And besides. I don't get into cars with strangers," I told him, making my way toward the halogen-lit island of gas pumps.

"Hey, I'm no stranger," Trey laughed gently. "I'm your grand-dad's yard guy. You know me. Hell, everybody knows me." And then, Trey Greyson proceeded to do the most embarrassing thing I've ever witnessed. He broke into song. *"Trust Greyson Bacon, that's the name, for crispy bacon, night or day! For breakfast, for lunch, or even dinner, Greyson Bacon—oink, oink!—it's a winner!"*

From over at one of the gas pumps, a fat trucker burst into applause and whistled.

"Forget the bus, okay? Buses suck. Let me give you a ride," Trey said. "I'm bored. I could use a little adventure. Hey, look, I know what you're thinking, but I'm not fucked up. Crazy, maybe, but I don't do drugs anymore."

"I think that trucker over there might beg to differ."

"Well, you just gotta take my word for it that I'm not on anything. Unless you wanna go find a narc to get me to pee into a cup."

"Gross, no."

"Then let me give you a ride," his voice softened. The cool spring breeze blew across the parking lot. The dark smell of a muddy field mixing with the sharp tinge of gasoline.

"Trey. Why should I trust you?"

"Because I've been through some shit, and I know what it's like to wanna get out of town." His eyes were clear. He wasn't fooling around.

"I don't know what I want." I bit my lip. I kind of just wanted to be back in my bedroom, where it was safe. My guts felt hollow, churning at the mere thought of the trip I was about to take. I felt like I was falling off into nothingness. But then I thought of Rory, and all the anger in me swelled up again, filling my chest. "All I know is I'm sick of being lied to. I'm sick of everybody treating me like I'm some little kid who won't understand anything. I'm sick of this place and I'm ready to get the hell out."

"I hear ya," Trey nodded. "But still. You don't wanna walk through Northside alone in the middle of the night. Unless you've got some hardcore death wish."

Dammit. He had a point.

"Trey, have you ever seen our nation's capital?"

three

IT WAS A SUNNY TUESDAY AFTERNOON, unseasonably warm for mid-September, but I was inside at Jay's. Music thumping out of her ancient, paint-splattered ghetto blaster, TV on mute, Jay scribbling away with a bunch of crumbled pastels, me, on the couch beside her, on beer number two. Or three. Wondering if maybe Leo was right.

"Don't let your granddad get to you," Jay said, reading my mind. "At least he cares."

"Whatever," I said, burping. Leo and I barely said two words to each other anymore. But before I left for Jay's that day, he lit into me. Didn't I care about my future. Wasn't I supposed to be working on finding a job, or a volunteer position, or blah blah blah. What happened to peer tutoring down at the computer lab. If this is what you're going to do with your life, sit around all day and drink beer with your friends, maybe you should just go on back to New Mexico.

"He's got a point, though," I said, knocking back some more of my beer. I kind of didn't like beer at first. But now that I'd tried a lot of different brands, I'd discovered that . . . well, that

I still didn't really like beer. I guess what I did like was being able to fuzz out and not think so hard about stuff for a while. The problem was, when the beer was gone, the stuff was still hanging around. Waiting to be thought about.

"And his point is?" Jay asked, looking up from her sketchpad to watch a Beyoncé video.

"Well . . . I mean, look at him versus me. When he was my age, he joined the Navy. By the time he was in his early twenties, his main job was to chopper wounded soldiers out of Vietnam under heavy fire. Like, forget working at the computer lab—that was his first job. He's still got shrapnel in his shoulder. Can't go through a metal detector in an airport to this day."

"Really?" Jay, for once, seemed genuinely impressed. "Shit. That's hardcore."

"I know, right? And here's me. Just a . . . mooch."

"You're not a mooch. You're a kid."

"I'm a mooch. I'm the mooching granddaughter of his ungrateful daughter, taking advantage of all his hard work and sacrifice. I'm eighteen now, you know. He could kick me out on my ass, and he'd be totally in the right."

"No, he wouldn't," Jay insisted. "By the way, how hot is Beyoncé in this video?"

"She's okay, I guess." Beyoncé was dancing, incongruously, to one of Jay's old mixtapes of girl bands from the nineties. Bikini Kill, Bratmobile, The Muffs. I had to admit, Beyoncé dancing to The Kelley Deal 6000 kind of worked.

"She's okay, you guess?" Jay took the beer out of my hand and set it on the coffee table. "That's it. I'm cutting you off."

"Huh?"

"Clearly, the alcohol is affecting your vision."

"Pfft," I laughed and grabbed the rest of my beer.

"Hey. Seriously, though. You can always stay here."

"Really?"

"Yeah. I mean, you can always crash on my couch. But if you really wanna move out, I've got a spare room. I'll rent it to you cheap."

"Thanks, but I can't even afford cheap."

"Whatevs," she picked up her pastels again. "It's there when you need it."

I should have been flattered that Jay wanted me for a room-mate. But it scared me a little. What if I really did just end up in Jay's dank little spare room, spending the rest of my life drinking too much crappy beer? Yikes. How un-Scully of me.

The truth was, I didn't want to move out of Janet and Leo's, even if it was weird and tense. I wanted to fix it, to make it like it was before, but I had no idea how to get us all back to normal. I sort of wished I'd never left. Sometimes you can't see how the stuff you do spirals out, like octopus arms, destroying everything in its path and . . . okay, that's a crappy metaphor. Octopuses don't really destroy anything. I had to do a biology report on octopuses once. Octopi. Anyway, they're actually really smart, loving animals, even if they do look like blobs. I'm no octopus. I'm more like a . . . like a big dumb puppy. Whipping around with its tail and its giant paws, making a mess, destroying everything without even meaning to, just trying to jump up on everybody's lap and see who loves me best.

TREY GOT WIRED ON RED BULL and drove all night. His car was an ancient Mercedes sedan with a Phish sticker in the back window. Tracy was in class until late afternoon, so Trey and I made a day of it in DC. It was a lovely spring day, the cherry blossoms in full bloom. I, of course, wanted to tour the J. Edgar Hoover Building, aka FBI Headquarters, but they weren't open to the public.

"Bummer, man," Trey lamented as we parked our tired selves on a bench out front. "We should just tell 'em we're friends with the Cigarette Dude."

"Excuse me?"

"You know, like on *The X-Files*? Did you ever see that TV show with the FBI agents, the dude and the chick, huntin' down UFOs?"

As it happens, Trey was a huge fan of *The X-Files* back in the day. Once he found out that I was a fellow Phile, I couldn't shut him up.

"Or, or—dude! Remember the one with the circus freaks, where Scully eats the bug? That's probably like, my favorite one of all time. Or, no, wait! Remember the one with Burt Reynolds? Oh, man. I saw that when I was tripping and I seriously thought Burt Reynolds was God."

"I think that's Tracy." I waved. We had agreed to meet outside the Hoover building, but I suddenly felt embarrassed. Me lugging Leo's old Navy duffel and Trey with his dreadlocks pontificating about how Burt Reynolds might actually be the Almighty. Everyone else around us seemed so professional. Dark suits. Neat haircuts. Briefcases and ID badges. Badass Feds.

"Tallulah Monroe! Girl!" Tracy swept me up into a hug. "I can't believe you're here!"

"I know! It's been forever!" Tracy was somehow even more beautiful than last time I saw her. She always called herself a mutt, because her dad was half-white, half-Filipino, and her mom was half-black, half-Colombian. But Tracy was, like, J. Lo-level gorgeous. I could tell Trey was checking her out. And what's weird was I was sort of checking her out, too. Ever since the thing with Sam, it was like I was running every girl I met through some test. *How about this one? Are you into her? How into her are you?* But even though I could see how beautiful Tracy was, she didn't make me feel like I felt around Sam Lidell. Like I just wanted to talk to her forever. Good gravy— even after the Humiliation, I still kinda felt all wavery, just thinking about Sam. *What's your deal, Lula, anyway?*

"Look at you! All grown up! And I love the hair!" Tracy was only two years older than me, but it felt more like she was my aunt or something. She finally noticed Trey. "Is this the infamous Rory I've heard so much about?"

"Ah, no. Tracy, this is Trey Greyson. He gave me a ride. Trey, Tracy."

"Hey! We sorta rhyme!" Trey exclaimed. "My pleasure, m'lady." Trey took Tracy's hand and bowed deeply. Tracy laughed.

"So, uh." I turned to Trey. This was going to be awkward. I wasn't sure how welcome I was going to be at Tracy's dad's, let alone with a guest in tow. "I guess I'm good here. Thanks for the ride."

"Oh, yeah. Thanks for the trip. I must say, I'm inspired by our nation's capital, and I never would've come here without you." Trey laughed. "Maybe I'll run for Congress!"

"Just tell them you didn't inhale. Here—take this for gas." I handed him forty bucks. It was a lot of my private investigator money, but gas was expensive.

"Seriously? Far out." Trey pocketed my money. "Well, I best be hittin' the horizon."

"Will you tell Janet and Leo that you saw me and I'm okay?"

"Sure thing, kiddo." He laughed. "Leo the Enforcer! Bet he's gonna be happy to see me again."

"Trey, you need a place to crash for the night?" Tracy interjected. "It's gonna be kinda full with us at my dad's, but I know some guys from school who could probably hook you up with a sofa."

"Nah, I'm good. I've got the travelin' bug now. Might truck on up to Jersey, see some of my old peeps at Princeton. Hit P. Rex for some car tunes and motor on back down the coast. I'm a free man, babies." Trey skipped off down the sidewalk, waving back at us. "Later days, T and T!"

"Okay," Tracy said when he rounded the corner. "When you told me you were coming to DC on the bus, I didn't think you meant the Grateful Dead bus."

As we took the Metro up to her dad's apartment in Cleveland Park, I told her the truth. An abbreviated version, because I was still humiliated. I told her that school was rough, I was having a hard time dealing with one of my teachers, that I'd had a falling out with Rory, and I had made up my mind to go live with my mom, who was probably up in New York. I just needed some money for a PI, and then . . . well, probably more money for the train or the bus or whatever. Traveling was more expensive than I'd realized.

"Wait, why do you need to hire a private investigator?" Tracy asked, unlocking the three—three!—locks on the apartment door.

"Because Leo won't tell me where she lives. I've tried every kind of computer search I can think of, but it always dead-ends. I need some kind of . . . next-level clearance."

"We could ask my dad." Tracy took my duffel bag and set it at the foot of the sofa.

"What good is that going to do?" Tracy's dad worked for the newspaper. He was the guy who had to read the articles and make sure all the punctuation and grammar was correct. I'd never actually met him before, but I imagined he was a boring old guy with glasses halfway down his nose and a perpetual disapproving look.

"Trust me." Tracy led me down a narrow hallway to a closed door. She knocked.

"What's the password?" A muffled voice called out.

"Vote Nader!" Tracy called back. Another lock flipped and the door opened. Wow. I am not kidding—Tracy's dad's office was like the Lone Gunmen's hideout on *The X-Files*. All this old reel-to-reel recording equipment, stacks of dusty books everywhere, mostly with "conspiracy" in the title. Piles of camera equipment, VHS tapes, notebooks, maps. A picture of Richard Nixon shaking hands with Elvis hung on the wall. Tracy's dad was typing on an actual typewriter. I felt a lonely pang in my chest—my first thought was *Oh my gosh, Rory, you have got to see this.* Then I remembered that Old Rory had recently been replaced by new Attack Rory, who had told me to fuck off and stop playing Mulder and Scully, so he probably wouldn't care, anyway.

"Dad, you remember Lula? From Drama Camp in Hawthorne?"

"Vaguely," he shook my hand, peering intensely over the rims of thick glasses. He was short, with spiky black hair and long, graying sideburns. "Welcome to our humble abode. Make yourself at home."

"Thanks for letting me stay."

"Dad, Lula's looking for her mom. She hasn't seen her in . . . how long?"

"Since I was three."

"Lula's done all the computer searches and nothing's turned up. Now she's thinking about hiring a private investigator. You got any advice?"

"Yeah, save your money. I'll do a search for you." Tracy's dad shoved a pile of papers aside to reveal a laptop computer.

"Dad! You said no computers at home!" Tracy exclaimed.

"Yes, I did. I'm trying to keep you from becoming completely zombified like the rest of your generation. Not to mention I don't want you meeting some maniac on Facelist or whatever." Tracy's dad pushed his glasses higher on the bridge of his nose. "But, computers do have their practical applications, even outside of the workplace." Mr. Perry booted up the laptop and began typing faster than I've ever seen anyone type.

"All right, I'm in. What's your mom's maiden name?"

"Allison Christine Monroe."

"Christine with a K or a C?" he asked. I spelled it for him.

"Date of birth?"

"April 18, 1965."

"Okay, hang on . . ."

"Here comes your next-level clearance," Tracy whispered.

"Allison Christine Monroe, according to these records, changed her name legally in 1986 to Christine Alexander, married in 1996 in New Mexico, changed her name again to Allison Christine MacKelvey. Driver's license, issued by the state of New Mexico to Allison Christine MacKelvey, vehicle registration, et cetera . . ."

"New *Mexico*? Are you sure?" I asked. All this time, I'd been picturing her in New York.

"I have an address here in Santa Fe and one in Los Angeles . . . the LA address has a suite number, though. Might be an office or an apartment." Mr. Perry was typing at a maniacal speed now. "Here she is again, recent news item from the *Santa Fe Reporter*, 'Christine MacKelvey welcomes Bill Wagner to Teatro del Santa Fe board of directors. . . .' Looks like she's some kind of administrator for a theater group . . . here you go."

He swung the laptop around. There she was. Just like in the Polaroid, but older. More beautiful. My mother, in a trim black blazer, smiling and shaking hands with a ruddy-faced man in a suit and a bolo tie. Her hair was the same ash-blond that mine used to be.

"You've definitely got her eyes," Mr. Perry said.

"How did you do that? I've been trying for years . . ." I couldn't stop looking at the picture. My mother. It was her. It really was.

"Trade secret."

I was too stunned to do much else except thank him. I had just found my mother. And, as far as Tracy and her dad were concerned, it was no big deal. Tracy and I drifted back out of the secret lair. She ordered a pizza and turned on the TV, the bleeped-out version of *The Big Lebowski*. Her dad stayed in his office, typing furiously behind the locked door.

"Hey, Trace, can I ask you a personal question?"

"Shoot."

"What made you decide to live with your dad? Instead of your mom."

"Easy." Tracy picked at a stray pepperoni. "He gives a damn about me. My dad always supported me, whether it was Drama Camp or the college I chose. Even all his crazy business about keeping me away from computers and cell phone radiation and stuff is just him trying to take care of me. All my mom cares about is herself and what she wants. When she ran off with that car salesman, I was like, forget it. Back in the day, you married this guy. My dad. You took vows. And now you're just gonna break 'em for Mr. BMW of Akron? No way. My dad may be kinda crazy, but he's for real."

"Huh." It had never even occurred to me to go looking for my father. I mean, I knew a lot of kids in school who either lived with their mom, like Rory did, or lived with their mom and stepdad. Tracy was one of the few friends I had with divorced parents who actually chose to live with her dad and he let her. Come to think of it, I hardly knew anybody who lived with their real mom and dad in a regular *Leave It to Beaver*-type situation. And, except for my mom, it's always the dad who leaves.

"Are you gonna try and find him, too?" Tracy asked.

"My dad?"

"Yeah."

"I dunno. I never really thought about it," I confessed. "I know even less about him than I do my mom. Janet only met him once, when she and Leo went out to LA to visit my mom. She said he seemed like such a nice guy, she couldn't figure out what happened. But . . . I guess I figured, even if I found him, why would he care? Guys are always walking out on their kids. It's what they do. Dads bail. Why should mine be any different?"

"My dad didn't bail. He fought hard to get custody of me," Tracy said.

"Well." I shrugged. "Mine didn't."

four

Janet and Leo were gone to Tango Night at the Y, and I was in the kitchen, heating up leftovers, when Rory called. It was the first time I'd heard from him since the Terrible Birthday, over a month ago.

"Hey," he said when I picked up. "It's me."

"It's you," I said. "What's going on?"

"Is it still Tango Night?"

"Yeah."

"I was wondering if I could stop by."

Right then, the microwave went *bing!*

"Yeah. Sure," I told him. "Come on over."

That was it. He hung up the phone. I made a mad dash upstairs to pick my dirty clothes up off the floor. I took a quick look in the mirror. Yikes. The refresher dye job Jay had given me a couple of weeks ago had already faded to a dull strawberry and my roots were showing, big time. I tried brushing it back, to no avail. Maybe I could raid Janet's closet for a hat. . . .

No time. The doorbell rang. That was *fast.* I raced down the stairs. Took a breath. Opened the door. Rory.

"Hi," I said.

"Hi," he replied. He wasn't smiling. He was wearing a Fighting Eagles sweatshirt, and his hair was damp and flowery-smelling. He must've just gotten out of the shower. I felt even more self-conscious about my hair.

"I'm guessing you're not just here to build a tower of furniture," I said, quoting one of his favorite episodes of *The X-Files*. He didn't even crack a smile. Uh-oh. This was not good.

"I just wanted to give this back to you." Rory had something in his hand. He held it out to me. My mother's backpack.

"Where did you get that?" I'd lost it somewhere on the trip. I figured I'd left it in Trey's car, or at Tracy's.

"They found it at the Flying J. The cops did. After you disappeared."

"Oh." I took the backpack. It seemed like something from another age. In a way, it was.

"You know, I didn't mean for it to get so crazy down here," I told him, forcing a chuckle. "I mean, I figured they'd just think I ran away, and . . ." I shrugged. "I didn't know they were gonna bring in the police."

"Huh." Rory jammed his fists into his sweatshirt pockets. "Well, that's what happens when somebody disappears without a trace. Police get called in. People freak out."

"Honestly. I thought Trey was on his way back down here. He was supposed to tell Janet and Leo that I was okay." I didn't know why I was going into all this again. I had already tried explaining myself on the phone and in an email. Little did I know, Trey never made it back to Hawthorne. According to the story I heard later, he took my forty dollars, drove to Princeton, and hooked up with some of his old druggie friends. Halfway to California on a stoned pilgrimage to find the Divine Burt Reynolds, his car broke down. After the drugs wore off, he spent the rest of the summer with his second cousin, working the Greyson Hot Dog stand at Kauffman Stadium, home of the Kansas City Royals.

"Yeah, that guy was reliable," Rory concluded.

So both of us were standing there, not saying anything.

"You wanna hang out for a while?" I asked. "I was just heating up leftovers."

"No, thanks. I just figured you'd want that." Rory turned to go.

"Hey, Rory!" I called after him. He stopped. He didn't turn around. "Come on. Don't be like that. I'm not mad at you anymore. So why be mad at me?"

"*You're* not mad? Why were you even mad at me in the first place?" Rory turned around.

"Why was I even—" I threw up my hands. "Because you lied to me! And you were mean to me about it. Do you even recall standing on your front porch, telling me to fuck off and stop playing Mulder and Scully?"

Rory was silent, staring at the ground.

"You were acting so weird and secretive and I didn't know what was going on with you. I was worried about you! And you were running around behind my back for who knows how long—"

"Six months," Rory said softly.

"Six months!" Six months! Half a year! "Geez, Theodore, I knew I was behind the times, but I—"

"You know, Lula," he interrupted. "Unbelievable as it may seem, not everything in the world revolves around you."

"But we—" I stopped. *We were best friends.* Rory looked hard at me, his brow furrowed.

"I didn't tell you about Andy and me because I was afraid you wouldn't understand. And I was right. Were you upset because I didn't tell you, or because you finally had to deal with the fact that I was never going to 'go straight' for you?"

Ouch, right in the heart. I opened my mouth, but I had no comeback at the ready.

"Forget it," Rory said, turning away. "Enjoy your leftovers."

He walked off into the night. I went back inside. In the kitchen, I took my plate out of the microwave. I scraped all the food into the trash and went to bed without wanting anything.

RORY KEPT EMAILING ME AFTER I left Hawthorne, but it was a while before I read anything he wrote. Mostly because I was still upset with him over lying to me. Upset over the fight we'd had. And, anyway, I was too busy working to deal with Rory Drama. I needed more money to make the trip to my mom's. I made up a minor lie and told Tracy's dad that I'd already graduated and was taking a gap year, traveling around and experiencing life, so he wouldn't get weird about me not being in school. (Tracy told me I was on my own with that one.) He offered to pay me to run errands for him, make copies at Kinko's, staple pamphlets, and make fund-raising calls for this project he was working on called—get this—*The Campaign to Arrest Dick Cheney for War Crimes.* (I'm still not sure how anyone could arrest the Vice President, even if they wanted to, but Mr. Perry was quite adamant that someone should. I did mention that his office looked like the Lone Gunmen's hideout, right?)

When I finally convinced Mr. Perry that the leaflets could benefit from a more streamlined design and it wouldn't kill us to use a computer just this once, I got online and took a peek at my inbox. I saw all of Rory's messages, but I left them unopened. What did he care if I gave him the silent treatment, anyway? Let him go frolic in the woods with his boyfriend, or whatever they do. Actually, the boyfriend was probably too old to frolic. He could break a hip.

I really did feel bad about Janet and Leo, though. I knew they'd be worried even if Trey the lawn hippie had told them that he'd taken me to stay with Tracy and I was okay. But I was afraid that if I actually called them, they'd drag me home before I even had a chance to find my mom. And, truthfully, as much as I love Leo, he does have his nuclear moods. I just needed more time. Okay, let's be honest—I was more than a little bit scared. Scared of Leo, but also scared of the trip I was about to take. It seemed too sudden, even after all this time. To show up at my mother's door. Just like that.

Then, one day, about three weeks after I'd left, I decided to finally read Rory's emails. And I immediately felt like a massive jerk. Everybody was freaking out in Hawthorne. The cops were involved and everything. I figured out that either Trey never made it back, or they didn't believe him, because they all thought I'd been abducted or something. And, I mean, I got it. To me, being out on my own, exploring a new city and everything, it felt like I'd barely been gone at all. But to my grandparents, just sitting around the house, waiting to hear from me, it probably felt like I'd been gone forever. I knew I really needed to call Janet and Leo now, but I was even more scared than before. And, to top it all off, my mom actually showed up in Hawthorne. By the time I read the emails, though, she had just left to go back to Santa Fe. I couldn't believe that Rory had met my mother, and I still hadn't seen her since I was a toddler. It made me more determined than ever to make the trip.

So, while it was a lot of fun eating Ethiopian takeout and listening to Tracy's dad rattle off all his theories about how the growth hormones in milk are turning us into a nation of supersized freaks, or how all the lore about aliens crash-landing at Roswell was just Cold War propaganda to make the Soviets think we were using ET technology, I knew I had to get a move on. And in another week's time, after half the DC phone book had hung up on me, and I'd folded so many Dick Cheney pamphlets that I was folding Dick Cheney pamphlets in my dreams, I had enough money to buy myself a one-way train ticket from Washington, DC to Santa Fe, New Mexico. I promised Tracy and Mr. Perry that I'd write, and I headed west, into the sunset, toward what I thought might be home.

five

I WAS DOWNSTAIRS WATCHING A MOVIE with Janet and Leo. *Hud,* the story of these cowboys on a ranch in Texas who . . . uh . . . have some cows or something. I wasn't really following it, to tell you the truth. Well, except for all the innuendo-y stuff between Paul Newman and Patricia Neal. Talk about UST—Mulder and Scully had nothing on those two. But, really, the fact of it was, I didn't want to sit in my room alone.

"So, what does your friend Jane study?" Janet asked me.

"Jay. Like the bird. Psychology, but she's also an artist."

"Oh, really? What kind of art? Painting, sculpture?"

"Painting and drawing, mostly. Although she has one of those pot-throwing things, out on her back porch."

"Oh, I always wanted to try that," Janet exclaimed. "What do you call those pot-throwing things? Leo, honey? Do you know?"

"You know," Leo growled. "Somebody in this room is actually watching this movie."

"Tsk." Janet patted Leo's arm. "Well, whatever it's called, it's nice that you've made friends at your new school. You should invite her over for dinner. I bet she doesn't get much home cooking."

"I'll ask her. Thanks." My attention was back on the TV. Leo was right; the movie was getting kind of interesting. How the strict grandfather wouldn't tell the boy, Lonnie, why he was so mad at Hud. And Hud seemed like such a cool guy, even if he was a total womanizer. Wonder what his big secret was. The silvery Texas clouds moved across the hi-def TV screen, and I thought about Santa Fe.

"It's called a potter's wheel," Leo muttered as the scene ended, fading to black.

After all those years of endlessly typing her name into every Internet search engine ever invented, finally, all I had to do was take a cab from the train station to my mother's address, written on the back of a Dick Cheney flyer. As the cab bumped along, I took in my new surroundings. I couldn't get over how everything in Santa Fe actually looked like all those cheapo art prints of the southwest that you see at Bed Bath & Beyond. With the blue windows and chiles hanging up on strings and everything.

It was weird how suddenly not-nervous I was, walking out to my mother's house. My. Mother's. House. This was huge. I hadn't even seen her since I was three.

There was a long driveway that went up a hill, fenced on either side. There were horses in the fields. The air smelled like woodsmoke and some kind of sweet, piney flower. I knocked like they were expecting me. Some old guy answered the door, and I felt a flash of panic—did I have the wrong address somehow? I mean, my mother was forty-three now. But this guy was practically Leo's age. His hair was totally gray and his face was tanned and creased. He looked like the Marlboro Man.

"You must be the daughter." He didn't even say hello.

"Um. Yeah. Lula."

"Lula. I'm Walter. The husband." His voice sounded like a growl. "Well, come on inside. Your mother'll be home late."

I walked into my mother's house, closing the door behind me. It was clean and cool. It smelled like bread baking. I followed Walter into the kitchen.

"You hungry?" Walter opened the oven door and grabbed a frayed blue dishtowel. He slid the top rack out and, sure enough, there was a loaf of bread sitting there. He folded the dishtowel in his hand and took the bread out of the oven, sat it on a painted tile on the kitchen counter. Before I could answer, he gave me a stern look.

"Now, right off the bat, I ought to tell you." He slapped the dishtowel against the counter. "I'm not your father. I met him once. But I'm not him. Maybe you already knew that. But . . . in case you didn't."

"No, I, uh—" Okay, pause, please. My brain was already exploding. First of all, who *was* this guy? Second of all, this guy knew my father? "I don't know anything about him."

"He was an actor. Friend of your mom's. I reckon she can, ah. Tell you more about him than I can."

"But, um—" Work, brain, work! "He's an actor? My father?"

"Not anymore. Last I heard, he's a teacher. Lives in Nashville, Tennessee."

"Oh." Huh?

"That's how your mother and I met, you know. Movies. I train picture horses. She was a set PA." He waved his hand. "These things, uh. Things happen."

"Oh," I said again. What was I supposed to say to all this? I was so completely floored, I was practically lightheaded.

"But it wasn't my idea for her to leave you." Walter looked me square in the eye. I was suddenly afraid to move. "Let's get that out of the way up front. I told her she could move you out here any old time she wanted. I still tell her, every year at Christmas, why don't you invite that little girl of yours to come on out here? But she's got her ways and I've got mine and we both learned a long time ago when to push and when to pull. You understand?"

"I . . ." I felt myself nodding, but I don't think I understood anything anymore.

"Well, I figured I'd . . . clear up any confusion you may have. Your mom could tell you more about him. Your father, I mean. Anyway." Walter coughed. "Go on ahead and make yourself at home. I've got a sick filly I gotta check on before it gets too dark. You can take that spare room down at the end of the hall, on the right. Bathroom's on the left, if you want to wash up before dinner."

"Okay. Thanks."

Walter nodded at me, like if he'd been wearing a cowboy hat he would've tipped it. Was this guy for real?

"And eat that bread while it's hot. There's butter and jam in the fridge," he called out as he walked outside, the door banging behind him.

I sat down for a minute on one of the barstools at the kitchen counter. Feeling dazed. Feeling totally knocked out by this new idea of a parallel life, completely away from not only the real one I'd been leading with Janet and Leo, but the one I'd always imagined, living in New York City with my mom, hanging out backstage at her plays, riding the subways together. Now here was a third option, a new existence in Santa Fe. And Walter was the one who wanted me there. This wasn't going to be like the kids I knew who hated their step-dads and had big fights all the time, threatening to move out. We could be a happy family.

Or a family, at least. I was still nervous about the happy part. Because, well, let's face it. My mother had never taken Walter up on his offer. What if she walked in the door, took one look at me, and walked right back out?

I MEAN, IT WAS STILL JUST weird. Leo sitting there in silence, swirling his scotch on the rocks around in its glass, while Janet chatted away. When I first came back to Hawthorne, I probably spent a solid month apologizing to them. Feeling genuinely sorry for how much I made them worry about me. I did every chore I could think to do: the laundry, the ironing, washing the dishes by hand. But Leo still wasn't talking to me. And Janet couldn't stop talking. Heaping pierogies onto my plate and asking me about my new college classes. Making this painfully obvious attempt at pretending that everything was totally normal when it wasn't, not quite. Normally I loved Janet's pierogies, but that night, they were just gumming up in my mouth like those wax lips you get on Halloween. The whole night had this melancholy in the air. It was getting cool and it would be autumn soon. I was missing someone or something or someplace, but I didn't

know who or what or where. I felt a million miles away from
Santa Fe. A million miles away from Janet and Leo, too, even
though they were sitting on either side of me. Then I real-
ized what it was. It had snuck up on me completely. It was
Friday. The night Rory and I used to get together and watch
The X-Files.

Rory. Rory. Rory. I'd started writing him a letter, but I
could never work up the nerve to print it out and put it in the
mail. Did he have any idea how much I missed him? How
sorry I was? Did he care?

"Do you guys mind if I turn in early?" I swallowed my
mouthful of pierogi mush. "Been kind of a long week."

"Are you sure you don't want dessert?" Janet asked. "I got
Neapolitan and Magic Shell. Your favorite."

"I know." God, I felt awful. Magic Shell was my favorite
when I was, like, four. Janet killed me sometimes. "Maybe I'll
come down later and have some."

"You know we're always open for midnight snacks. Come
here, you." I bent down and Janet smooched my cheek. I
patted Leo's arm as I passed. He didn't say a word.

It was ten to nine. Back in the day, Rory would be making
his place on the floor, propping himself up on pillows, and
I'd be setting up the DVD player. The room was so quiet
now. I could hear the train far off outside, a low, ghostly
whistle. I looked at my solid row of *X-Files* DVDs and I turned
on the computer instead. Maybe my fellow Philes at the
Friday Night Live Chat would make the melancholy go away.

But first, a quick check of the email. And, I'm not kidding—
right then, a split second after I'd opened my inbox, a new
email popped up. And it was from Rory. The subject heading

was *Season Five, Episode 20: The End*. The body of the email was just one line: *wrote this last spring. just rewrote the ending now.*

There was a file attached. This was weird. If he was sending me his latest entry for the *Guide*, he was a good season ahead.

I opened the file. Good gravy, it was almost five pages long. Rory started his review by explaining how "The End" was the final, cliffhanger episode of the fifth season, the last episode before the summer when the first *X-Files* movie came out. Then, the usual plot summary—after a six-year-old chess prodigy narrowly escapes assassination, Mulder and Scully get involved and find out that the boy's a psychic. And he's psychic because he has alien DNA. So of course the Cigarette-Smoking Man and the rest of the Syndicate are after him. But, worst of all, Mulder and Scully are joined on the case by the mysterious Agent Diana Fowley. As the episode goes on, things get botched, the assassin gets assassinated, Mulder gets blamed and almost creates an international incident, and the whole X-Files might end up getting shut down. But that's nothing compared to how Fowley wedges herself between our beloved Mulder and Scully. Or, as Rory put it:

> But of all the sickening kicks in the gut in this episode, the absolute worst, by far, is the introduction of Diana Fowley, one of the most sinister villains yet. Fowley's very presence threatens to sever the delicate bond of trust forged these past five years between Mulder and Scully. Throughout the episode, she quietly attempts to usurp Scully as Mulder's partner, and Scully is unable to do anything but stand by and watch.
>
> At first, all Scully knows is that Mulder and Fowley worked together back in the day, before Fowley was reassigned overseas. But then Scully consults the Lone Gunmen, and Frohike (in

bulletproof pajamas, no less) tells her that Fowley used to be "Mulder's chickadee" when he first got out of the Academy. Scully takes this new information in her usual good stride. So Mulder has an ex he never told Scully about. And why should he? They're co-workers, not fiancées. Even if she is an ex who, according to Byers, was there when Mulder discovered the X-Files, and supported his wild paranormal theories instead of constantly debunking him with actual scientific facts.

Scully goes back to the institution where they're holding the psychic kid for observation. She's got big news for Mulder—the Lone Gunmen found an anomaly in the MRI that may explain the kid's psychic abilities. Scully walks down the hall toward the kid's observation room where Mulder's waiting . . . and keeps walking. She takes a few steps down the hall, then turns, pauses, and walks back out. As she leaves, the camera angle reverses, and we see what she saw, through the window to the observation room. We see Mulder, not observing anything except for Fowley, who is holding Mulder's hand and gazing lovingly into his eyes!

Cut to the parking garage. This is where it all happens. It's the briefest of scenes. Unlike climactic scenes in other season finales, nothing blows up. Nobody jumps onto the top of a moving train. What happens is this: Scully gets into her car. Her face is half-hidden in shadow. And she just . . . sits there. Taking a moment. We take that moment with her. We comprehend what she's just seen. We comprehend everything. After this series of simple motions—passing by the door, that moment of decision in the hallway when she chooses to walk away—we are brought to an unnerving stillness.

In the book An Actor Prepares, there's a scene where Stanislavski talks about physical immobility. He says that just because an actor is sitting on the stage, not moving, it doesn't mean they're passive. An actor who isn't moving might still have a sort of inner intensity, and inner intensity is more artistic, anyway. While one could argue that Gillian Anderson (as Scully) is "just sitting in the car," what is, in fact, occurring in this scene is a fairly dramatic series of internal realizations and negotiations.

Everything that's happened—the abduction, Melissa, the cancer, even the Pomeranian, for Pete's sake—all of it happened to Scully because of her dedication to Mulder's crazy quest. In that silent moment in the car, Scully tries to convince herself that it doesn't matter if he holds some other woman's hand, if he's had some whole other relationship that he never told her about. Just because she and Mulder trust each other with their lives, it's not like they're married. Nothing's been promised. They're partners on an assignment, and that's all. Two people who were randomly paired up by a bunch of suits at the FBI. This connection between them, maybe it never really existed. Maybe it was no connection at all. Maybe it was just dedication to the job, all along. Dedication she mistook for love.

Maybe she's silently cursing herself. She's a scientist and an FBI agent, not one to get carried away by girly love stuff. Still, it's a kick in the slacks. And what's worse, she's the last to know, when she should have been the first. That Fowley knows Mulder in a way that Scully doesn't, even though Scully's closer to him than anyone else, is bad enough. But Scully has to hear it from the Lone Gunmen, not from Mulder himself. She has to sneak up on it in the hall, happening right under her nose. It's not that there's no relationship between Mulder and Fowley anymore, or that it's too minor to mention. It's that Mulder thinks it's none of Scully's business.

So, the typically pragmatic, reliable Agent Scully can be forgiven for turning and walking away from Mulder and Fowley. For deciding, on her own, to act. After that moment in the car, when she is finally able to pick up her phone and call Mulder, she can be forgiven for lying to him, for telling him to meet her back at the office, for not telling him she was just downstairs in the parking garage. She can be forgiven for not knowing how to do her usual job with this new, unusual third party involved. And that's what they should've been doing, Mulder and Scully. Their usual job of finding the truth amidst cover-ups and lies. Except that Mulder allowed himself to become distracted, distant, losing sight of all the work he and Scully had done together, the alliance they'd forged.

Maybe it was easier for Scully to turn around and walk away and let Mulder think that she was nowhere near him. Maybe she needed more time to figure out her next move. Because, after all those years of being together, but not really together, Scully finally knew the answer for certain. In that brief, still moment, she knew for certain that she loved this man, and that he did not belong to her.

And it's crushing. It's awful to feel alone in the world. Everyone wants to belong to someone.

Even someone as kickass as FBI Special Agent Dana Scully.

I saved the file and closed it. I got online. I sent Rory an IM.

BloomOrphan: just read 5x20. it's beautiful.

I waited there, chewing at the edge of my thumbnail. He was still online. But the cursor was just blinking in white space. I logged in to the *Phorum*, but he wasn't in the chat room. I logged out, came back to the IM. Still blinking. Still blank.

BloomOrphan: really, it might be your best work.

Blink. Blink. Blink.

BloomOrphan: rory. thank you.

Almost a half an hour later, I turned off the computer. I turned off the light. I stumbled over to the bed and cried for a while until I fell into a deep, empty dream.

six

So this is my mother.

Mom. Mother. Mama. Ma. None of these words felt right. She was like an iceberg. Floating and cold and distant. She was so far away still. She was standing right there in front of me. For nine months I was in this woman's womb. We were once connected by actual flesh. This was a completely alien concept. Completely abstract. She was a dream to me. A flickering image I only barely remembered.

And now there I was with the real thing. My mother. She was tall and slender and reminded me of a roughly chiseled sculpture that sat outside the First Carolina Bank on Dalton Street. Her eyes looked like mine as they looked at me.

"It's you," she said.

"It's me."

She had an armload of books and three-ring binders that she slunched onto the dining room table. She dug a BlackBerry out of her purse and dialed a number. She's making a call, at a time like this?

"Leo? It's me, Chris. Call off the dogs. Yeah, she's here." My mother handed me the phone. "Talk to your grandfather."

I blanched, shaking my head. No way. He would kill me. Through the phone, somehow. Phone bullets.

"Leo, she's a little freaked out, but she's fine. You're fine, right?" She was speaking to me. My mother was speaking to me. I nodded my head. "She says she's fine. Yes. Yes. I'll have her call you later, okay? She just got here. Yes—why would I? . . . Now you're being ridiculous. I said yes, didn't I? Okay, goodbye." She tossed the BlackBerry back in her purse.

"They're worried sick about you." She rapped her fingers against the kitchen counter. "You're going to have to call them, you know."

"I know." *Memorize her! Memorize her! She'll go away!*

"What were you thinking?"

"What were *you* thinking?" I parroted. No, no, that was all wrong. I wasn't angry anymore. I loved her. Look at how cool she was. That silver ring on her thumb. Her cowboy boots. She was so fucking cool. She was the coolest woman I'd ever laid eyes on. I couldn't believe this was my mom.

"Oh, brother." She sighed and flipped her hair with her hands. "Listen, I'm starved. Can we wait until after dinner to get into all the psychodrama? I assume you're staying for dinner."

Of course I was staying. I had already staked my claim, put my duffel bag in the spare room and taken a shower with her weird narcotic soap, and I'd been sitting there at her kitchen counter eating hot bread for a good half hour by the time she got home. I was staying. She wasn't getting rid of me.

"Now, ain't that a picture?" Walter came in, stamping his boots on the gnarly braided rug. "Mother and child reunion. Whaddaya say let's eat?"

JAY WAS IN MY ROOM AT Janet and Leo's and suddenly I felt completely inadequate. I had the sneaking suspicion that Janet only invited her to dinner because she was trying to keep tabs on who I was hanging out with. As for Jay actually agreeing to this supremely awkward grandparent dinner/ inquisition, I guess she figured after I drank her beer all the time, the least I could do was pay her back with gargantuan quantities of free Polish food. We'd retreated upstairs while Janet put the finishing touches on the meal.

"Man, it's like a shrine in here." Jay glanced around my bedroom walls. "I had no idea they made Hobbit wallpaper."

"Well, they're actually posters—"

"I was being sarcastic."

"Right . . ." I felt strangely off-balance with Jay there. Like suddenly my room was smaller than usual, or something. "You're into *Lord of the Rings*?"

"Never seen it. Well, I saw part of one of them on TV once at my cousin's house."

"Seriously? You've never seen, like, any of them? At all?"

"Yeaaah, I'm not really into, like . . . wizards and shit."

"But, Jay! It's not just about wizards and shit! I mean, wizards are awesome, Gandalf's the coolest, but . . . it's all about humanity and like, good versus evil."

"And beardy guys with swords?" Jay asked, eyeballing my Aragorn posters.

"That's Aragorn. He's like, this total badass. He's just, like, roaming the forests, carrying this tragic, impossible love for Arwen, but they can't be together because she's an elf and he's a man, and, meanwhile, he knows he's the king, and he doesn't let on, because he's too lovesick to even deal with it. Seriously, he's the hotness. You have to see the trilogy. It's epic. I'll bring over my DVDs."

"Mmm, can't wait." Jay picked up a book from my shelf. "You're reading Sam Shepard?"

"That's my mom's."

"I had to see *Fool for Love* for this playwriting class I took back at Smith . . . not my cup of tea. All that macho cowboy stuff." Jay shrugged and put the book back.

"Oh, it's not all macho cowboys. Most of his stuff's really weird and funny. Like, in *The Unseen Hand*, there's a—"

"Wow. Really?" Jay interrupted, holding up my Mulder and Scully action figures, still in the original packaging. "Just when I thought you'd told me all your deepest, darkest secrets, the truth comes out. Wizards. Elves. Kirk and Spock. Mulder and Scully. Lula, you're a *nerd*!"

"First of all, those are collector's items. Second—"

"*Nerrrrrrd.*"

"It's not like I carry around a Klingon–English dictionary." I knew a kid who did that. Steve Meese. Now *that* guy was a nerd.

"So you won't be mad if I crack this open—" Jay flipped the Mulder figure over, her hands around the protective plastic casing.

"HEY." I reached out and grabbed it out of her hands. "Not cool!"

"Nerrr-errrrd." She sang softly.

"Okay, yes, I am a bit of a geek. I enjoy escapist entertainment. Listen, I'd rather watch a bunch of elves and wizards trying to save Middle Earth from the forces of evil than, I dunno, the *Bachelorette* or the *Real Housewives* of wherever getting their butt fat injected into their lips."

"Point taken," Jay laughed, gazing up at my wall of *X-Files* posters. "How'd you even get into this, anyway? This show came on when you were, like, two."

"Reruns." I put action figure Mulder and Scully back in their places on my shelf. "Rory and I started watching it together. It's one of our things. Or, it used to be." Past tense.

"Ahh, now it all comes together." Jay lay back on my bed, her hands behind her head. "You've seen one unrequited white hetero love story, you've seen 'em all."

"What's that supposed to mean?"

"I mean I totally get it. You thought your buddy Rory was the Mulder to your Scully."

"Well . . . yeah." I sank down into my desk chair. "But, no."

"Or, wait, did you think, what's her name again, Sam? Was she supposed to be the Scully to your . . . other Scully? . . . Scully's the chick, right?"

"Please don't tell me you've never seen *The X-Files*."

"Honestly, I tried, a million years ago, back in junior high when it first came on. Not into UFOs, not into unrequited heteros. I did get into *Buffy* for a while, but just for Tara and Willow."

"Jay. I'm coming to your house with all nine seasons and you are not going to see the sun for three months. *X-Files* is literally the best show ever."

"Dude, *The Wire* is the best show ever, and we are done talking. But, back to my question. Rory. Sam. You. The fact that Ms. Adorable Pouty Redhead is duking it out with the Beardy Swordsman over there for bedroom wall supremacy. Did it ever occur to you that maybe you're not gay or straight? Maybe you're bisexual."

"First of all, Ms. Adorable Pouty Redhead? That's Special Agent Dana Scully you're talking about. Who is not only an FBI agent but also a medical doctor."

"So she could arrest me and tell me whether or not I should start watching my cholesterol?"

"And perform an autopsy, if the need arises."

"Impressive," Jay remarked. "You know you're allowed to be an FBI agent-slash-doctor and be adorable at the same time, right?"

"Sure, I'm just saying. Agent Scully occupies a place of honor in my bedroom wall pantheon because she's a total badass, not just because she's some cute chick. And anyway, I thought you said one time that bisexuals don't really exist."

"Oh, I only meant, you know, sometimes people say they're bi when they're really just too scared to commit to being gay. Listen, you can't take everything I say while we're watching *Dr. Phil* at face value. I'm sure there are some legit bi people out there."

"And you think I'm one of them?"

"Well, your average lesbian probably wouldn't deliver monologues about the 'hotness' of Mr. Pointy Cheekbones from *Lord of the Rings*. On the other hand, Agent Scully notwithstanding, it sounds like you made a pretty definitive effort toward initiating the sexytimes with your lady teacher. So . . . there's that."

"Yeah, there's that," I sighed, sinking down into my desk chair. "Can I be honest?"

"Please."

"I don't think I really wanted to sleep with Sam. But I liked her. I like her. I mean, I . . . care about her life, and stuff. I don't really care that much about any of my other teachers. Like, I don't bear them any ill will, or whatever. But I don't get to school on Monday morning and think 'Hey, I wonder if Mrs. Dalrymple got up to anything fun over the weekend.'"

"Lula, there's this fascinating social concept called 'friendship,' where you're allowed to be interested in another person without having to declare some kind of sexual allegiance. You're even allowed to be interested in one of your high school teachers. Beneath all the fangs and gore, they're regular people just like you and me."

"Fangs and gore?"

"I'm trying to speak to you in your idiom. Listen, seriously, I think I'm starting to get it now. You're trying to figure out what flavor of queer you are, if any, and you've got Scary Leo downstairs running interference, so you're, like, couching it all in TV shows instead of going out and actually dating people."

"First of all, I'm not not dating people because I'm scared of Leo. Nobody at my school was ever even remotely interested in me. My nickname was Weird Girl. Second of all . . . Leo's scary, but he's not that scary."

"Dude. You practically saluted him when we walked in the door."

"I'm not . . . I wasn't . . ." I trailed off. Jay stared at me coolly. "You're right. I'm afraid of him. I'm afraid of what he thinks of me now."

"Well, he hasn't kicked you out of the house yet, so he's one up on my dad," Jay said softly.

"I don't think he'd kick me out just for being gay. Leo's always saying how civilians waste too much time worrying about gays in the military when they ought to worry about veterans not receiving adequate healthcare and stuff. Plus, he's like, really into Barbra Streisand."

"Now *that's* gay."

"I know, right?" We both laughed. I dug the toe of my sneaker into the carpet. "But I'm scared of him thinking I'm . . . ruining my life or something. I'm scared of him not being proud of me."

"Everybody's scared of that with their parents," Jay said gently. "You just have to do your best. That's all."

"I'm scared of other stuff, too, Jay."

"Well no wonder. You sit up here alone watching all this alien abduction, wizard apocalypse stuff."

"No, I mean . . . like, when I went to meet my mom. I haven't . . . told anybody this. She was saying how my dad . . . how they were friends but they didn't really love each other. It wasn't meant to be."

"Ah. You were an accident baby."

"Yeah. But, more than that. Apparently, um. My dad was gay."

"No kidding." Jay sat up. "Huh. And you can't figure out if you're gay like him or not. This is all kinda starting to make sense now. You know it's not genetic, right? You can't inherit being straight or gay. Otherwise I'd be a happy hetero just like my mom and dad."

"I know. It's more like the whole . . . him not really loving her thing. It doesn't feel too good. I mean, I knew she didn't want me when she left me here with Janet and Leo. But to have it confirmed. That I was just this, like, error. I mean, not like a minor error, like they were so crazy about each other they couldn't wait for the wedding night, or whatever. I mean like, these two people never even really wanted to sleep with each other in the first place. They were just . . . I don't even know, drunk and lonely and trying to pretend they actually loved each other. And then I came along. This mistake that neither of them saw coming. That neither of them wanted."

"But, Lula, come on. So what if they didn't plan to have a baby? You're here now; your grandparents love you—even if your granddad is scary. They plastered the whole town with flyers when you left."

"I know, I know. It's not that, it's just . . . lately I've been thinking, what if I'm always going to be this superfluous person, roaming the planet all alone, never fitting in, never connecting with anybody because I wasn't supposed to be here in the first place? You know how, like, when two people are in love, and everybody says, oh, it was meant to be? It was written in the stars? Lately I can't help thinking: what if I'm not meant to be *with* anybody because I wasn't even meant to *be*?"

"That is . . . one of the most depressing things I've ever heard in my life." Jay sighed. She got up off the bed and knelt down in front of me, her hands on the arms of my desk chair, holding me steady, so I couldn't turn away.

"Lula. Look at me. You're just a kid. Just because you haven't met the Mulder to your Scully yet, or the Scully to your other Scully, or whoever it is you're looking for, it doesn't mean you're superfluous."

I looked down at my shoes. I didn't want Jay to see that I was on the verge of tears.

"Lula. Forget your parents. Forget their intentions. You exist. Okay? That's really important. You're here now, and you're the one who gets to say what's a mistake and what isn't. Your parents not loving each other doesn't negate you as a human being. This is your life, and it fucking matters, okay? Are you hearing me? You are here, and *it fucking matters*. You're the one setting the intentions now. Don't punk out just because your parents couldn't get their shit together. Kiddo. Don't despair." Jay leaned in, and whispered in my ear. "You're not going to die a virgin."

I almost laughed. Jay leaned back and tipped my chin up. I wiped my nose on the back of my hand. Yuck. So much for being cool. Jay must've thought I was such a gross, snotty kid.

There was a knock on the door. Janet. Jay stood up hastily, jamming her hands in her back pockets.

"Who's ready for klopsiki?" She looked at me and Jay. "Polish meatballs!"

"Sounds delicious," Jay said.

"Lula, honey?"

"Klopsiki," I managed to smile. "Sure. Fine. Whatever."

seven

WALTER COOKED THIS AMAZING MEAL. AND I don't even like Mexican food all that much.

"It's Southwestern," he corrected. Blue cornbread, green chile enchiladas. Maybe it was because I'd been eating Amtrak food for the past two days, but this was the best meal I'd ever had in my life.

It was also kind of like an out-of-body experience. I mean, there was my mother. *My mother.* I kept saying this to myself, hoping it would sink in.

"You're, what, sixteen now?" Walter asked. So far, he was the one doing all the talking. My mom was periodically checking her BlackBerry at the table. Which was officially Bad Manners in our house, but then, we weren't at Janet and Leo's anymore, Toto.

"Seventeen," I told him. "I'll be eighteen in August."

"Seventeen. What is that, eleventh grade?"

"Yes, sir. Going into twelfth."

"You've just about served your time."

"Yes, sir."

"You don't have to keep calling me sir, you know," Walter gave me a sideways smile. "This ain't the Navy."

"Okay," I replied.

And then another long awkward silence. My mother stared at me coolly. I stared back. Walter chewed determinedly.

"Fourteen years," I said.

My mother raised her eyebrows at me.

"Fourteen years since we've seen each other."

"Fourteen years," she repeated. "So what do you want from me? Exactly?"

"Chris," Walter muttered.

"It's a legitimate question. I've had to deal with Leo calling up and interrogating me every day for the past few weeks because of you—I think I'm entitled to ask a few questions. Is it money you're after? Or just a place to hide after you've embarrassed yourself in front of your friends and your teacher?"

Oh, God. I could feel my ears turning red-hot. She knew the whole story. How did she find out? Did everybody know? Did Sam tell? Rory told me in one of his emails about the cops taking my computer, but still. I buried my journal deep in the recesses of my hard drive, in a file marked "Algebra II Study Questions, Chapter Four." I was seriously never going home again.

"Lula, you know you can stay here as long as you like," Walter said, as if he were reading my mind. Did he know, too? Somehow that was even more embarrassing.

"I don't want your money," I said, keeping my voice steady. Why would I want her money? I stabbed my enchilada. "And I have plenty of places to stay."

"So why show up on my doorstep now, after fourteen years? What do you expect from me?" My mother sat back in her tall wooden chair and folded her arms.

"I just wanted to know—" I stopped. She was too cool. I just wanted to know you. That was what I wanted to say. *I wanted to know you, and I thought maybe you could help me figure out who I am, too.*

"Know what?" She was impatient.

"Know about you. You and me. I wanted to know—Walter said he told you that I could come and live here with you guys anytime. So why didn't you send for me? I want to know how it all broke down. I want to know why you left me with them. I want to know why you never . . . why you never wanted me around." By the end of the sentence, my voice had trailed off to a whisper. My mother looked at Walter. He wiped his mouth on his napkin and gave her a stern look. Kind of like he wanted an answer, too. My mother cleared her throat.

"Lula, listen. It's nothing personal. I was young, I was broke. Living in LA, going to one audition after another. I was barely making ends meet, taking any job I could get. That's how I ended up on the movie where Walter and I met. I was a set PA; I spent all day putting batteries in walkie-talkies and thanking my lucky stars I wasn't waitressing that week. And your father was in the same boat. Financially speaking."

"So, that was it? You guys couldn't afford me?"

My mother and Walter exchanged a look.

"It wasn't purely financial. Your father met someone else. We were at the end of our . . . relationship. When I got pregnant. He tried to be there for you, but it was better for all of us if . . ."

"Wait, but, if my old man bailed on you for some other chick, couldn't you sue him for child support? Alimony or whatever?"

"We weren't married."

"I think she means palimony," Walter explained quietly.

"Whatever," I said. "So my dad's some total bastard—"

"He's not a total bastard," my mother insisted.

"Chris—" Walter reached for her hand.

"Yeah, he's a bastard. He left you and then you left me."

"It's not that simple and it's not—" my mother's voice got loud. She stopped, tightening her fist around her fork. "It's not something I talk about."

"Okay, *granddad*," I said. She set her fork down and looked at me.

"You want full disclosure? All right. Your father was not a bastard. Your father was gay. But he was too deep in denial to admit it, even to himself, and I was too young and naïve to see what was right in front of my face. He thought—we both thought he could change, but he couldn't. He met someone else before he knew I was pregnant, but when he found out, he tried to make it work anyway. But it didn't work. He met his true love, and it wasn't me. You think this is something I like hashing out over enchiladas?"

My mother's look was a dare. I didn't want to take it.

". . . My dad's gay?"

"Yeah. He is."

I let that sink in. My dad was gay. Wow. Weird. Wow. . . . Really weird.

"He's worried about you, you know," my mother told me.

"He is?"

"I called him after Janet called me. When she told me you went missing. We thought you might have gone to find him. Since he's closer. He's in Nashville. He teaches acting at Vanderbilt."

"I didn't know. I don't even know his name." My head felt prickly, trying to take everything in. "But I guess he didn't want me, either."

"It wasn't that he didn't want you. Peter—your father's name is Peter—he loved you. He loved taking care of you. Singing you back to sleep when you woke up in the middle of the night, changing your diapers, the whole bit. But he was at a different place in his life. He was older, and, aside from coming to terms with the whole gay thing, he was facing the fact that his movie career wasn't going to pan out. He wanted to go to grad school so he could teach, and he and Dale were trying to make a life together—Dale's his . . . partner."

"Why didn't he come visit, or something? I mean, Nashville's like, a day's drive away from Hawthorne."

"Fear, probably. His mother disowned him when he came out. And Leo was . . . Leo. They met once, and Leo was pretty intimidating toward him. But that Stanislavski book you've been toting around was Peter's. He ran this little acting workshop on the weekends—that was where we met." She smiled, remembering. "He gave me that book for inspiration. Sometimes I think he was the only person who believed I had any talent." Her voice was quiet. Walter touched her arm. My mother's BlackBerry buzzed. She looked at it, then silenced the call.

"I'm sorry you never knew his name. I thought Janet

would've at least told you who he was."

"I don't think you realize the extent to which Leo has obliterated your existence in our house. Not to mention my father, or anyone else vaguely you-related."

My mother rolled her eyes to the ceiling. "Leo . . . you know, this is why I can't even come home for a holiday. He makes everything so . . . goddamn impossible sometimes."

"Tell me about it."

My mother looked at me, biting her lip. Walter finished his enchiladas in silence.

"I still think it was the right thing, though. For him and Janet to raise you," she said, after a while. "My life was no place for a baby. Or a little kid. After the break-in, I knew it for sure—"

"The break-in?"

"Boy, they really didn't tell you anything about me, did they? And you'd think this would be the most important thing for you to understand. The whole reason I gave you to them. You don't remember it? Not at all?"

"I don't think so."

"I'd just moved to New York. You were three. A friend of Peter's, actually, got me a part in this off-off-Broadway thing, and I loved it and thought I'd stay. Of course, the only neighborhood I could afford was really awful. One afternoon, I had a rehearsal, and the babysitter was sick, so I took you with me. And while we were there, our apartment got robbed. Not just robbed, but . . . *utterly demolished*. I'm glad you don't remember this. It was such a terrible feeling. I mean, it's bad enough some creep comes into your place and takes everything you own, but what's the point of destroying the rest?

What's the point of breaking every dish? What's the point of turning all the furniture over, taking every picture off the wall and smashing it? What had I ever done besides live there?" My mother paused. Her BlackBerry buzzed again. This time, she ignored it.

"But the worst part of it," she went on, "was wondering what would have happened if I'd left you there. Maybe nothing would have happened, right? Maybe if someone had been home, there never would have been a break-in. But what if it had happened anyway, and the babysitter couldn't protect you? What if those creeps had taken you, or hurt you, or . . ." My mother stopped. It was almost like she got choked up. Walter put his hand on hers. "So I called Janet and Leo. I didn't know where else to go. I didn't have insurance. Leo bought me a plane ticket and met me at the airport. When I saw how happy they were to have you there—especially Leo, my God. And you could grow up in a nice condo, in a quiet neighborhood, with all the trees and lawns. It wasn't like all those crappy military bases we lived on when I was a kid."

"Trees and lawns?" I blurted out. "Seriously? I mean, I get that you didn't want to raise me on the mean streets of New York City. I get that you'd think I was safe with Leo, what with all the guns in the basement and everything. But I don't get . . . I still don't get how you could bail on your kid."

"It wasn't bailing. It wasn't my original intention to just . . . leave you behind. I was leaving you in more capable hands so I could get my life together. It wasn't easy, Lula. It was not an easy decision." My mother looked down at her plate. Walter was still holding her hand. "But it was the right decision. I know it was. Some people just aren't mom material. I found out that I'm one of those people." She gave me a sort of half-smile. "Try not to take it personally, kiddo." My mother's BlackBerry buzzed, and this time she checked the caller ID and sort of thought about it for a second before she hit the silence button again.

"Who wants ice cream?" Walter stood up, clearing our plates. Neither of us answered him.

"I don't get why you just ran off, though. Why you couldn't at least let them know where you were going? Just a note, just a 'Hey guys, I'm gonna leave my kid with you, I'll be in Santa Fe if you need me, keep in touch.'"

"They knew I was in Santa Fe. Leo didn't tell you because he was trying to protect you, probably. He didn't make it easy for me. I never meant for it to get so . . . extreme, but . . . look, put yourself in my place. Every time you want to call up and say hi to your kid, you get blasted with the third degree from Drill Sergeant Daddy about why you're not there, what's so important about your *career* . . ." My mother frowned and picked idly at her placemat, at a slender thread unraveling from the edge. "Anyway, I had a lot to deal with. I didn't know how things were going to work out. Where I'd end up. Walter had become a good friend. I called him after the break-in, and he told me that if there was anything he could do to help, he would. He offered to let me stay at his place until I got back on my feet. Neither one of us anticipated . . . each other." She got this faraway look, talking about Walter. The old guy. Yuck.

I looked up at him, rinsing dishes in the sink and chunking them into the dishwasher matter-of-factly. The determined look on his face. It was almost funny, really. The resemblance.

"You know you married Leo, don't you?" I whispered.

"Just because he's older, he's nothing like—" My mother gave me a look, but she knew what I was talking about. "Tch. Don't be gross."

eight

"YOUR FRIEND'S IN THE PAPER," LEO said from behind the morning paper.

"Jay?"

"No. Theodore." He folded the newspaper back. "Your old school's undefeated. Says here 'Quarterback Seth Brock is on pace to break Hawthorne's all-time single-season passing record. The addition of senior Theodore Callahan has made the Fighting Eagles' offensive line nearly impenetrable to every defense in the region.'" Leo sipped his coffee. This was a far cry from our old breakfasts, where Leo and I traded the sports page and the funnies, then shared the high points of *Peanuts* and praised Bobby Cox's managerial decisions with the Braves. But still. My grandfather had actually started a conversation with me. Leo speaks! Alert the press!

"Mmm. Impenetrable, huh?" I sat there behind my cereal bowl, doing a bang-up job of pretending this was all just the usual breakfast chitchat.

"What do you hear from old Rory these days?" My grandfather snapped the paper back open.

"Nothing." I walked over to the sink and chucked the rest of my Corn Flakes down the garbage disposal. I stuck the bowl in the dishwasher and wiped my hands on my jeans.

"I'm gonna be late." I grabbed my backpack. "Tell Janet I'll probably stay over at Jay's tonight."

"Will do," Leo said, but I could tell from his voice he wasn't happy about it.

I WENT TO HIS HOUSE. RORY'S. Maybe this time I'd catch him on his way to school. Maybe this time he'd be in a good mood from his football wins, and we'd joke about everything, finally put it all behind us. Maybe we'd—

"What do you want?" Rory's mother came to the door. Patty the Pickle. She was already soused, at eight-something in the morning. Or maybe she was still hungover from the night before.

"Hi, Mrs. Callahan. I'm, uh. Looking for Rory?" God, Patty made me nervous. I mean, you know. Drunks. Who knows what they're going to do next?

"He dozzen live here anymore."

"He dozzen?"

Patty the Pickle closed the door in my face.

LATER THAT AFTERNOON, STARING OUT THE window during Concepts in Earth Science, listening to Mr. Badfinger ramble on about plate tectonics, I had a brilliant idea. It was Friday. I'd go to the football game. I could see Rory. Just see him. Ask him what the hell was going on. Tell him good for him, moving away from his messed-up mother. Not like a major confrontation or anything. Just dropping in to cheer on the home team. We could exchange fucked-up-mom stories. We could reminisce about the old times.

That is, if he would speak to me. I mean, if I could get over how pissed off I was, then surely he could get over his—

"Miss Monroe, is there anything you'd like to add?" Add to what? Uh-oh. Badfinger could tell I wasn't paying attention. He'd been gunning for me ever since I'd slipped and called him Mr. Badfinger to his face. It'd been his nickname since the *seventies*, for Pete's sake. His real name was Mr. Bodinger. I mean, what do you expect?

"Uh . . . plate tectonics. Are what happens when plates move. Tectonically."

The rest of the class tittered. Badfinger stood there at the white board, glaring at me. His big, meaty hands methodically uncapping and re-capping a dry erase marker. Badfinger also taught automotive repair at the tech school. Which is a step up from having a gym coach as a teacher. I guess.

"Little Miss," he drawled. "You realize there's going to be a test on this material at the end of the week, don't you?"

Little Miss. That was what he called me when I annoyed him. And I annoyed him frequently. It had crossed my mind more than once that, if I'd just stayed put at Hawthorne, I'd either be in Conceptual Physics II or AP Biology right now. Instead, because of the college's ridiculous freshman year requirements, I had an auto mechanic lecturing me about the mysteries of the San Andreas Fault. At least they'd let me skip to Earth Science. But, yeah. I reckon I missed a little.

"A test," Badfinger went on, "that will count for a good percent of your final grade this semester."

"A good percent?" I paused, letting my next sarcastic rejoinder rest on the tip of my tongue. It was just too easy to mess with this guy. I would've felt bad, if I wasn't so appalled by his dismissal of me as some twerpy little girl who couldn't possibly grasp the infinitely daunting realms of . . . Concepts in Earth Science.

"You are on thin ice with me today, Little Missy," Badfinger warned, turning around to face the dry-erase board. "Thin. Ice."

"But I do know the point at which it freezes," I chirped. "In Fahrenheit and Celsius." A couple of kids in the back snickered. At least somebody was amused.

THE HORSE TWITCHED ITS TAIL, SNORTED. It turned its massive head around and looked at me out of the corner of its gigantic dark eye, as if to say, "You cannot be serious." Walter stood there, holding the reins.

"Go on, put your foot in the stirrup. He won't rear up."

"Can I take a pass?"

"Take a pass?"

I hesitated. Walter was turning out to be a cool guy. My mom had left for work at the crack of dawn, so he spent the day showing me around the ranch, introducing me to the cowboy guys in the fields and the two girls in the office who took care of getting jobs for the animals—the horses actually had headshots!—and telling me his whole story. Walter grew up in LA; his family were movie people, set designers—his dad even worked with Orson Welles. But Walter spent his summers working on this very ranch, which belonged to his uncle at the time, and he'd always liked Westerns, so that became his main deal. Training horses for movies—picture horses, he called them. Which had a kind of poetic ring to it, I thought. Walter pointed out the horses I would recognize if I'd seen this movie or that miniseries, like they were real celebrities or something. He was so proud of them. Truthfully, I couldn't tell the difference. I was like "there's a brown one" and "there's a black one" and, honestly, I never in my life needed to know what the term "gelding" meant. I guess I could appreciate that these horses were magnificent beasts and all. But now Walter expected me to climb onto the back of one and do what, exactly? I mean, as cool as it would've been to go charging off to Rivendell on my noble steed like Arwen rescuing Frodo in the movies, in real life, these suckers were huge!

"I'm sure he's a nice horse and all, but, seriously, Walter. I'm not feeling it."

"You're not feeling it?"

"I, uh . . ." I stood there in the smelly barn in my Converse high tops, wanting to fit in, really wanting to love the ranch. But I'd never been one of those girls who fantasized about riding horses. I knew those kinds of girls back in elementary school. But I never understood the allure. I mean, it's a big stinky animal. So what?

"I really appreciate the opportunity," I explained, "and I appreciate that you're taking time out of your day, but, really—I'm just not a horse girl."

Walter wiped his nose with a bandanna he kept jammed in his back pocket. He frowned at me.

"You are your mother's child, you know that?" He didn't make that sound like a compliment, but I was secretly pleased. "What're you so afraid of? Afraid you'll fall off? You won't. Gingerbread here ain't exactly a rodeo pony. We just used him in the background of a Stetson cologne ad. All he's good at is standing real still."

"It's not that."

"Then what is it?"

"I don't know. Why do you care? I don't want to do it, that's all." I turned and started walking back to the house, vaguely aware of the farmhands or whatever who were watching this scene play out. This whole thing was getting lame fast.

"Hey, you're starting a real disturbing trend here, you know that?" he called after me. I looked back. Walter tied Gingerbread's reins to a post with a loose knot and followed after me.

"How is not wanting to ride a horse a disturbing trend?"

"Is this how you're gonna live your life? You're gonna run away when things get a little hard? When there's something new and unfamiliar and scary?"

"Walter." I stopped. "You remember how the first thing you said to me was that you're not my father?"

"I'm not speaking to you as a father, I'm speaking to you as an adult who's been on this planet longer than you have. Sometimes you have to stick it out. You have to be willing to do things you wouldn't normally—"

"I did that already, didn't I? Just because I don't want to ride some big smelly horse doesn't mean I don't take risks. What do you think I came out here for? This whole trip was one big risk, and I was scared out of my mind, but I did it because I had to. I couldn't hang around that shithole town anymore wondering why—wondering why she left me there—" I stopped. Good gravy. I was about to cry.

Walter squinted at me. Why was I standing in the middle of a field, telling my problems to the Marlboro Man, anyway? *Because I don't want to go back home. Because I want to be home right here. Because I don't want to be Lula Monroe anymore, Weird Girl, holed up in her room at her grandparents' house in the retirement community, watching* X-Files *with her gay best friend who doesn't love her.*

"It's not you. You know that, right? She doesn't even know you."

I nodded. I knew. My mother didn't even know me. The Marlboro Man pulled me in close to him and held me while I cried into his shirt.

AFTER THE BADFINGER HUMILIATION, I WENT to the computer lab to check my email. Rory was online. What was he doing online in the middle of the day?

Okay, this was nothing, right? Communication. Just go for it, give it a shot. What's the worst that could happen? He could ignore me. He's already doing that.

BloomOrphan: hey

Is it possible for a cursor to blink for a thousand years? So he wasn't speaking to me. Fine. I minimized the screen and opened an email from Jay that had a link to a YouTube video of Le Tigre. This sort of disco-like girl band that she liked. I put my headphones on to listen. Instead, *bing!*

SpookyKid: Hey yourself.

He's speaking to me! Now what?

BloomOrphan: how's it going?

SpookyKid: Crazy busy. Senior year. How's it going with you?

BloomOrphan: ok. I went by your house this am. patty said you moved out.

SpookyKid: Something like that.

BloomOrphan: everything ok? (dumb question?)

SpookyKid: Bit of a SNAFU at first, now ok.

BloomOrphan: oh. good.

Well, what did I expect? That he's going to go into this whole dramatic story with me over IM?

BloomOrphan: Leo saw you in the paper this morning. undefeated.

SpookyKid: I know. Weird, right? Furman U in Greenville SC offered me a scholarship. Coach M says hold out for more schools.

BloomOrphan: congrats!

I was already bored with the small talk. I wanted to talk to him, really talk to him, like we used to. But what could I say in a stupid IM? How does it feel to be undefeated? I mean, really. But then:

SpookyKid: XF2. Mulder with a beard.

BloomOrphan: aieee!!! I know, right?!

SpookyKid: I knew you would freak out.

I almost jumped for joy, right there in the computer lab. This was major. This was huge. Not only was Rory speaking to me, he was speaking to me about *The X-Files*. This meant that, on some level, we were back. Something was smoothed over, forgiven. This would probably seem silly, if you didn't understand us. If you didn't understand the way we spoke. There were times when talking about *The X-Files* was actually more important than talking about ourselves. I mean, it was the way we talked about ourselves. It was the two of us saying, all right, we can't even approach the real stuff, can't even begin, but we have this shared love, and, yes, it's just some television show, but it's *our* television show. It was this language that we spoke, that only the two of us understood. If you knew me like Rory knows me, you would know that our first topic of conversation after the credits rolled on the second *X-Files* movie would not have been the plotline, the cinematography, or the special effects. It would have been the fact that, holed up in his snowy hideaway for all those years, Agent Mulder has grown a crazy exile beard.

We're simultaneously shallow and intense this way.

> *SpookyKid: gotta run end of study hall*
>
> *BloomOrphan: nice typing with ya*
>
> *SpookyKid: :)*

WALTER FINALLY GOT ME ON THAT damn horse.

"Now, I don't wanna say I told you so," he said. "But what'd I tell ya?" We rode the horses up a small mountain, through a wooded trail. Just when we'd come to a clearing near the top of the ridge, the gray clouds that had clotted the sky all day suddenly broke apart. Shafts of dark amber light seemed to pour out of cracks in the horizon as the sun began to set off in the distance, over the twinkling city lights.

"It's okay. You're right. This is the most beautiful—this is fucking amazing." It was, truly, one of the most breathtaking things I'd ever seen that wasn't CGI.

"You, ah—" Walter cleared his throat. "You use that kinda language in front of your grandma?"

"No," I snorted. Then I got it. I didn't even have any sarcastic comeback. "Sorry." He was right. There was no reason to drop the f-bomb, especially in front of such an incredible sight. Go ahead and laugh, but it felt spiritual. Really, it did.

"Hey Walter, are—are you religious?" I asked him all of a sudden. I don't know why I cared.

"Religious?" Walter barked a laugh. "What brought that on?"

"I dunno. Sorry, forget I asked."

"I'm not a regular church attendee, if that's what you mean. Are you?"

"Me? No. Not at all."

"But you get it, don't you?" He looked at me with a sort of Gandalf-like twinkle in his eye.

"Get what?"

"Being up here. Feels like you're getting the point, don't it?" Walter crossed one hand over the other, ruminating. "You can spend your day running from here to there, busying yourself with all these things you're convinced are so important. It's easy to lose your sense of being alive in it. Easy to forget that you're still part of all this . . . all this life. You're just another animal, and you're right here in it with the bugs and birds and trees and mountains, on this little rock spinning around the sun. Doesn't seem possible to forget that, but somehow we all do." Walter scratched his long, sunburned nose. "The first time I ever came up to these mountains, when I was just a kid, I had this crazy idea that this is where God lives. But on the other hand," he squinted out at the epic, molten-lava sunset, a half-smile on his face. "Maybe it's not all that crazy."

"Maybe you should bring my mom up here sometime," I said. "If you can pry her off the BlackBerry."

"Oh, your mom's seen the sights." Walter smiled to himself. "Sometimes you gotta be patient with her. She's got a lot on her plate. But once you get to know her better, you'll see. She's amazing, Lula. Sometimes I wonder why she even gives raggedy ol' me the time of day. I just thank God that she—" Walter stopped. "I suppose that's your answer, right there. You wanna know if I'm religious? I sure haven't made a dent in the pew, but boy do I thank God. For every morning I get to wake up and my coffee's hot and your mom's right there next to me at the breakfast table. I thank God I get to work this ranch for a living instead of having to put on a necktie and commute to some office. I get to smell sage and piñon instead of traffic exhaust. Somebody or something made a beautiful place in this ugly world, and saw fit to put me right in the middle of it. Now, whether there's some old fella with a beard floating on a cloud up there or just some . . ." Walter waved his hand, "cosmic energy or whatnot, I got no idea. But whatever God is, wherever He lives, I thank Him because, I tell you what, I can look back on ever minute of it, good and bad, and I can tell you that I've had one hell of a life." Walter laughed. "Pardon my French."

I felt the horse shift his weight beneath me. I took a deep breath. Smelled the prickly-sweet pine smell and the sharp, musky sage. Smelled horse hair and leather. My own sweat.

Thank God for this. Thank God. But I didn't know who or what I was thanking. Did anybody know? Janet was Jewish, or at least she had been once. Leo was raised Lutheran, but he'd given up on religion after Vietnam, and Janet had followed his lead. Most of the kids at school, except me and Rory, went to the big First Baptist church in town, or their basketball rivals over at First Methodist. I went to the Baptist version with Jenny once, but I didn't get it. A bunch of guys in shiny suits giving me earnest, toothy smiles like an army of Bill Clintons, shaking my hand with both of theirs and saying emphatically "We're just so *glad* you're here. God bless you, we just *love* you." Who was this "we," I asked Jenny skeptically, and why do they love me when they don't even know who I am?

But I wanted to feel like Walter did. Like there was something or somebody in charge, watching over us, who had put me here for a reason. When I was all old and crusty like Walter, I wanted to look back and say I had one hell of a life. Pardon my French.

"I reckon that all sounds pretty corny, huh?" Walter chuckled. "Y'ask an old man about religion, you'll get an answer, one way or the other. Come on." He slapped the slack reins against his horse. "We better get back home before it gets too dark."

"Okay. How do I . . . um . . ." My horse was just sitting there. "Where's reverse?"

"Gingerbread!" Walter whistled sharply and clicked his tongue. Gingerbread craned his neck and, slowly, turned and followed.

"You're looking pretty good up there," Walter remarked.

"You think so?" I leaned back in the saddle as we began our descent.

"One ride and you're already a pro," he called back over his shoulder.

"Beats driving a car, that's for sure." Gingerbread's hooves made dry claps along the rocks.

"Not much of a driver, huh?"

"I don't know how," I confessed.

"You don't know how to drive a car?" Walter was mildly incredulous. "Shoot, time I was fifteen, I was driving horse trailers all over California."

"Janet and Leo were too nervous to teach me on the Cadillac. I signed up for Driver's Ed at school last fall, but there was only one period where you could take it, and it was the same time as Advanced English."

"Maybe your mother could teach you. She's pretty good behind the wheel."

"Sounds like a bonding experience to me."

nine

THE FRIDAY NIGHT FOOTBALL GAME WAS the absolute last place on earth I expected to find Samantha Lidell. I'd successfully avoided her ever since the Humiliating Incident last spring. And now there she was, smoking discreetly behind the Booster Club tent.

"Tallulah Monroe." She said my name. "Didn't expect to find you here. Long time no see."

"Likewise," I muttered, having a hard time getting the words out.

"I heard you got your GED. How is college life treating you?"

"I um. It's okay." *I um. It's okay. Dum de dum dum.* Listen to me. I was like some monosyllabic mouthbreather. Did she have to be so cool? Just . . . standing there like that? "So what are you doing here?" I blurted out. Not very cool at all.

"I'm rooting for the home team." She displayed her Fighting Eagles sweatshirt. "I'm Rory's Senior Year Advisor. He's been having a bit of a rough go lately, so I'm here for him."

"Well. That's nice of you."

"His mother threw him out of the house. You knew that, didn't you?" She gave me the patented Mrs. Lidell Withering Stare, so lethal it's banned in twelve states. I wanted to crawl under the bleachers and die. "He—" Her mouth was moving, but I couldn't hear anything over the marching band.

"He what?"

"You heard me." She exhaled smoke.

"No, actually, I didn't." The band was playing "Smells Like Teen Spirit," if you can believe it. The Nirvana song. Since when did it have a trumpet solo? "What did you say?"

"He came out to his mother. Not on purpose. It happened during the summer, right before you came back. She caught him out on a date with a boy from UNC. And she told him not to come home."

"Oh my God." I felt terrible. And Sam was staring at me as if I were the one who'd thrown the kid out. "Is he all right? Does he have a place to stay?"

"He's not out on the street," she said. "Not anymore. I don't know if I should tell you anything else."

"What? I mean, I heard you this time—why not?"

"You know why not. Because of everything he went through. Rory was barely holding it together when you left. And you just went blithely along on your trip, never thinking once about who you hurt, or what it cost. You couldn't leave a note, or pick up the phone just once? Return an email?"

"I already had this lecture from my grandparents, thanks," I muttered, turning to leave. "I messed up. Well aware. Thank you."

"No, Lula. I don't think you are aware. We all care about you." She grabbed my arm. I stopped. "You can't just make people feel . . . feel so much concern for you, then act like it's nothing when they get upset."

"I didn't think I could make you feel anything for me," I said, surprised. She was concerned? For me? "Let alone feel upset."

"Just because I didn't have feelings for you like you wanted doesn't mean I don't have feelings at all." For a second there, our eyes locked. Finally, she flicked her cigarette butt to the ground and stomped it. Shrugged toward the field. "Why don't you go down there and find Rory? It's halftime."

OKAY, SO, YOU'RE PROBABLY WONDERING WHAT exactly went down between me and Sam—Mrs. Lidell, to you—and why that whole exchange was so awkward and fraught with hor- ribleness. And you're probably wondering why I was hiding out in the girls' bathroom instead of hanging out by the side- lines trying to catch Rory's eye. The answer to the second one is that people were staring at me like I've got antennae coming out of my head. Seriously, it was like they'd never seen somebody who ran away from home before. I couldn't believe I actually wished it was like it used to be, when they all just ignored me and acted like I was invisible. Now it was all staring and "Hey, Lula, glad you're back" from these ass- holes who used to call me Weird Girl when they thought I was out of earshot. You jerks aren't glad I'm back. You could care less. If you knew what kind of tremendous screwup I truly am, you'd wish I'd stayed gone forever.

And on that note, let's climb into the wayback machine, and I'll tell you exactly what went down between me and Sam.

Not that I'm jumping up and down to revisit last spring. The end of eleventh grade. What a shitty time. But maybe if I tell you where I was, then you'll understand where I am. Which is in the third stall down on the left. Trying not to cry.

Samantha Lidell singlehandedly kept eleventh grade from totally sucking. She was the coolest teacher Rory and I ever had. Maybe we were inclined to like her just because she shared a first name with Agent Mulder's long-lost sister. Maybe it was because she was younger than our other teachers, or maybe it was because she had lived in Paris. Or maybe she was just naturally cool. Like the time I ran into her in the parking lot after school and asked her to bum a smoke. I don't know why I did it—I hate cigarettes. But Sam Lidell even made smoking seem awesome.

"I don't think you'd like these," she said, not even shocked that I asked. "They're strong. Gitanes."

"Gitanes?"

"They're French."

"Why do you smoke French cigarettes?" I asked.

"Because my friends in France send them to me," she said, exhaling, considering the cigarette between her fingers. "And because they make me feel like Jean-Paul Belmondo."

"Who's Jean-Paul Belmondo?" I asked.

"Look it up," she said, giving me her usual half-smile. Mrs. Lidell was always dropping little hints, saying "Oh, you know, it's just like so-and-so," then telling us to look it up when we asked who or what so-and-so was. And of course Rory and I always did. It usually turned out that she was talking about some foreign movie or an old band. Sam would—huh, that's funny. I just realized that when I thought of her in school, as a teacher, I always thought of her as Mrs. Lidell. But when I thought about her any other time, I just thought of her as Sam.

And I did think of her. Outside of school. You might have noticed my tendency to go a little overboard on the research. I admit it: when I'm into something, whether it's a movie or a TV show or my own mother's whereabouts, I go whole-hog. I want every detail I can find. Well, last year, Samantha Lidell was one of my prime interests. Some of the research, like figuring out who her name-drops were, I did with Rory. But some of the research, like looking up her home address, I did by myself.

I don't know why I did it, or why I didn't want to tell Rory. I guess I knew I was crossing a line, somehow. I looked up her address and then, one afternoon, I rode my bike past her house. I just wanted to know where somebody like her lived. I mean, I couldn't even believe she lived in our *town*, let alone right there in a regular old split-level on Loblolly Court. It seems kinda crazy and stalker-ish, I know. But I didn't plan on doing anything else with that information besides my one brief bike-by. It's not like I was going to . . . I dunno, show up at her house in the middle of the night. Completely uninvited and unannounced.

I blame Rory.

Okay, I don't *really* blame Rory. I take full responsibility for all of my insane, foolhardy behavior. But maybe what happened between me and Sam would never have happened if Rory had trusted me. If he'd just been honest with me from the start.

Actually, he was honest, in the beginning. I mean, at least he told me he was gay. He was so upset when he first came out to me, back in tenth grade. So afraid that I'd stop being his friend. Bullshit, I'd said. We're best friends no matter what. So what if he liked boys? So did I; it was one more thing we had in common. It was a relief to both of us, at first. He could be himself and we could still be friends. We could crush on David Duchovny together. No big deal! But then things got weird. As they often do.

At first, I felt like, theoretically, sure, I could understand how a person could be gay. It was probably easier being with someone of the same gender, right? Like, sexually and stuff, you'd know how their body worked. And you could share clothes! Thrifty and fun, the whole gay experience. But as far as actually feeling attracted to other girls, I never looked at, like, Mandy Coleman coming down the hall in her cheerleading outfit and felt compelled to yell, *Whoa, watch your backs, everybody, hot babe alert!* like that paragon of chivalry Mike Landy would.

To be honest, most of the girls at Hawthorne High seemed terminally uninteresting, obsessed with boyfriends and manicures and Youth Group ski trips. (Not that the boys were that much better, but, even though I wasn't into jocks, for instance, I could totally see how Sexy Seth Brock got that nickname.) But maybe I was never able to fit in with them because I'd never been very good at being a typical girl, myself. When I was little, Janet still had a job working as a receptionist in a dermatologist's office. Leo was the one who ended up looking after me, and he didn't have any idea how to relate. He let me help him paint his model airplanes and watch *M*A*S*H* reruns and movies like *The Magnificent Seven.* By the time I started school, I was completely inept at relating to girls, too. Girls liked shopping for clothes and drawing pictures of horses. I could quote freely from Lee Marvin movies and hold my own in a Phil Mickelson-versus-Tiger Woods debate. You'd think I would've fit in with the more tomboyish girls, but I was terrible at both soccer and lacrosse. Aside from Tracy at Drama Camp and Jenny Walsh, who was quiet and shy and became my friend because she needed protection from the older girls who smoked under the bleachers after gym class, I was lousy at making female friends.

Fast-forward to eleventh grade. Enter Samantha Lidell. She smoked French cigarettes and didn't have a manicure. She kept a picture of Bob Dylan tacked to her office door and she once got in trouble for saying "bullshit" in class. When she was fifteen, her mom bailed on her just like mine did. I found myself thinking about her a lot. Not, you know, sexually or anything. But I'd see something on TV or read something, and get this urge to call her on the phone and ask her what she thought of it. I wanted to tell her things. I kept signing up for tutorials with her so I actually could tell her things. It was kind of freaking me out, the amount of time I spent thinking about her. Was this, like, a gay thing, or was it just that she was the coolest person I had ever met? I tried to suss out how much obsessing over her was too much, and I thought Rory could help, even though I felt too weird about the whole thing to just come right out and say it. I asked him one time, how did he know for sure he was gay, before he even slept with a guy? Was there some kind of tipping point, a moment he knew for certain one way or another?

"I just knew," he shrugged.

"Yeah, but . . . I mean, *how* did you know? What happens now if you finally do it with a guy, and then you're like, 'You know what? I kind of prefer the other.'"

"Look, you're still a virgin, right?"

"Thanks for bringing it up."

"Sorry. What I mean is, you don't have to have sex to know what you want. Like when we watch *Lord of the Rings*. You might be a virgin, but you know you're attracted to men because the person that catches your eye is Viggo Mortensen and not Liv Tyler or Cate Blanchett."

"And, let me guess, the person who caught your eye was Orlando Bloom, and that made you suspect something was up?"

"Well, Hugo Weaving, but, essentially, yeah, that was how I figured it out."

"You figured out you were gay from watching *Lord of the Rings*. Won't Peter Jackson be surprised."

"It wasn't just that one movie. It's everything. It's not just thinking some man is attractive. I feel like . . . it's just who I am, you know?" Rory shrugged. "I've been different my whole life, and I didn't know why. It wasn't just the kind of books I read or the characters I identified with, or the movies I watched or the fact that I sucked at soccer. It was something deep down inside . . . I've known it was there for a long time. But I'm just now able to say it. Able to say it to you, at least."

Hm, okay. The next time we watched *Lord of the Rings*, I tried checking out Arwen and Galadriel. . . . Nope. Nothing. I couldn't really picture myself taking an elf out to the Regal 7 on a Friday night. Eowyn was pretty badass, but she was no Aragorn. Great. That was *no* help. I tried looking at other girls in movies and on TV, but ultimately, no matter how badass they were, no fictional character was as cool as Sam Lidell in real life.

I tried again with Rory, when we were over at his house, dyeing my hair. I asked him what would happen if he met someone he really liked, but they just happened to be the wrong gender. I thought he could tell me. If I was or I wasn't. Gay, I mean. Or maybe I really was just trying to make him jealous all along.

And this is where it gets really wacko. Because even while I was obsessing over Sam Lidell, Rory was the one I thought was my soul mate. What sucks is, I didn't even realize I had feelings for him until he came out. There I was, trying to be the Supportive Female Buddy, and all the while, my mind had started wandering into restricted areas. Wondering what it would be like to hold him. Kiss him. And various other activities. I even dyed my hair red in an attempt to look more like Gillian Anderson, aka Special Agent Dana Scully, who, according to Rory, was the Greatest Actress Ever to Grace Stage or Screen. I figured, you know. Just in case he might be leaving the heterosexual window open for redheaded girls.

But all this muddle didn't reach Maximum Awkwardness until the spring of our junior year. Rory started spending more and more time at his job at Andy's Books and Coffee. At first, I thought it was good for him. The guy, Andy, took him on all these trips, book-buying and even camping and hiking and stuff. Rory needed a guy like that in his life. A stable, sober adult. A father figure. But Rory was spending more and more time away, and it wasn't all work-related. He kept making excuses why he couldn't come over, or why he had to leave early. He was working out all the time, trying to lose weight, and suddenly he decided to try out for the football team, of all things. Sweet, sensitive Rory, on the *football* team. How many linebackers do you know who wax rhapsodic about Shelley and Keats?

Then there was the night he came over, a complete wreck. He said he'd been fighting with his mother, but there was no way. He fought with Patty all the time; he was used to it. This time, the kid was a mess. Was he on drugs? I didn't ask. He got into bed with me and we held each other for the longest time. It was so perfect, and we didn't even do anything but just lie there together. He was warm and strong and when he fell asleep, he looked so sweet. Like a lion cub. Like a hibernating bear.

But all of that was just the tip of the Weirdness Iceberg, compared with the day we were studying for our Chemistry midterm. All of a sudden, out of the blue, he asked me if I'd consider being a surrogate mother for him. He assured me that we wouldn't actually have to have sex. (Gee, thanks, Rory.) No, I'd just be the carrier for his offspring, which he would raise with his Boyfriend To Be Named Later. I tried to play it off, like I'm totally cool with being asked to bear the non-love-child of my best friend and possibly the love of my life. But what I really felt, for the first time ever with Rory right there beside me, was alone.

Fast-forward to the night I left town. Nothing seemed out of the ordinary that night. I biked over to Rory's to study for Mrs. Lidell's infamously insurmountable midterm exam. The house was dark—his mother was either gone or passed out. But Rory's car sat in the driveway. Hmm, odd. I was parking my bike in the garage when, through the small, grimy back window, something caught my eye. Something moving. Even from far away, I knew what I was looking at. A three hundred-pound kid running across a lawn doesn't really look like anything else.

I stepped out of the garage just in time to see Rory disappear into the woods. I don't know why I didn't call out to him. There was something strange going on here; I felt it. I looked around. Was he running after some animal? No one was following him. Patty the Pickle wasn't chasing after him with a butcher knife. So what's going on?

I hurried to catch up. When I did, I followed at a safe distance. We came to a clearing by the stream that ended up being a backyard. I crouched behind a rhododendron bush and watched Rory walk right up to the house, an A-frame with a kayak tipped on its side on the patio, and a big sliding glass door. Rory knocked on the glass and waited. He knocked again. Maybe he really was doing drugs, and this was his dealer. My heart raced. Maybe that was the reason for all the weirdness, all the excuses. Maybe it was the football team. Maybe he was already high on steroids. Finally I saw a skinny figure on the other side of the glass—it was his boss, Andy. Huh, that's strange. Why wouldn't Rory just drive over to his house? Why cut this crazy path in the dark when we were supposed to be studying, anyw—

Oh. *Oh.* I watched them kissing. I mean really kissing. And then.

So much for that father-figure theory.

Now I knew. This wasn't a phase Rory was going through. He was sure. And it didn't matter what color I dyed my hair. Rory and I had been alone in the dark plenty of times. But we had never done that.

Okay, I whispered to myself. *Okay.* Now I understood. And understanding felt like an instrument, a vehicle, a machine, some metal bulldozer or something was inside my throat, and then my chest, burrowing a hot hole down to my stomach. Understanding was raking me out, turning me hollow and machinelike. I don't know why I kept standing there, except that I was suddenly too heavy to move. It was as if hot liquid metal had been poured into my newly hollow, understanding self. And I would be stationed there for all eternity, watching the boy I loved love someone else. I wanted him to love me, but it was too late now. There was no "me" anymore, just this statue. This leaded metal thing. Hollowed and bronze. Real feelings bounced right off. I was Han Solo, frozen in carbonite. My mouth twisting out "No, stop" for the rest of my days.

I don't know how I found my way back. It was so dark outside. I ran through the woods, not caring how much noise I made. I got my bike out of Rory's garage. Everything seemed smudged out of focus. Was I crying? It had been forever since I'd cried over anything. I wasn't a crier. Hey, where was I going, anyway? Not home. Not back to Janet and Leo's, to my bedroom without him. Where else could I go? Everything had closed. Jenny Walsh was away at a special school for girls with eating disorders. Maybe her parents would be home. *Hi, I don't know if you remember me, but I used to be friends with your daughter. I know it's been a while and I look different now. It's because I'm a statue.*

A car almost hit me twice. I mean, two different cars. Before I finally remembered where to go. By then, I wasn't crying anymore. It was almost like I was outside myself, acting out some script. I couldn't believe the things I was doing, but there I was. Doing them.

"Lula?" Samantha Lidell opened her front door. She was wearing scrub pants, the kind doctors wear, and a faded T-shirt that said PRETENDERS EUROPEAN TOUR. Even her pajamas were cool. "Are you all right?"

I shook my head no, and I was crying again, harder than before. Sam pulled me inside, pulled me into her, hugging me, patting my back, not seeming to care at all that I was getting tears and snot all over her Pretenders T-shirt. I held on to her.

"Hey. Hey, you're okay now," she whispered. "What's going on? Lula? Are you hurt? What happened?" She pulled back, looking hard at me. She picked a stray leaf out of my hair. "You're a mess."

"Nothing. I'm fine. I just needed—" I gulped, trying out my voice. Broken, but not bad for a statue. "I needed to see you."

"Why? What's going on? Is it your grandparents? Did something happen between you and Rory? Kiddo, hey. Tell me what's the matter."

Where could I start? With Rory and Andy, Rory and me, me and no one, me and my mother, gone, me, alone, just me. Me and her. Mrs. Lidell. Sam.

"Here, sit down." She led me into the burgundy living room, to a mod-looking Ikea couch. "Chill for a second. Let me get you a glass of water."

She walked off to the kitchen. I sat there, pulling myself together, surveying the scene. Wow, there were all these guitars. And books, too, but that was less of a surprise. The walls were decorated with movie posters, all the titles in French. The TV was paused on an image of George Clooney making one of his "I'm sexy, yet concerned" faces. A pile of our last in-class essays covered half the coffee table, next to a half-full glass of red wine. I couldn't believe I was here.

"Drink this." Mrs. Lidell reappeared, handed me a glass of water and a handful of Kleenex. I sipped the water and blew my nose.

"Sorry to interrupt your evening. I was, um. In the neighborhood."

"Don't worry about it. I was just waiting up for Mark." She clicked the TV off. Oh yeah. Mark, her husband, was a Doctor Without Borders. She told me about him once, when I asked her about living in Paris. She met him there, when he was on a layover from helping child amputees in war-torn Iraq. They moved back because he was born here, and he'd always dreamed of coming back to help the poor kids of the rural South. In the meantime, she didn't even seem to care that I'd looked up her address and shown up here like a total stalker. In fact, she was sitting next to me, rubbing my back in little circles.

"We can talk about it, if you want to. Or we can not talk about it," she said.

"I want to," I said, my voice cracking. "I wish I could tell you . . ."

"Tell me what?"

"Everything." I looked up at her. I really wanted to tell her everything. I'd already told her a lot. But I wanted to stay right there on her weird pointy sofa and tell her everything in my hollowed-out heart. I wanted to hold on to her and breathe her in and be like her and have her tell me how to do that, how to become some entirely other person, some Not-Lula, someone who had a real life and went to Paris and had mysterious Southern doctors fall in love with her on their way home from Iraq.

But I knew that was impossible. I was stuck in myself. That was always the problem. Even back in Drama Camp. I could memorize the lines, I could put on a costume and some silly wig. But at the end of the day, underneath it all, I was still Lula. The surplus baby. The kid who got left behind. I wanted to ask her if it would always be this way. If I would spend my life waking up disappointed. Never smart enough, never delivering the punch line on time. Was I always going to be Weird Girl? Why is it that I don't feel so weird with you, Sam? Would she tell me that? Would she call me kiddo again? Would she explain to me why Rory would rather make out with his creepy old boss than with me? Would anybody ever hold me the way his creepy boss held him? Would anybody ever want me like that? Would she?

So, I don't know. I kissed her.

I'd only ever been kissed on the mouth once before. Daniel Casey, right after the eighth grade dance. It was gross. He had lips like a snake. This was not like that. This was not like that at all.

"Lula!" She laughed. "What are you doing?"

I opened my eyes. We weren't kissing anymore. Instead, this woman that I adored was, well, recoiled in horror. Looking at me like I was nuts. Worse than nuts. Looking at me like I was the creepy lightning kid in that episode of

The X-Files. Looking at me like she was Scully and I was the tail-baby guy who shapeshifted into Mulder in order to seduce her. Except I forgot to shapeshift into somebody handsome first. I was just some girl from the back row of Advanced English 11. *Some girl.* Wow, does this mean I'm gay now?

"I'm sorry," she shook her head, touching the back of her hand to her mouth. Wiping my spit off her lips. "I didn't mean to laugh at you."

"No, I shouldn't have—"

"Lula—"

"I should go—" I stood up and accidentally knocked the glass of water all over the in-class essays.

"Shit," Mrs. Lidell swiped the papers out of the way. I righted the glass.

"Here," I gave her the Kleenex I hadn't used. "I'm sorry—"

"Wait, wait a second." She slopped the papers down on the far end of the table. I waited. I don't know why.

"Is this why you came here tonight? To put the moves on me?" When she put it like that, it sounded awful.

"No—not exactly. I didn't know where to go. Rory and I were supposed to be studying. But he . . . was with somebody else."

"Somebody else?"

"He had a date."

"I see." Sam sighed, her hands on her hips. "So this is revenge or something?"

"No." It was weird how calm I felt all of a sudden. I was already getting this feeling. It was kind of like that script feeling I had before. A feeling like I already knew what was coming next.

"I wasn't using you to get back at him, if that's what you mean," I explained. "I keep thinking about you. I don't know why I like you so much. It's weird. Because I like him, too."

"Rory?"

I nodded. "I mean, I think I love him. I even slept with him. I mean, we didn't have sex. But we slept in the same bed. I thought, maybe, that was even better somehow. But . . ."

"But he's dating someone else?"

"Dating." I kind of laughed. "Something like that. Rory is fucking his boss."

"What?" Now Sam looked really incredulous. "Doesn't he work for Andy Barnett? Andy's Books and Coffee?"

"Yeah. He does."

"Lula. I know Andy Barnett. He's divorced with two kids; one of them is almost Rory's age."

"I saw them. I saw them . . . *together.*"

"Maybe you misunderstood a friendly gesture—"

"Sure, if you call sticking your hand down somebody's pants a friendly gesture."

"Lula."

"You think I'm lying." I said quietly. It struck me suddenly how quiet the house was. In that quiet moment, I wanted to memorize every detail I could about Sam Lidell. The way she stood, with one hand on the curve of her hip. Her dark hair curling behind her ears. Her almost Scully-esque look of skepticism. I wanted to file it all away for later. I was over-whelmed by this certain feeling that I was never going to see her again.

"Actually, I don't," she said. "I don't think you're lying. That's the problem." She rubbed her forehead, closing her eyes. "Jesus, kiddo. You're kinda blowing my mind, here." She laughed softly. "I should call Rory's mother."

"Good luck. Maybe if she sobers up, she'll remember she even has a son."

"Then I'll call Andy Barnett. This isn't right. Rory's underage."

"So am I," I said for no good reason. I looked up at her.

"Oh, Lula, don't. Please don't do this."

"Don't do what?"

"Fall in love with me."

The dark corners of her living room felt like they were squeezing in on me. I wished I could be swallowed into the Persian rug, into the hardwood floor. It occurred to me that I still had to take her midterm. I had to sit there in class with her in front of me and Rory beside me and pretend I'd never kissed her and I'd never seen him kissing Andy Barnett and lying about it. Pretend I still believed him. Pretend I still looked at her and felt . . . what did I feel? I didn't even recognize myself anymore. I didn't recognize any of us. Rory and I weren't the people I thought we were. We weren't Mulder and Scully, bonded in trust, telling each other everything. And Sam and I weren't—well, we weren't anything. Not even friends.

"What if we just pretend this whole night never happened?" I asked. "What if I agree to, like . . . evaporate?" I wished I really could. Just vanish into a puddle of goo, like one of those shapeshifting aliens. Those damn shapeshifters again. Lucky jerks.

"That's not what I mean," she insisted. "Don't be melodramatic. It's just that—Lula, I'm straight. I'm married. And, above all, you're my student. My seventeen-year-old student. What did you expect?"

"I don't know. I didn't plan this." I really didn't. "I just . . . didn't want to be alone anymore."

"Lula." Samantha Lidell cringed as if I'd hurt her. "Don't say that. You're not alone. But you shouldn't be here."

"Then where should I be?" I asked.

"Home," she said, softly. "You should be at home, studying for my midterm."

Ha ha. I gave her half a smile. Home. Where's that, anyway?

"Trust me on this, will you?" she sighed. "Go home and write this down. You're still keeping that journal I assigned? Just go home and put this in it. Put everything in it. You don't ever have to show it to me if you don't want to. You can tear it up and burn it, for all I care. But, before you do anything else, will you please promise me that you'll write this down?"

Write this down. I almost laughed.

"Will do, Teach." I gave her a little salute, and turned quickly, darting out the door. Feeling like I already had evaporated. I walked back the way I came, pushing my bike alongside me. The air was cool and damp. I felt, oddly, like something was clicking into place. Like I had truly shed every last bit of my skin. My guts, my muscles, my blood. I was plain bones walking around now. Walking without a shadow. *Just write it down.* Okay, Sam. You want a chronicle, you got it.

ten

I WALKED ALONG THE EDGE OF the school parking lot, my hands jammed into my black hooded jacket. The game was won. Everybody was leaving. Cars in a line, headlights on, honking. Maybe one of them would hit me.

"Lula! Tallulah Monroe!" Somebody yelled out of one of the cars. I kept my head down. The car caught up to me. A big old Buick station wagon with wood panels on the side. I knew it by heart. Rory's car. The Beast. The guy in the passenger seat calling out to me was Sexy Seth Brock, the Fighting Eagles' undefeated varsity quarterback.

"Yeah?"

"Need a ride?" Sexy Seth asked.

"No, thanks." It was only ten more feet or so until the break in the fence. I could slide in and cut through the woods.

"Are you sure? We don't mind taking you home," Seth chirped. I looked over at him, leaning out the window with his floppy blond surfer hair, his perfect cheekbones, his long, sunburned nose. Rory kept his eyes on the road. The line of traffic stopped. I kept walking. Then I stopped. This was why

I came, wasn't it? To talk to Rory. To try and fix this. Isn't this what I wanted? I never knew what I wanted.

I turned back around. Walked to the car, opened the back door. Next thing I knew, I was climbing into the backseat of the Beast, shoving aside a pile of cleats and helmets and sweaty shoulder pads that smelled like wet goat.

"Sorry about the mess," Seth apologized. "So . . . how's college?" *How's college?* Weird. Why was Sexy Seth speaking to me as if we were friends or something?

"It's . . . fine, I guess." What was I supposed to do, get into a whole long thing about community college? Rory inched the car forward. He looked different. Older, maybe. He'd grown a little scrap of a beard, just some chin scruff. I wasn't sure how I liked it. A car blew by, going the other direction, blasting music and honking the horn. A girl leaned out the back window and shrieked Rory's name. Rory gave a little wave and beeped the horn.

"Man, you guys are like rock stars." I couldn't believe some random girl just shrieked Rory's name. *My* Rory.

"People love football," Seth said, attempting modesty. "Hey, we're having some people over—you wanna come? Just, you know, kick back, celebrate the win."

"Oh my God, are you serious?" I leaned forward and smacked Rory on the shoulder. I couldn't help myself. "Theodore, are you hearing this? Weird Girl is being invited to a Sexy Seth party. Has the polarity of the earth shifted? Might pigs actually fly?"

Sexy Seth actually laughed. "What did you call me?"

"Sexy Seth. Come on. You have to know. It's what everybody at school calls you."

"Sexy Seth? Man." He chuckled. "I thought it'd be Stupid Seth or Slovenly Seth or Smartass Seth. Sexy is a step up. I can live with that."

"You don't wanna come over." Rory finally spoke. "You won't like it."

"Maybe I will. Maybe I'll have the time of my young life. I think I'll take you up on that offer, Sexy."

"Right on. It's a party now."

The car lurched forward. There was finally a break in the traffic, and Rory wheeled the roaring Beast out into the street.

THE PARTY AT SEXY SETH'S WAS not at all what I expected. There were about fifteen or twenty people down in the base-ment, playing Wii Tennis and pool. There were Foo Fighters songs playing really low in the background. Nobody was drinking or smoking. There was fruit punch and pizza and healthy snacks. Seth's mom and dad were upstairs, chaperoning. It was all so civilized. Rory immediately busied himself at the pool table, taking charge of a very competitive mini-tournament. Meanwhile, Seth was going completely overboard trying to make me feel welcome.

"Can I get you another drink?" he asked. "We've got tea upstairs. We don't drink soda, but I think there's some Dr. Pepper one of the neighbors brought last time we had a barbecue."

"I'm fine, thanks. You guys really don't drink soda?"

"Nah, my mom's all about organic food, no high fructose corn syrup. Hey, my iPod died, so I was gonna run upstairs and get some CDs. You wanna come see the house?"

"Sure." Did I want to see the house? What am I, a real estate agent? I didn't really care what Seth's house looked like, but I couldn't help feeling like he had a room full of supermodels in a hot tub hidden away somewhere. I followed him up the basement steps. "I gotta tell ya, Seth. I always thought these post-football parties were like, total Roman Empire debauchery. I'm a little disappointed I'm not being ravaged by linebackers right now."

"Nah," Seth laughed. "That's Speed's deal. I mean, he doesn't ravage anybody. But he's a serious party guy. You know Speed Briggs, right?"

"Everybody knows Speed." Speed Briggs was probably the only guy on the team who was bigger than Rory. His nickname was a testament to the notion that even a football dumbass can grasp the concept of irony.

"Yeah, he's definitely Mr. Popularity. Hey guys—Mom, Dad, this is Lula. She's a good friend of Rory's." Seth paused outside the den and introduced me to his parents, who were parked on the sofa in front of an old Regis Philbin-era episode of *Who Wants to Be a Millionaire*. "Lula, these are my folks, Sherry and Don."

"Hi Lula, nice to meet you," Sherry waved. She was so pert and blond, like the mom on *The Brady Bunch*. Seth's dad was older—they both were, but not as old as Janet and Leo.

"What is the Colorado River?" Seth's dad shouted at the TV.

"Honey, you don't have to answer in the form of a question. That's only on *Jeopardy*." Seth's mother patted his arm.

"Right, right."

"Say hi to Lula, honey."

"What? Oh, hi Tallulah Honey. Rory's friend, right?"

"Yes, sir," I answered.

"Glad to have you back in town."

"Regis, I'd like to phone a friend," the contestant on the show said.

"See you guys later," Seth ambled up the stairs.

"Nice meeting you." I caught up to him.

"Sorry about that," he said over his shoulder. "You can't talk to my parents when they're watching *Millionaire*. Even in reruns."

"It's cool. Your dad's funny."

"Yeah, he's awesome. Anyway, Speed's the one who throws the huge parties. I've been a couple of times, but it gets *rowdy*. You, like, wake up at four in the afternoon the next day, face down in the backyard. And you don't even know whose backyard it is."

"Ahh, male bonding."

"I know, right? I figured I was either gonna get arrested or end up in the hospital if I kept going to Speed's, so I started doing my own thing, having a few friends over, you know, keep it simple. It's mostly kids I know from church. Anyway, here's the upstairs. Not much going on. That's my parents' room down there. Bathroom. That's my brother's room. And that's Rory's room. This one's mine."

"Rory's room?"

"Yeah." He flipped the light on in his bedroom. "Rory came to live with us when his mom threw him out. I thought you knew."

"No, I didn't. So." Wow. Okay. "How long has he been living here?"

"I dunno, couple of months? Since the summer." Seth flipped through a tall stack of CDs on his desk next to his laptop. His room was immaculate, the furniture dark wood, the bedspread dark green. There were posters on his wall of football players—Tom Brady, Tedy Bruschi, David Garrard, Drew Brees, the names in bold, all-caps print. And then there was—

"Is that . . . a Guided by Voices poster?"

"Yeah! You like GBV?" Seth brightened. "My brother gave me that poster, right before he died. They're basically my favorite band of all time, ever. How do you know about Guided by Voices?"

"Um, there used to be this DJ who played them, on the college station—"

"Midnight Pete?"

"You've *heard* Midnight Pete?"

"Have I heard Midnight Pete?" Seth exclaimed. "Dude! I've *met* Midnight Pete!"

"No way!" I couldn't believe it. I thought it was basically me and ten other insomniac losers listening to Midnight Pete. He used to play all this old stuff like the Pixies and Pavement and eighties REM, and really old stuff like Elvis Costello and the Ramones. Sometimes he'd even play these crazy rockabilly songs from the fifties, or some random sixties stuff like Herman's Hermits. Almost every night of the week from junior high through sophomore year, I fell asleep with my clock radio tuned to Midnight Pete.

"My brother actually took me to hang out with him in the studio one time," Seth told me. "I can't believe you used to listen to Midnight Pete."

"I can't believe you *met* him. How much did it suck when he finally graduated and left us with Midnight Steve?"

"Dude. Midnight Steve bites the big one. All he ever plays is, like, stale emo."

"Don't remind me," I sighed, leaning back against Seth's bureau. "So, what did he look like? I mean Midnight Pete." I'd always been curious.

"He kind of looked like a fat version of that guy from The Cure," Seth said, still in obvious awe. I giggled. "Seriously. Donnie met him at this party, right after he moved back home, and they hung out a bunch before he got too sick. The night Donnie took me to hear Pete do the show was like going to the Super Bowl or something."

"Right awwwn, man," I imitated Midnight Pete's drawl. Seth laughed. "But, uh, seriously," I said. "I'm sorry your, um. Your brother died."

"Thanks. Uh. It's been a few years now. He was twenty-six. Twelve years older than me. I was the Accident Baby." Seth gave an apologetic half-shrug. "You wanna see his room?"

"Um. Okay," I said. Seth walked across the hall, opened the door to his brother's room, and flipped on the light. I hung back. This felt a little strange.

"My mom and dad call it the guest room now, but they left all his records here. I guess they sorta did it for me." Seth walked in. I followed. I couldn't believe my eyes. It looked like a cross between a record store and a museum. There were tall shelves full of real record albums, racks of CDs and cassettes. Faded posters covering the walls. I recognized some of the names as the old bands Midnight Pete used to play. Yo La Tengo. Teenage Fanclub. Superchunk.

Liz Phair. Pavement. Guided by Voices. Guided by Voices. Guided by Voices.

"Donnie was a total music nerd," Seth explained. "He went to school in New York just so he could intern for Matador, the record label. I still come in here and listen to 45s on his stereo. It's kind of like hanging out with him, you know? He used to talk about how, when he got better, he was gonna take me to my first GBV show, because they were, like, the best live band ever. But we never did make it . . ." Seth trailed off.

"You could go see them now. I'm sure that's what your brother would've wanted," I said.

"Except that they broke up, like, right after he died." Seth shrugged. "It sucks pretty hard, but I'm optimistic. Bob Pollard, you know, pretty much the mastermind of the band, he has this new group, Boston Spaceships. Their album just came out and it's pretty awesome, so . . ." Seth shrugged again. Optimistic or no, he looked like he was trying not to cry.

"Maybe they'll play an all-ages show at Cat's Cradle or somewhere."

"Yeah, maybe."

I hesitated. "How did he die? Your brother, I mean."

"Don't laugh. Testicular cancer."

"Who's laughing? That's terrible."

"He never got it checked out, and it metastasized. The worst thing about it is, you don't have to die of it. I mean, look at—" Seth stopped, catching himself. "Donnie used to get so sick of people saying, 'Look at Lance Armstrong,' but, seriously. Look at Lance Armstrong. That guy had it, and now he's won, like, seven Tour de Frances. When I first made the team, junior varsity, I was telling some of the guys about him, saying, like, hey guys, you gotta check your balls and make sure there's nothing crazy going on down there."

"You told the guys on the football team to check their balls?"

"I know. They just about laughed my ass outta the room. But you know what?"

"What?"

"Just last winter, this guy Darryl Harris—you remember him? Played right guard? He was a senior when we were freshmen. Anyway, he called me up from college, out in Texas." Seth had this very serious look on his face as he related this story. "Sure enough, dude found a lump on one of his balls. Cancer. They caught it in time, and now he's totally healthy. He even started in the game last Saturday."

"Wow," I tried not to cringe.

"So, there you go. My brother may be gone, but he already saved one life. I try to look at it like that because otherwise. You know." Seth exhaled, looking around the room. "I just miss him too much."

I was afraid that Sexy Seth was indeed about to cry. I reached out to give him a friendly pat on the back. And then somehow, all of a sudden, he hugged me. My face was pressed against his Fighting Eagles sweatshirt. He smelled clean and familiar. It took me a minute to remember. My mom's soap. Made out of organic hemp.

"I bet you think I'm so weird right now," Seth said into my hair.

"No, this is totally normal. I'm into random hugs and stories about testicles."

"Sorry about that." We pulled apart. "Am I grossing you out? Some girls get grossed out."

"No, it's actually enlightening," I told him. "Just for you, I'm going to go home and check my balls." Seth laughed. "For real, though. I'm really sorry about your brother. I'm sorry for you. I really am."

"Thanks." He looked at me. I mean, he *looked* at me. For, like, a ridiculously long time.

"Maybe we should, um." I cleared my throat. "Maybe we should get back down to the party."

"Yeah. Lemme grab those CDs." He flipped off the light, and we left his brother's room, closing the door behind us. I looked at the other closed door down the hall.

"How did Rory end up living with you? If you don't mind my asking."

"He showed up at my dad's church," Seth said, crossing the hall back to his bedroom. "My dad's the minister at the Unitarian church—you know that church in the building where the old library was?"

"Sure. I used to love that library."

"You should come by sometime. It still smells like books," Seth said, turning his bedroom light back on. "Anyway, they've got a support group down there for gay teens. Well, gay people of all ages who don't feel welcome in more conservative churches, or fall out with their families, or whatever. So, Rory came in. He came to a couple of meetings before somebody figured out he was living in his car. My dad, like, flipped out and insisted that he come live with us. Especially since we're on the same team and everything. And it's been really cool. Kind of like Instant Brother."

"Oh." I didn't know what to say. I felt horrible. It should have been me. I should have been the one to take him in.

Even if I was gone, why didn't he come to Janet and Leo's? I sank down on the end of Seth's bed, feeling too bad about Rory to even appreciate the weirdness of sitting on Sexy Seth's *bed*.

"But enough about Rory. We have serious business to discuss." Seth gave me an all-business look as he took a small handful of CDs off of the shelf by his desk. "What's your favorite Guided by Voices album?"

"Well, I don't actually . . ." I could feel myself blushing. "Truthfully, I only really know one of their songs."

"Just one? Lemme guess: 'Hardcore UFOs'? That was a Midnight Pete favorite. I could see you digging that song. Rory told me you guys were into that *X-Files* show. He showed me those articles you wrote."

"He—Rory did what?" I felt my stomach drop to my toes. Sexy Seth knew about the *Guide*.

"He showed me your, uh, *Guide to* The X-Files, the blog you guys did?" Seth opened one of the CD cases, closed it, then chose another. "I never watched the show, but those articles were pretty funny. I like the "point/counterpoint" one about the liver-eating mutant guy, where you and Rory were arguing and he kept making you all mad."

"Oh yeah. The liver-eating mutant guy," I echoed weakly. My ears were so hot, I was afraid my hair was going to catch on fire. I couldn't believe Seth had read all that goofy stuff we wrote.

"So that's why I guessed 'Hardcore UFOs.'"

"Huh?"

"Your Guided by Voices song. Did I guess right?"

"Oh, the song . . . it's, um. Actually, it's 'Teenage FBI.'"

"Man! That's a great song, too! Do you have the album version, or the EP version?"

"I'M NOT SURE. IT WAS . . . on the *Buffy* soundtrack." Just when I thought it was impossible to be any less cool, I went and admitted to Sexy Seth Brock that I owned the *Buffy the Vampire Slayer* soundtrack. I was blushing so much that I felt like Madeline Kahn in *Clue*. "Flames. Flames . . . on the side of my face." Extra flamey.

"*Buffy* had a GBV song on the soundtrack?" Seth asked. "That's awesome. I might have to go back and watch that show now." He knelt down to a lower shelf and pulled out more CDs, seemingly unfazed by my uncool confession. "The EP version is like, rawer, but it's awesome. I love 'em both. Some people say *Do the Collapse* is too polished, you know? Too slick. But I love that album. I love the lo-fi stuff too, though. Even when it sounds like it was recorded straight into a tape recorder—it probably was—but the songs are so good, it doesn't matter. *Under the Bushes Under the Stars* is maybe my favorite album of all time. Even though *Isolation Drills* is the one I usually listen to before games. I know, I'm supposed to say *Bee Thousand* is the best, and, I mean, don't get me wrong, it's awesome, but—" he paused, gave me one of his patented Sexy grins. "I'm not making any sense right now, am I?"

"Yeah, I kind of need to phone a friend right now," I admitted. Seth laughed.

"I tend to get sorta carried away when I talk about Guided by Voices. It's just—their songs are like magic to me. Some of 'em get me so psyched up, I feel like I could leap tall buildings, be all Superman. And then the very next song, I go and get all choked up—" Seth paused, kneeling on his carpet. He shook his head. "Why do we love this stuff?"

"What, music?"

"Anything! Why do we love anything? I mean, my brother played plenty of other bands. Good bands. There was music coming out of his room all the time. But this one time on a long car trip, he let me listen to some GBV on his headphones, and that was it. I had to hear it all."

"You woke up one morning and said, 'I know: dolls.'"

"Do what now?"

"It's, uh. Sorry, kind of random. It's from this *X-Files* episode. Clyde Bruckman . . . he's a psychic, and he's wondering why this woman they're investigating was a doll collector. Like, why do any of us become obsessed with the stuff we become obsessed with? The stuff that kind of defines who we are. Is it some kind of destiny, or more like a flash of inspiration? Like, was it a series of unavoidable events, all through this woman's childhood, leading her to accumulate all these dolls? Or did she just wake up one morning—"

"And say, 'I know: dolls!'" Seth laughed. "Exactly! Like, *Under the Bushes*—the first time I heard it, I didn't even like it that much. I felt like it was too long and there weren't enough songs that stood out. I kept going back to *Alien Lanes* and *Bee Thousand* instead. But then one night, the summer after Donnie died, I was lying here watching the sun go down. For whatever reason, I put on *Under the Bushes Under the Stars*. It was one of those nights, before school started back. Even though I was psyched about the football season, I was feeling kind of bummed out about summer being over. You know how it gets right before night in the summer, when the trees are dark, and the sky behind them is all fire colored and dark blue, and you feel this sort of . . . melancholy?"

Sexy Seth Brock, popular football star, looked out at the trees at dusk and felt melancholy? Are you kidding me? Was I being Punk'd? I would've assumed a guy like Seth would look out at the trees at dusk and feel like, I dunno, doing a keg stand.

"Yeah, actually, I do," I said. "I think I know what you mean."

"And right then, this song came on, 'Acorns & Orioles'— you got a minute?"

"Well, I should get back to this fabulous party I've been invited to, but," I shrugged, "for you, I've got a minute."

Seth grinned. He stood up, opening a CD case. He slapped the disc into the little portable stereo on his bureau and skipped tracks until he found the one he was looking for. I heard plaintive, minor-key acoustic guitar, quieter than the one other GBV song I knew. The first verse sent a sort of chill fluttering through me. By the time the song got to the chorus, *I can't tell you anything you don't already know*, I knew how Seth felt.

"Like the weather changed."

"Huh?" Seth turned the volume down a little.

"It's like—" I hesitated. "The first time Rory and I watched *X-Files*. Normally we talk through whatever we're watching. But that first episode we watched, we were dead silent. And afterward it felt like the weather had changed. Like the clouds had rolled in, even though they hadn't. But it was like we . . . went through the wardrobe or something." I trailed off, feeling like a weirdo, as usual. "It's a really good song."

"Isn't it? Like the weather changed . . . that's a good way to describe it. What do you reckon it is," Seth mused, "that makes us see something all of a sudden? When we've passed by it a hundred times, and it suddenly jumps out? All of a sudden it's not just music that you're listening to, it's a feeling that you're . . . feeling. And next thing you know you can't stop listening to the record without all the catchy tunes on it, or out of all five hundred channels, you can't stop watching that one old show. Why do we love the stuff we love? Especially when it doesn't make no regular sense."

"Maybe love never makes sense," I said. The song was fading to an end. Seth popped the CD player open.

"You know, back before I knew him, I thought you and Rory were going out," Seth said, putting the CD back in its case.

"We were just friends. Best friends. But we . . . had a falling out. He didn't tell you?"

"Rory's kind of private about stuff. Not like me," Seth smiled. "He said the same thing. You guys had a falling out. But he talks about you all the time. Me and Lula used to do this, Lula always says, Lula this, Lula that."

"He does?" I felt myself blush again. "Bet that gets boring."

"Any friend of Rory's is a friend of mine. Anyway, whatever happened, I don't think he hates you or anything. You guys can work it out." Seth went back to his CD shelf. I hoped he was right. That Rory didn't hate me. I didn't know what to say. I still felt the melancholy of the song, that feeling like dark trees at dusk in the summertime. It reminded me of Rory, of our Friday nights.

"I guess these'll do," Seth broke the silence, gathering up a stack of CDs. "Sorry, didn't mean to get off on a big GBV tangent."

"It's okay. I really like them. I mean, I like what I've heard so far. You should tell me which songs to download, and I'll get some more," I said, trying to break up the melancholy. I didn't want to further my embarrassment by admitting to Seth that I'd just stopped at the one Guided by Voices song because I was more intent on making a mix CD for Rory. Who didn't even care enough about music to realize that I'd found all these songs that seemed to be written just for us. "I looked them up online, but there were, like, a hundred albums. I didn't know where to start."

"Probably more like a thousand albums! I swear, Bob Pollard writes more songs than Lil Wayne. Anyway, you can't download GBV." Seth became very professorial all of a sudden. "I mean, you *can*, if it's the only way you can hear them. But they're one of those bands where it's better when you can, like, hold the albums in your hands. Almost all the covers are Bob's collages . . . they're so awesome. Next time you come over, we'll spend some quality time with Donnie's collection. He's even got an original *Propeller* on vinyl!"

"Well, uh—okay." I was too busy trying to make sense of the suggestion that Seth and I were going to spend some "quality time" together to wonder what on earth a propeller on vinyl was.

"In the meantime, I'm gonna make you a mixtape!" Seth went on. "I've got all their albums, plus Donnie's old EPs, Bob's solo stuff, Tobin Sprout's solo stuff, all of it. In fact, it's gonna have to be mixtapes, plural. Prepare yourself, Lula Monroe, 'cause you are fixin' to get bombarded with GBV."

"I hate to tell you, Seth, but I think I've been vaccinated against that sort of thing."

Sexy Seth laughed again. He stood up, tucking the CDs under his arm. He gave me one of those classic Sexy Seth smiles, and, I have to admit, I could see why my fellow female classmates tended to turn into complete idiots around him.

"Has anybody ever told you you're pretty funny, Lula?"

"Many times, as a matter of fact, but I think they meant funny-strange, not funny-ha-ha."

"Huh. Well. I think you're pretty funny-ha-ha." Seth looked down at the stack of CDs in his hand, raking his hand through his hair. He seemed nervous or embarrassed or something, all of a sudden. His room was quiet except for the dramatic *dum-da-da-da-DUM!* music coming from *Millionaire* on the TV downstairs.

"Maybe we should get back to the party," I suggested.

"Yeah. These oughta keep us busy for a while, don't you think?" He flipped the light out.

"For a little while, anyway." I stopped in the doorway. "Hey, Seth? When you said you and Rory were on the same team, did you mean—"

"Football." Seth said. "What'd you think I meant? Ice hockey?"

eleven

MY MOTHER AND I WERE WALKING around downtown Santa Fe, on our way to meet Walter for dinner. The night air was cool and the sidewalks were threaded with tourists bearing shopping bags, their wrists stacked with turquoise bracelets. We had just made a lame attempt at bonding by going to the opening-night screening of *The X-Files: I Want To Believe*.

"I'm just surprised, that's all. I thought it would be a lot more suspenseful. Wasn't this show about government conspiracies? It wasn't even scary."

"You weren't scared? Not even when they had Mulder out in the barn with the axe?" I kicked a loose pebble down the narrow street. I was already writing in my head, trying to compose an entry for the *Guide* about the movie, but my mom's complete lack of shrieking hysterical excitement was making it hard to concentrate.

"Come on," she scoffed. "You know they're not going to chop up one of their principals. I can't believe you're defending this movie. It was sort of homophobic, don't you think? Not to mention trans-phobic. Evil gay mad scientists chopping up bodies for bizarre transgendered Frankenstein experiments? Predatory gay pedophilic priests? I thought your best friend was gay."

"Yeah. He is." What was I supposed to say? My mother was seriously raining on my *X-Files* parade. She didn't even care about Mulder's Exile Beard, or that he and Scully were living together, but they were still too wrecked to be normal and married and happy. And we even got to see Skinner come in and kick some ass. Everything else was, well . . . secondary.

"And what about you? You weren't offended?"

"Me? Offended?" On the contrary. I got to see Mulder and Scully on the big screen—I was delighted. But I didn't say that. My mother's disdain was actually making me feel embarrassed to love *The X-Files*. Thankfully, there was Walter, standing on the corner, giving a big wave.

"Walter!" My mother seemed relieved, too.

"Lucky me, two lovely ladies on my arm." He and my mother kissed. I looked away. "Hey there, sport. Did you two have fun together?" He gave my shoulder a little punch.

"Yeah, we had fun." I sounded a little too chipper.

"Come on in," he opened the door for us. "Our table's ready. Now, I won't tell you what to order, but I believe they've got the best tamales in town."

The dinner was indescribably boring. My mother kept talking to Walter about some guy they knew who was divorcing his wife and who would get the gallery they co-owned and the wife was having an affair with some artist who blah blah blah. Walter just nodded and chewed his tamales. Which were insanely good, by the way, but it wasn't like I'd eaten a lifetime of tamales for comparison. I kept wishing I was with Rory; we would be at Federico's Pizza right now, going insane, already planning on going back to the Saturday matinee. I wondered where Rory was right now, who he was seeing the movie with.

"Did your mother tell you that the oldest-known church in America is right here in Santa Fe?" Walter said when she'd gotten up to go to the bathroom. "You'd think it'd be in Boston or some such, but it's just a few blocks away, matter of fact. Spanish explorers came up here through Mexico, years before the Pilgrims."

"Huh." I tried and failed to sound interested.

"I figured that'd be right up your alley. You're looking for religion."

"Who says I'm looking for religion?"

"You did. Didn't you?" Walter leaned back in his chair. I shrugged.

"I don't know what I'm looking for," I admitted, and it hit me how true that was. All of a sudden, though, I felt like I was going to cry. My mother came back from the bathroom and sat down, shaking her napkin out like a matador and landing it in her lap.

"Should we order dessert?" She looked at my plate. "Are you finished? We could get them to wrap that up."

"Don't rush her, Chris."

"It's fine. I'm done." I wiped my mouth.

"Walt, you wouldn't believe this movie we saw. So gruesome."

"Huh." Walter swirled his beer bottle around and took the last swig. "I thought it was an adaptation. Something off TV."

"You remember that show, *X-Files*?" Mom tried to jog his memory. "Mid-nineties? FBI agents investigating UFOs?

Kind of *Twin Peaks* meets *All the President's Men*." Walter squinted, trying to remember.

"Sounds familiar . . . sorta like *Kolchak: The Night Stalker*, but with a guy and a girl, right?"

"Right. Same cast, but this time, instead of UFOs, it was about a serial killer who turned out to be decapitating girl's heads so that he could attach the head of his dying gay lover to their bodies and re-animate them."

"Shoo," Walter winced. "That's gruesome, all right." He cocked a look at me. "You like horror movies?"

"Not really, no."

"What would you call that, then?" my mother challenged. "It was certainly horrifying."

"But it wasn't about—I mean, it was really about them. About Mulder and Scully, working together again. If you were into the show, that's all that matters—"

"Is it?" My mother arched her eyebrow. "So you're postulating that plot has nothing to do with your overall enjoyment of a piece of cinema, as long as you like the main characters? That's interesting."

"No, I meant—"

"Because you have to admit, it was not a pleasant viewing experience. It was dreary, visually unappealing, credulity-straining at every corner—you have to admit that it simply wasn't very good."

"Why do I have to admit anything?" I felt my stomach knot up. Walter picked at the label on his beer bottle with the edge of his thumbnail. "Why can't I have my own opinion? I mean, yeah, I would've liked it better if it'd been about the mythology arc, but whatever. They used to do stand-alone episodes all the time. They call it Monster of the Week. Maybe you just don't understand—"

"Then enlighten me, daughter." My mother sat back and folded her arms. "What do I, after a lifetime of working in film and theater, fail to *understand* that you, in your infinite fangirl wisdom, fully comprehend? I mean, I've seen the posters on your bedroom walls, and I gotta say, kiddo, I don't have a lot of faith in your ability to give a fair, objective critique of anything that involves an hour and a half of David Duchovny's puppydog eyes."

I stared down at my half-empty plate, willing myself not to cry. Okay, so this is how it was going to be. We weren't going to bond. We weren't going to go to the Georgia O'Keeffe museum together and stand arm in arm in front of the big flower paintings. She wasn't going to be impressed by the endless Internet articles I'd read on Stanislavski and method acting or Ingmar Bergman's use of Jungian dream imagery or magic realism in the plays of Sam Shepard. We were going to sit here in a crowded restaurant with the forks clinking against the plates and hate each other silently, one of us for leaving, one of us for showing up.

"Christine," Walter whispered. "It's just a movie. Take it easy."

The waitress came with her tray. "How we doin' over here? You guys ready for some dessert?"

"I think we'll take the check," Walter told her.

I stood up and pushed past the waitress, walked out of the restaurant, to the sidewalk outside. This line from one of my mom's books came into my head. From the Liv Ullmann book. *To return is not to revisit something that has failed*. It was underlined. I always hung on to that line, thinking it meant that someday, somehow, my mom would come back. Now it dawned on me that I could take it for my own. That maybe it meant I should go back home. It would be mortifying, for sure. But maybe the embarrassment would hurt less than this.

I found Rory outside, sitting on the low brick wall that edged the patio, texting somebody on a brand new phone. Maybe the Brocks bought it for him. Maybe Seth was texting him right now. *Dude, your friends are weird*. Or maybe he was texting the old guy from the bookstore again. Planning another secret rendezvous.

"There you are," I said.

"Here I am." He snapped the phone closed.

"The enigmatic Theodore Callahan. Hey, nice Exile Beard."

"This old thing?" Rory smiled absently, rubbing his chin. "I was getting all broken out from the chinstrap. On my helmet. I'm gonna shave it as soon as the season ends."

"It makes you look older," I said, not wanting to admit that I preferred clean-shaven, baby-faced Rory. I noticed his pinkie finger, wrapped in strips of white tape. "What happened to your finger?"

"Oh." He flattened out his hand as if he was seeing the taped finger for the first time. "Got dislocated."

"You dislocated your finger? You're allowed to play with a dislocated finger?"

"I don't block with my pinkie." He laughed softly. "Anyway, it just happened tonight. It's no big deal."

"No big deal?" I jammed my finger playing basketball in gym class once, and it hurt like a bitch for at least a week. "I guess they're making a tough guy outta you yet."

"It doesn't hurt that much, that's all." He opened his Gatorade bottle and took a drink. "Having fun?"

"Yeah, it's been, ah—" Okay, all sarcasm aside, yes, I was having a good time. Some of Seth's church buddies started a huge game of Uno, which I hadn't played since I was, like, seven. I know. Uno. Go ahead and laugh. I'm uncool, whatever.

"It was fun. Seth's friends are nice. Seth's nice. We had a weird, um—" I hesitated. For some reason, I felt like I shouldn't tell Rory. But, what the heck. We used to be best friends, once upon a time. "He told me about his brother's testicles, and then he hugged me." I stopped at telling him about the song, or Seth's melancholy trees and musings on the nature of love.

"He gets pretty emotional about Donnie," Rory agreed. "The first night I lived here, he told me the whole story, and he was crying and everything. Then we stayed up till, like, 3 a.m. listening to Guided by Voices. I don't think his parents like to talk about Donnie dying, so it's like any chance he gets, you know?"

"Makes sense." I stuck my hands in my jacket pockets. "How's it working out? Living here?"

"It's nice. It's different. Seth's folks are cool. They're older." Rory looked up at the house. "It's nice that everything stays the same."

"What do you mean?"

"I mean the furniture doesn't move." We both laughed. "You know what's weird, though? I miss her." Rory sniffed. "I miss my mom."

"Patty the Pickle? Come on," I sighed. "Even without being a crazy inebriated homophobe, she's nuts. Remember that time she wouldn't let you throw out the shower curtain because she thought the mold pattern looked like the silhouette of Dick Cavett?"

"I guess no matter how old you get, you still want a mother," Rory mused.

"You can have mine," I offered. "She totally ruined the *X-Files* movie for me. We were supposed to be bonding or whatever, and we had this huge fight afterward because she was, like, adamant that it sucked."

"She seemed pretty hardcore."

"She was. She is." I kept forgetting that Rory had met her. This conversation was making me nervous somehow. "So, did you go see it with, um, with Andy?"

"No. We broke up. I saw it alone." Rory twisted his Gatorade cap again.

"Oh. Sorry to hear that. That you broke up." Was I sorry? Not really. I didn't even know the guy. I hadn't even known Rory was in a *relationship*, for Pete's sake—how could I feel sorry? But I wished I'd been there for him. I was so far out of Rory's life, I didn't even know how long it had been since the breakup.

"It probably would've happened anyway," Rory shrugged. "He's moving to Salt Lake City to be closer to his kids. He already sold the bookstore and everything."

"Geez, that's . . . that sucks." I didn't know what else to say.

"Um. Anyway. I'm gonna head home, but I just wanted to say, you know, if it doesn't work out over here, you can always come stay with me at Janet and Leo's. We've got the pullout bed and you know how Janet loves to cook, so." I cleared my throat. "Of course, we don't have Sexy Seth sleeping in the next room. Just raggedy old me."

"Just you, huh." Rory looked at me. Good gravy. He and Seth must get together and practice their Intense Stares on each other.

"Yeah. Just me." I said. "Well. See ya 'round, Rory."

"See ya, Lula."

I started to walk away, then I stopped. I wondered if Seth was telling the truth, if Rory really did talk about me all the time. I kicked at the edge of the patio wall. *Dammit.*

"Rory, hey. I'm sorry."

"What?"

"I said I'm sorry. I really am sorry about you and Andy breaking up. I'm sorry I wasn't there for you after Andy, or when your mom threw you out. I'm sorry about leaving and not telling you. I'm sorry I didn't reply to your emails or call you or anything. I was really angry that you didn't tell me about Andy. I was mad that we fought about it. But that's no excuse." I stopped. Faint voices drifted out of Seth's basement, laughing, a whole other world.

"It was a shitty thing to do, for me to leave like that and not tell you," I went on. "And I'm sorry. I'm really, truly sorry, and I wish that I hadn't acted like I did. I wish I'd confided in you. I wish I'd been honest with you about leaving. It should have been the easiest thing in the world to send you an email as soon as I left, and tell you not to worry, that I was okay. But . . . it wasn't. You don't have to be friends with me if you don't want to, but I just want you to know that . . . I'm sorry I hurt you. Okay?"

Rory stared straight ahead.

"I'll take that under advisement," he said finally.

twelve

I WALKED HOME TO CHECK IN with Janet and Leo, but they were sleeping already. I didn't feel like trying to sleep, so I got on my bike and rode over to Jay's. When I got there, Jay was standing on the front porch with a fat woman I'd never seen before. Not that I'm like, size-ist or whatever—I mean, look at Rory, he's huge, and he's adorable—but this woman was, like, *noticeably* fat from a distance. And way bigger than Jay. Jay was a little on the skinny side, but standing next to this woman, she looked like a pipe cleaner with a head.

I stood there in the shadows across the street, not really spying on purpose but just hanging back because I could tell, even from far away, that they were in the middle of an intense discussion. Then, they hugged. The fat woman kissed Jay's hair and pulled away from her, and Jay reached out for her hand. And I realized that this must've been Carol, the infamous Carol, the one who'd wrecked Jay so much she had to drop out of school. I waited until Carol's car was all the way down the street before I clicked my bike across and

knocked on Jay's door. When she came to the door, her face
was puffy and wet from crying.

"Hey—is everything okay?" I asked. Jay looked at me for
a second, her eyes filling with tears again. She shook her
head and sort of crumpled, and then she was crying into
my shoulder. Really sobbing, her entire body shaking with
it. I held her in the doorway for a few minutes, then I took
her over to the couch. There were two wine glasses on the
coffee table, still full. A ring, a thick band of silver with a
notch of a diamond chip in it, sat on the table next to the
bottle of wine.

"She said she had to see me," Jay said, swallowing and
sniffling. "Carol."

"That was Carol?" I asked, still not quite believing it. I'd
been picturing someone . . . less plus-sized.

"You saw her?"

"She was driving away—" I backpedaled, not wanting Jay
to think I was spying.

"Yeah, that was Carol." Jay narrowed her eyes at me.
"So what?"

"So . . ."

"I mean, you say her name like you're all surprised. Why,
just because she's black?"

"What?" Like I'm supposed to be shocked that Jay prefers
ladies of color? After her endless Beyoncé monologues? Not
to mention the fact that the only decorations in her whole
house were a poster of the cover of Janet Jackson's *janet*
album and a framed one-sheet from the movie *Foxy Brown*.
Nah, I was just trying to get my mind around the physics of
the whole thing, given Carol's substantial mass and Jay's

considerable lack thereof. "No, I don't care if she's black. But I thought she . . . lived all the way up in Massachusetts."

"She flew down here. She called me from the airport." Jay crossed her arms. "I thought maybe she was finally—I thought she'd changed her mind. But she—" Jay blinked up at the ceiling, trying not to cry. "She flew all the way down here just to tell me that she finally worked everything through in her head. Once she had some time to think. She wanted to say goodbye and give me my ring back in person. She wasn't even here long enough to drink the wine."

I stood up. Jay grabbed my hand.

"Where are you going? Don't leave yet, okay?"

"I'm just going to get you some Kleenex."

"I don't have any. There's toilet paper in the bathroom."

I went into the bathroom and emerged with a roll of toilet paper. Jay had already downed one of the glasses of wine and was halfway through the other when I came back. I handed her the toilet paper roll. She put the wine glass down long enough to blow her nose loudly.

"You want some?" She handed me the bottle. "It's really good wine. Really top notch stuff. No sense in letting it go to waste."

I had a glass, and then another one, just so that Jay wouldn't drink the whole bottle herself, but I didn't feel like drinking. We sat there on the couch for a while, Jay talking about Carol and Kendra, Carol's kid. The things they did together. How much Jay wanted to have a family, since she'd pretty much been kicked out of hers for being gay. After a while, I went into the kitchen for a glass of water. And for a break. I'd been listening to Carol Stories for nearly two hours, and maybe it made me a crappy friend, but what I really wanted now was to go home and go to bed.

"So why were you out and about tonight, anyway?" Jay drifted into the kitchen.

"I went to a football game. Back at my old school."

"You went to a football game?" Jay snorted. "How was it? A totally vile display of pseudo-masculinity?"

"It was a veritable who's who of people I never wanted to see again," I sipped my water. "But I ended up going to a party with Rory and his quarterback. This guy Seth. He told me all about how his brother died, and now he sits in his brother's old room and listens to his music. And then we—" I hesitated again. "We had, like, a moment. He hugged me. It was weird. But it was really nice. *He's* nice."

Jay laughed softly, slouching in the doorway. "So now you're making out with the quarterback. Next in the line of completely unattainable people you fall for. That makes sense."

"We weren't—"

"Lula, you're so dumb," Jay said. I was too surprised to say anything. "Why did you come over here tonight?"

"I—I dunno, I thought we'd hang out."

"I don't think you know anything. You don't know what you want. Why don't you go back to the quarterback's house and get knocked up?"

"Gee, that's nice. Who said I wanted to get knocked up by a quarterback?"

"You think you're so outside everything, but you're so typical," Jay kept on talking. "You're just too scared to act on it. You're too scared to feel something real for a real person. I mean, for somebody who's not a movie star on your wall."

"I'm going home," I muttered. I was too tired for this.

"No, wait a minute." Jay grabbed my arm again. I waited for her to make sense. "When did you realize you were in love with your gay best friend? Before or after he'd come out to you?"

"What?"

"And your little come-on to your teacher. You think it's a coincidence that it happened on the same night you saw your gay crush with his real boyfriend? You honestly think that what you did had anything to do with real love? You just needed to find somebody outrageous, to get What's His Name's attention. You needed to cause a scene. You found the safest possible person—married, straight, your teacher— the *most* unavailable. You knew she'd rather keep her job and not be ridden out of town on a rail than sleep with you. So it was easy. You acted out, but you didn't have to act on it. I mean, *really* act."

"What is this? You're putting me on trial because I can't get a date?" I realized she was still holding my arm, and I jerked out of her grip.

"I'm not putting you on trial—I'm—Jesus, I can't believe I told you anything. You don't know what love really means. You have no idea. You don't know what it's like to put yourself out there, to put it all on the line—you think you do, but you don't. You were so proud of yourself, *Ooh, Jay, look at me, I made out with my English teacher and then I ran away from home.* You're so *affected.* Big fucking deal. Lula, you're a child. A simple, sheltered child. So why don't you stay in your room, with your TV set and your DVDs and your computer, and stop pretending like your pathetic bratty outburst is somehow *meaningful*. I mean, all this handwringing you do. *Am I gay? Am I straight?* You're too scared of anything you can't turn off with a remote control to be anything at all."

Jay, you're drunk, is what I started to say, but then she kissed me. And I realized a few things, right there in that kiss. One was that Jay was probably right, that I wasn't really in love with Sam, and maybe I wasn't even truly in love with Rory. I just loved him, but I didn't know how to draw the lines yet. To love him like Seth did. Like a best friend. Like a brother.

The other thing I realized was that maybe Jay didn't know any more than I did. I mean, she spent plenty of time here in her house with her stereo blasting, hiding out from everything that had happened at her old school. Not dating anybody or hanging out with anybody but me. And not dealing with Carol, either. What was she waiting for? Maybe she was the one who was using me.

Jay pulled out of the kiss, looking coolly at me. A look like a dare.

"You wanna prove something," she said, "then stay here with me tonight."

"No," I said softly, shaking my head.

"I knew it." Jay held up her hands. "Fine, then. Go home to Grandma and Gramps. Go home where it's safe."

"I'm going home because you're drunk," I told her. "And because I'm not the person you wanted to stay with you tonight."

It also occurred to me that Jay was acting out, just like she said I was acting out when I went over to Sam's. She knew, deep down, that I wouldn't sleep with her tonight. So it was safe, to kiss me like that. Because it wasn't me that she wanted. She was just trying to make Carol feel as lonely as she felt. Just like I'd wanted Rory to feel alone, last spring, and I couldn't see any other way to make him feel as alone as I had except to leave town completely.

I went outside and got on my bike, feeling pretty smart. Being able to see it all like that, so clearly, for a change.

IT WAS STILL DARK WHEN I got home. I stood there in my room, listening to the faint hum of Leo's breathing machine from down the hall, the one he used for his sleep apnea. I didn't feel afraid or tense or angry or anything, really. I didn't even feel drunk. I felt clear. I felt like the future, the immediate future, was a glowing neon arrow in front of me, straight and solid and bright.

The last time I felt afraid—I mean, really, truly afraid—was the night I left. I was halfway to town, my shoulder already aching with the weight of my full duffel bag. I was almost at the highway overpass when I heard a truck shifting gears, growling behind me. I walked to the farthest edge of the grass, away from the road, but the truck still shook me as it passed. I stayed shook; by the time I reached the Flying J truck stop, I was trembling like it was thirty degrees out. My stomach was churning. It wasn't too late to go home. But somehow I couldn't make myself turn around.

I walked into the Flying J and made it into the bathroom stall just in time to puke my guts out. I was drenched in sweat, but cold at the same time. My hands vibrated, hanging on to the toilet seat. I couldn't do this. I had to call Janet.

Leo. Somebody. *I'm too small for this. Too weak to be out here alone. Come get me. Come take me home.*

But I knew it was false and I knew I wasn't home. I wouldn't be home until I went all the way, until I found her, until I stopped going along with Leo, pretending she didn't exist. His own daughter. My own mother. All of this other stuff— Rory, Sam—it was small ball. She was the one I needed to confront. If I was ever going to know who I was, who I *really* was, then I had to know who she was. Until then, I was nothing. A shadow. A character. Nobody real.

Blindly, I took my sweaty clothes off and opened the duffel bag and changed. I didn't realize until later that I'd spilled my mother's things out of my own bag and left them there, on the Flying J floor. But it made sense, when I thought about it. Without even knowing it, I was getting rid of the props. I was getting ready to make her real.

Now I stood there in my bedroom at home. I was really at home. At Janet and Leo's. Finally. This is where I'd grown up. This is where I was from. Maybe I had to get rid of the props here, too. Maybe Jay was right. Maybe she wasn't. Anyway, it seemed like a good idea at the time. I stood on my desk chair and started at the top corner. The first *X-Files* poster came down with a satisfying rip, tiny flecks of black paint coming away with the tape, leaving white pinpricks beneath like fledgling stars. Once I started, it was hard to stop. It was like some Christmas morning in reverse, opening the packages to find nothing underneath. I peeled away the pages I'd ripped out of sci-fi magazines. I tore away the one-sheets, let them float like autumn leaves into a pile on the floor. Afterward, I surveyed the scene. I felt the same way I had when I changed clothes and walked out of that bathroom stall. Like I didn't know who I was. Like I might not have even known my name if someone had asked. But I also felt like I was at the beginning of some endless possibility. And that maybe I was bigger and stronger than I ever realized.

The familiar faces were gone. No more Aragorn, no Gandalf. No Lone Gunmen. No Mulder and Scully. The wall in front of me now was blank, black, a vast space. Maybe I'd just leave it that way.

thirteen

I SAT BEHIND THE WHEEL OF Walter's pickup truck. Walter sat beside me, holding the keys. My mother kept making excuses, finding reasons why she didn't have time to teach me to drive. So Walter finally took me under his wing.

"The object of the game," he explained, "is real simple. Get from here to there without running anybody over or smashing into any of the other cars."

"Aye aye, captain." I reached for the keys. Walter jerked them up out of my reach.

"Now, don't get crazy here. This truck is not a toy."

"C'mon, Walt. We're driving in a straight line from the gate to the barn. I think I can handle it."

"Hey, listen up, Geronimo. Every time you get behind the wheel, the odds that you will die a gruesome death increase exponentially. You have to respect the odds. I'm about to put you in charge of two tons of metal, here. I need to know that you understand the gravity of the situation before I put these keys in your hand."

"I promise," I held up my hand in a scout-ish salute. "I will do my best to kill myself in the most un-gruesome way possible." He wasn't budging. "Walter, come on. I'll be careful. I promise."

"I hope so." He finally handed me the keys. I put them in the ignition and started the motor.

"All right. Now, just like I told you. Ease off the clutch, slow on the gas, but not too slow—"

Right away, I stalled the engine. "Whoops. Sorry."

"That's okay. Just turn it off and start it again."

This time, I got it in gear. We puttered off down the road, bumping along the jagged gravel.

"There you go! It's just like the horse. You're a natural." Walter approved! I made it all the way to the barn, picking up speed. The barn was suddenly very, very close.

"Now what?"

"Brake! Brake!" Walter exclaimed. I slammed on the brake, and we both jerked forward. Then the motor stalled again.

"Maybe you should teach me on an automatic," I suggested.

"Nonsense. Everybody ought to know how to drive a stick. Now, start 'er up again, and this time, put it in reverse." I did as Walter said and backed the truck away from the barn.

"Don't hit the water tank. Now, easy does it, shift back into first—yep, just like that." And we were on our way again, bouncing off toward the gate. We made the crooked loop again and again, until Walter didn't even have to remind me to go easy on the clutch.

"You're getting the hang of it, kiddo!" Walter grinned and ruffled my hair as I drove. "See, the thing about driving is, you can understand it intellectually, but your body has to learn, too. You gotta get used to the sound of the gears, get your hand-eye coordination to where you know how quick to put on your brakes. That's what's good about learning on a stick shift, too. When you're young, you get so damn excited by the thing, you wanna get out on the open road and go faster than your reflexes are ready for. Having to shift gears keeps you honest. These kids today, their parents buy 'em some speedy little number where all you gotta do is put it in "D" and punch the gas. Next thing you know, they're wrapped around a goddamn tree. Artificial acceleration. These kids, their bodies wanna move faster than their brains."

"Or their hearts," I murmured.

"Huh?"

"This is one of those driving-as-a-metaphor-for-life speeches, isn't it?" I asked.

"I hadn't thought of it that way, but I reckon it is a rite of passage," Walter mused. "Watch out, now, there's the barn again."

I slowed down, reversed, and turned us back toward the gate. Beyond the gate, there was the house, and my mother's Subaru parked outside. She was back home, probably for lunch. I pulled the brake on the truck and rested my hands on the wheel.

"Walter, can I ask you a question? Not about driving?"

"Sure, what's on your mind?"

"When I first got here, you said you're not my father." I turned and looked at him. "Are you sure about that?"

Walter shifted in his seat. Sniffed. Rubbed his forehead like it hurt.

"Tallulah—"

"I mean, are you really, one hundred percent sure? There's not a chance that it might have been you, and not this other guy? I mean, he was gay, right? Maybe he couldn't even, you know, perform."

"Hey now." Walter made a puckering face. He looked back at the house. At her car. "Listen. When Chris told me she was pregnant with you—" He exhaled hard. "I didn't even have to ask. We didn't have, ah . . . we didn't have that kind of a relationship. Not back then. But I wish—I wish I could sit here and tell you—" Walter looked back at me. His voice was almost a whisper. "You're a good kid, Lula. I would've been honored to be your dad."

"If I'm such a good kid," I said, clearing my throat. "Then why does she hate me so much?"

"She doesn't hate you. I don't like how she treats you, but she doesn't hate you."

"Then why is she so mean to me all the time? We can barely say five words to each other without her making fun of me or making me feel stupid. Does she really think I'm so dumb and awful?"

"She doesn't know what to think. You want my opinion?" Walter scratched his chin. "She's angry at herself. Your mother's a perfectionist. You're the one thing in her life she didn't do right, and she knows it. Everything else she didn't succeed at—her movie career, being an actress— she can blame it on the whims of Hollywood or what have you. But when it comes down to you, she's the last man standing. She wants to be the best at everything she does, and being a mother is the one thing she's been the worst at. If you ask me, though, the best thing she ever did for you was to leave you with your grandparents. They raised you into a fine young woman. A little smart-mouthed, but you're brave and you speak your mind and stand up for yourself. That's important stuff, kiddo. Just standing up to your mother the way you do. You don't let her bully you, honey. You're doing a lot better than you think. Better than I'd do, in your shoes."

"Then why do I . . . feel so bad all the time?"

"Because it's hard." Walter looked at me. "She's your mother. You want to get along with her. But she loves you, deep down. She really does. I know it."

I don't know who Walter was trying to convince, me or him. We both stared out at the house, at the sun glinting off her car.

"Walter, can I ask you another question? This one isn't about driving, either."

Walter just nodded.

"Could I come to work for you?"

"Work for me? What for?"

"I want to save up some money. I'm gonna buy another train ticket. I'm gonna go home. Back to Janet and Leo's."

Walter looked at me. He touched my hair. "You can stay here as long as you want. You can work for me if you want to, stay the rest of the summer if you like. But whenever you're ready to go, you just say the word, and I'll drive you home."

"It's a long way."

"I've driven it before."

"You'd have to go back all the way by yourself."

Walter nodded. His voice caught when he spoke. "Yeah, I reckon that'll be the hard part."

We both just sat there in the truck for a minute. It was quiet.

"Do you mind," I asked, "driving us back down to the house? I'm kind of tired right now."

"Sure." Walter got out and I slid over to the passenger side. The door opened and Walter got in, got behind the wheel.

"You wanna hand me my sunglasses? They're in the glove box, there." He started the engine. I opened the glove box and saw his glasses in a flat black case. Also, a couple of cassette tapes. The same girl singer that my mom had a tape of, that she'd left behind for me a hundred years ago. Laura Nyro.

"Are these my mom's?" I asked him, holding up one of the cassettes.

"No. Those are mine." Walter put his sunglasses on and gripped the gearshift. "Your mother hates driving this truck."

Janet knocked twice and then just came on in.

"Lula, honey. Did you forget about your haircut?"

I rubbed the crust out of my puffy eyes and sat up. My haircut? Oh yeah, my haircut. Janet was going to take me to get my lame hair fixed, finally.

"I guess so." My throat was rough. Last night came back to me in floating pictures, hazy jigsaw pieces. Rory and Seth. Sam at the football game. Seth's brother. Jay and Carol. Jay, drunk. Me, coming home. Okay.

"You took your pictures down," Janet said, eyeing the pile of shiny poster paper on the floor. "I thought I heard something last night."

"Sorry about the noise," I said.

"I'm glad it was you." Janet ruffled my hair. "I was afraid we had a rat."

I usually hated haircuts, but this one wasn't so bad. Janet's hairdresser, Frank, snipped the dead ends and didn't try to convince me to get some tacky little asymmetrical bob or streaky highlights like everybody else.

"We could dye it again, if you like the red," he offered. "Otherwise, we can just strip it. Take the color out."

"Let's get rid of the red," I decided. "I'm going for the natural look." Would Frank understand if I told him I was putting my Scully days behind me?

"Your wish is my command," Frank said. An hour later, I walked out into the sunshine with Janet, looking like the old self I didn't feel like anymore.

"What would you say to a little lunch?" Janet said, unlocking the car.

"Hello, little lunch," I supplied the punch line. Janet laughed. That was an old one.

"How about the Tea House? I could go for a chicken salad sandwich."

"Sure." I stared out the window as Janet cranked the car. She backed out into the road, singing along with her Dionne Warwick CD in her off-key smoker's voice. Good old unflappable Janet.

"I think it's cute," she said. "Your hair. You don't like it?"

"It's hair," I shrugged.

"You usually complain that nobody cuts it the way you want, not even Frank."

I shrugged again, unable to muster up much comment. I had more on my mind now than hair. "I guess he finally got it."

"Everything all right?" Janet asked. "Did you and your friend Jay have a fight?"

"Mm. Sort of. A misunderstanding. I'll give her a call later. It's no big deal."

"We don't mind if you want to have her over to the house. You know that, right? We're trying to be supportive of your . . . life choices."

"Thanks," I said.

"Leo might seem a little prickly about it, you know, but he'll come around. He's just old-fashioned. But you know we just want you to find someone who makes you happy."

"Wait a minute—you guys think Jay's my girlfriend?"

"You mean she isn't?"

I laughed.

"Well, you were always sleeping over! And she's sort of— you know, not a tomboy, but what do you call it? Anti . . . uh. Ambidextrous?"

"Androgynous?" I couldn't stop laughing.

"Don't laugh at me! This is all very new."

"I'm not laughing at you. It's just the idea that—I mean, it's a wonder Jay even speaks to me. She'd never go out with me in a million years."

"Oh, that's not true. She was giving you the flirty-eye all night that time she came to dinner."

"The *flirty-eye*?" I laughed harder. Then I remembered last night. Maybe Janet was on to something. Maybe Jay wasn't just trying to get back at Carol. No, that was crazy. Jay was too cool for me.

"She seems like a nice girl. I think you'd be good with one of those creative types. Not that I didn't like Rory. But I think you've got an artistic streak, like your mother. You should explore it."

"First of all, Rory wasn't my boyfriend, either. And second of all . . ." I looked out the window at nothing much going by. A blank field, a cemetery on the horizon, a Family Dollar beyond that. "I'm not anything like my mother."

"I meant it as a compliment," Janet said quietly.

"I know." I bit the edge of my fingernail. "Do you think Leo's ever going to stop being mad at me?"

"He's not mad at you, honey. He loves you."

"Yeah, yeah. Deep down inside, right?"

"No. He loves you right up close to the surface. Maybe you don't even realize. When you came to live with us, he'd just retired. Fifty years old and didn't have any idea what to do with himself. He'd been in the Navy since he was eighteen, can you imagine? Decades in the service, and suddenly he didn't have anybody to answer to. He didn't have any orders. Not to mention we just moved into the condo and we were probably the youngest people in the retirement villa at that point. I thought Leo was going to go out of his mind. Your mother leaving you with us is the best thing that ever happened to him. He just lit right up. He didn't get to enjoy your mother when she was little. He was off fighting that war. Didn't know the first thing about babies. Kids. You gave him a second life. He'd never admit it, but taking care of you kept him going."

I closed my eyes. I wasn't sure I wanted that kind of responsibility.

"I know how badly I messed up. But I still don't know how to fix it."

"Honey, your granddad sits up half the night thinking the same thing."

WHEN WE GOT HOME THAT AFTERNOON, there were two messages from Leo on the kitchen counter, and a stack of mail. The first message read: *Jan—gone to Ralph's. New putter's ready. L.* The second: *Lula—Jay called. 13:35. Call her back.*

"This came for you," Janet handed me a postcard from the stack of mail. It was a picture of Santa Fe taken from up high, almost the same view that I'd seen that day I'd gone riding with Walter. My heart skidded—my mom! I flipped it over. Read the blockish script.

> *Lula,*
> *I saw this in town and it reminded me of you. How's your driving coming? I just wanted to let you know you're missed here at the ranch. Hope you'll come back for a visit sometime. Maybe Thanksgiving or Christmas if your grandparents don't mind. Hope you're well.*
>
> *Sincerely,*
> *Walter MacKelvey*
> *P.S. Gingerbread says hello.*

"Lu, honey? Is everything okay?"

I nodded quickly.

"Are you sure?"

I swallowed hard. I was thinking of my severely restricted pay-as-you-go phone. "I'm sure. Hey, Janet—"

"Mm-hmm?" She smoothed my hair.

"Can I use your phone tonight to make a long-distance call?"

"Sweetheart. Of course you can."

fourteen

My bag was packed. Walter and I were getting an early start tomorrow. Five a.m. My mother wouldn't be joining us for the drive. Things to do. People to see.

"You like beef jerky?" Walter asked. He was packing a cooler and a brown bag full of snacks for the road.

"Gross. No." I laughed. "What part of the beef is the jerky, anyway?"

"Smart aleck. Hand me that tin foil, Lulabelle."

I slid the drawer open. I couldn't believe I'd gotten so used to being here, I knew where the tin foil was. Or that Walter had already saddled me with this dumb nickname. Which I secretly kind of liked, but only coming from him. My mother wandered into the kitchen, yawning, BlackBerry in hand. She plugged it into the charger, getting ready for the next shift.

"I thought you two were getting an early start," she said. "You're still up."

"We are. Just taking care of a few last-minute food items." Walter looked at my mother, then at me. "Which reminds me, I have to go—check on something in the truck. Excuse me, ladies."

Boy, was that a lame excuse. *Okay, Walt. Here we are, alone.* Me and my mom. Did he really think we were finally gonna bond during my last eight hours in Santa Fe? *Nice try, buddy.*

"I was going to leave this for you," she said. She pulled something out of her back pocket. It was a photograph, slightly creased, of a younger version of my mom, her mouth wide open, laughing, with her arms around some dark-haired guy in a shiny paper hat that said HAPPY NEW YEAR! The guy looked vaguely familiar, though I couldn't place him. "It's kinda goofy, but it's the only one I had of the two of us together. Me and your dad."

"Whoa," I whispered as it suddenly hit me. That's where I knew him from. From *me.* We had the same ears. The same mouth, the same chin. He was shorter than her, short like me. I felt a hot tear nibbling the edge of my lashes and I wiped it away quickly, swallowing.

"Technically," she cleared her throat. "It's the three of us. I'd just found out I was pregnant with you. So, there you go. Family portrait."

Huh. Some family. I flipped the picture over. The name Peter Hubbell was written on the back, in pencil, with a phone number.

"In case you want to give him a call," my mother explained. "I told him—I talked to him recently, and I told him you might be getting in touch. He said he'd love to see you some-time. If you ever wanted to meet him."

"Oh." *Peter Hubbell.* My father. My dad. My old man. *Lula Hubbell.* None of that sounded right at all. But he wanted to see me. Maybe he'd be cool, like Tracy's dad, or Walter. Or maybe he was a big selfish jerk. Still, it probably wasn't easy for my mom to call him. Being her ex and all. "Thank you for the picture. And also for calling him."

"No sweat. He's a good guy. Complicated, but a good guy." She smiled to herself. "Tell Janet and Leo I said hi."

"Will do." I sniffed. I put the picture down on the kitchen counter. Tucked my thumbs into my back pockets.

"It was . . . interesting," she said. "Having you here."

"Thanks. Thanks for having me. Thanks for being interested."

"I hope everything works out for you. With your friend Rory. And school and everything. You'll be graduating this year. Heading off to college and all that."

"Yep." Okay, oh my God. I was going out of my mind. College, really? Small talk, now? *Mother, hello, I'm walking away from you! I'm leaving! Do something real, now! Say something meaningful! Love me! I'm here right now! Don't just give me this picture and say good luck and then walk away! Do something! I'm right here!*

"I feel like I ought to make some speech or something. But I—" she crossed her arms. Smiling, a little sheepish. "I don't know. I wasn't cut out for this."

"I know. You've mentioned that. You're not mom material," I reminded her. "I'm not a little kid, you know. I mean, you don't have to take me for my shots or cure me of the croup, or whatever. I'm pretty much grown up. So . . ."

"Pretty much grown up, huh?"

"Uh-huh." All right, so maybe I wasn't so grown up. Fine, let her take me apart. *Here we go.*

"You know, ah. I've been meaning to tell you. That backpack of mine. The one you had. With the books and everything."

"Yeah?" The one I'd lost on the trip. The books I'd studied for so long.

"I didn't leave it for you. I mean, I didn't leave it on purpose. It was the only thing I had that didn't get stolen, but it reminded me too much of . . . it reminded me of everything that didn't work out. I wanted to forget all that, but I didn't mean . . ." She ran her hand through her hair and sighed. "Sometimes you think all you need is a change of pace. A fresh start, get back on your feet. And the next thing you know, you're caught up in this whole other life and it's easier to just . . ." She kind of threw up her hands. "I guess what I'm trying to say is, I didn't mean for you to be like that stupid backpack. You know. Just some old piece of baggage. That I left behind."

"Okay," I said, slowly understanding. Was that an apology? I'd take it.

"Okay, then." My mother nodded. We must've looked like a couple of gunslingers, standing there in the kitchen. Waiting to shoot.

"So what am I supposed to do now?" she asked. Because I may not have been a little kid, but I wasn't really an adult, either. Not in her mind. I didn't care about galleries and affairs. I couldn't defend my interests and inclinations with deliberate intellectual . . . deliberation. I was her daughter. What was that? A person who wanted something. Wanted what, exactly? Some piece of you you didn't want to give. Some piece of you I already had.

I looked at her. She looked at me. Was she seeing me, seeing how I looked like her? Did she see how we both had Janet's cheekbones, that we had the same eyes? Did she know I had her hair, before I dyed it red? Maybe I just reminded her of the mystery dad, maybe she was tired of the way my mouth looked like his. Or maybe she was tired of my gangly hands and my too-big nose, because those were straight from good ol' Leo.

"What are you supposed to do now?" I repeated her question. Shrugged, looked at her. *Family*. That word again. Mostly meaningless. At least when it came to me and her.

"You just . . . say 'Have a nice trip,'" I suggested. "And I guess we could hug goodbye."

She nodded and took a step. We both sort of silently decided to raise our arms at the same time, and we hugged. We hugged like a pair of badly articulated action figures that only bent at the elbows. After our nanosecond of bodily contact, my mother, in her piney aura of hemp soap, pulled away.

"Have a nice trip," my mother said. She let the briefest of smiles flicker across her lips before she turned and shuffled back down the hall to her bedroom alone.

LOW CLOUDS HAD ROLLED IN AND a light rain had begun to fall. Jay was slouched down on the porch swing, the hood of her sweatshirt pulled low over her eyes. She looked like Obi-Wan Kenobi. Except, you know. Hungover.

"Hey," I said, brushing water off my raincoat.

"Hey." Her voice was rough. There was a cigarette in between her fingers, smoked down to the filter tip. I sat down next to her on the swing, careful not to jostle it too much.

"I was an asshole last night," she said, clearing her throat. "I'm sorry. Are you mad?"

"Not really. But thanks for apologizing. How's your head?"

"Mean."

I nodded. I wasn't feeling all that hot myself, and I'd only had two glasses.

"Wine fucks with me," Jay admitted. "I don't know why."

"It's the sulfites. Leo can't even drink red wine anymore. He says it gives him heart palpitations."

"Leo," she murmured. "He's cool. Even if he is a little scary."

"Yeah," I agreed.

"You're lucky. You've got a good family."

"Good grandparents, at least."

"That's more than most people get." Jay finally dropped the cigarette onto the porch and stubbed it out with her bedroom-slippered foot. I put my head on Jay's shoulder. I wasn't sure why. I wasn't a real touchy-feely person. But it seemed like the thing to do.

"Maybe it just takes time," I said.

"Maybe." She leaned her head against mine. "You're a good kisser."

"Really? You're only, like, the third person I've ever kissed in my life."

"I guess you're a natural."

"I've got mad lip skills, yo."

"You're a dork," Jay laughed.

"And you're friends with me, so, hey."

"Some friend. I thought I could get back at Carol by sleeping with you."

"I guess I should be glad somebody wants to sleep with me, even if it is just to get revenge," I reasoned.

"You're pretty cute," Jay said. "I'd probably sleep with you anyway."

"Seriously?"

"Seriously." Jay nudged my shoulder. "Why else do you think I've been letting you hang around?"

"So Janet was right! She thought you were giving me the flirty-eye at dinner that night!"

"The flirty-eye?"

"You know." I demonstrated. Jay cackled and gave me a shove. I shoved her back.

"Janet was on to me," Jay said. "I kind of wanted to kiss you that night in your bedroom, but you were so distraught. I was afraid it might mess with your head."

"You did?" I couldn't believe it. Jay actually entertained the thought of not only kissing but actually maybe even sleeping with the likes of *me*, her bratty eighteen-year-old hanger-on? I was flattered and surprised. Surprised because, even though I thought she was so cool and good-looking and everything, I didn't feel all overwhelmed sitting next to her, or even when we kissed the night before. I didn't feel the same flutter of thrill in my chest as I did when I kissed Sam. Or the same warmth I felt holding Rory in my bed. I thought about Seth up in his bedroom with his sad songs. *Why do we love what we love?* Or who we love. I was nowhere close to figuring it out, but I was pretty sure I wasn't in love with Jay, even though I liked her a lot.

"All this time I thought you thought I was a joke," I confessed.

"A joke? Why?"

"Because, I dunno. I thought you thought of me as naïve and everything. Because I'm not all that . . . experienced." Jay was quiet. I listened to the soft, padding sound of the rain on the grass.

"I've been really dismissive of you," Jay said. "And I'm sorry. It hurts to be dismissed."

"Seriously, I'm not mad about last night. People get drunk. Shit happens."

"I'm not just talking about last night. I mean, you came to me for, like, guidance. And ever since we started hanging out, I've been disregarding your experience. Sometimes I forget that not everybody figured out they were gay when they were seven years old. It's totally okay for you to still be figuring it out. I'm sorry I haven't been more . . . receptive to your struggle."

"It's not so much a struggle as it's been just me going around being a dumbass, but thanks all the same," I said. "Seriously. I'm really glad I've had you to talk to."

"So we're good?"

"Yeah. Duh. Of course we are."

Just then, her cell phone chirped. She pulled it out of her pocket and looked at the number.

"It's Carol." Jay bit her lip, looking at the phone.

"Go ahead, answer it," I said.

Jay put the phone back in her pocket.

"Maybe later. I was gonna do some drawing. You wanna come in and hang out?"

I looked out at the rain. A chill was setting in.

"No thanks. I gotta get home. There's some stuff I wanna work on, myself."

I was waiting. On purpose. So that when I finally got up the nerve to dial the number, there was a good chance she wouldn't be home.

"Hello?" Walter's voice came through the coiled wire of the kitchen phone in Santa Fe, bounced off a satellite somewhere in space, trickled through Janet's cell phone into my anxious ear.

"Hiya, Walt." I was afraid he wouldn't remember my voice.

"Lulabelle!" That stupid name. But I didn't mind. "How you been?"

"I'm okay. How are you?"

"Plugging along. You just missed your mother. She's at her Saturday yoga."

"Oh. I guess I forgot about the time change."

"I'll tell her you called. How's everything? You back in school?"

"Yeah. Sort of. I took the GED. I'm over at the community college now."

"Hey, smart cookie! Your mom'll be real proud to hear that. Real proud."

"Huh. Yeah." I sort of laughed. "You don't have to lie for her, you know."

"It's not a lie." I could hear Walter shuffling around, hundreds of miles away. "She wants you to do well."

"Anyway," I changed the subject. "I got my learner's permit. Janet's been letting me drive the car."

"Great news, honey! What'd I tell you? You're a natural behind the wheel."

"Um, also. I was thinking. Remember that jalapeño corn-bread you made that time?"

"Sure do. Your favorite, if I recall."

"Do you think I could get the recipe?"

"Well, now." I could almost see Walter giving me one of his stern looks. "That's an old family recipe. I don't go passing it around to just anybody, you know."

"Oh. Okay." I wasn't sure if he was being serious or not.

"So. You got a pen and paper?"

fifteen

RORY AND SETH STOOD IN THE parking lot of the
Hawthorne Unitarian Church, looking like mismatched
brothers. They both wore khaki pants and blue blazers,
but Rory's was too big for him, his fingers barely peeking
out of the sleeves. As big as he was, he still looked like a
little kid. And me, I must've looked like the biggest dork
on the planet. Wearing this ridiculous skirt-and-blouse
combo Janet bought me for some Tennis Club luncheon.
It had giant flowers on it. Not exactly the Dana Scully
Power Suit.

"Hey, what're you doing here?" Seth seemed baffled at my
presence. Maybe this was a mistake.

"I wanted to see if you were right. If it still smells like
books." I was suddenly afraid that Seth had forgotten our
whole conversation that night at his party. Rory just stood
there, examining me beneath the cloudy sky.

"Right on," Seth nodded, and I felt relieved he wasn't
laughing at me for showing up out of the blue. "Let's get
inside before it rains."

I somehow managed to get shuffled into the aisle between Rory and Seth. Seth's mom, sitting at the end of the pew, gave me a little wave hello. Seth's dad sat up at the front, beside a simple wooden lectern. I looked around. It was different from the First Baptist Church, that was for sure. Smaller and more casual. Some kids—and even some adults—were wearing jeans. I recognized a few of the guys from the Uno game at Seth's party. Our seventh grade science teacher, Mr. Brantley, was singing in the choir. They sang a few songs, we stood up, we sat down, we stood up again. A woman with her hair in a long gray braid stood up and reminded us to donate to the food bank's can drive. Then Seth's father stood up and began his sermon.

There I was, with Rory on my right and Sexy Seth on my left. I was trying to pay attention to what Seth's dad was saying, but I couldn't really focus. I kept wanting to stand up and yell out: *Aren't either of you going to acknowledge how awkward this is?* It was the first time I'd been this close to Rory in forever, and it was in a church, of all places. But then, a funny thing happened. I realized that I wasn't thinking impure thoughts about him. I wasn't angry at him. I didn't want anything from him except to be friends again. And if we couldn't be friends, I was glad that he had Seth, and Seth's family, looking out for him. *Okay, God. Wherever you are. I'm officially releasing Rory to your care. Just make sure he stays in school and eats a decent meal every once in a while, okay?*

Was that a prayer? Was I even allowed to pray? Maybe I could ask Seth's dad about it after the show. I tried to focus on the sermon again, but I was too busy thinking about myself. *Typical Lula.* But then, another funny thing happened. I actually started thinking about God. Actually, I was thinking about *The X-Files. Again, typical.* But I remembered how, on the show, it's a big deal that Scully was raised Catholic, and she maintained her faith in God through the whole thing, but she never believed in extraterrestrial life until the end of the series, when she grudgingly admitted that she'd seen too much not to believe. Mulder believed in aliens, but did he ever end up believing in God? Not that I could remember.

Why was it so easy for some people to believe in God, like Jenny and her family? They just got up every Sunday and did the whole shebang, dressy clothes and hallelujahs. But some people didn't believe in anything they couldn't see. And frankly, I could sympathize. I didn't want to believe that the mysteries of the world were unsolvable. On the other hand, it seems the best stuff is always so nebulous. I thought back to when I first went horseback riding with Walter, and we watched the sunset through the clouds. If I had to, I could've recited back facts to explain it all. I could've made Mr. Badfinger's head spin with everything I knew about clouds and the atmosphere and the tilt of the earth from the sun. But no equation on a page ever made me feel like I did in that hushed clearing, watching the sun turn the sky the colors of fire, the fields beneath us glowing like the glassy underneath of the sea.

I thought about Walter, who thanked God for my mother and black coffee every day. Who felt sure that God had put him in the exact place he was supposed to be, despite the fact that he had no idea whether God was some all-seeing humanoid overseeing our daily meanderings from a high-altitude Fortress of Solitude, or some cosmic force on the level of black holes or solar flares that caused regular joes like him to fall in love with prickly, emotionally unavailable women like my mom. I thought about Janet and Leo. Rory and Andy. Jay and Carol. Sam Lidell and her husband, meeting in an airport. My own mom and dad. Did God bring people together, or was it fate? Accident or luck? Love was a pretty nebulous thing, too. Had I ever really been in love? Would I ever know if I was or not? Was there an equation for love? Was it quantifiable? Or did it just move through you somehow, like some spirit breath?

Okay, one day in church, and already I was noodling away on some trippy spiritual nonsense. I glanced over toward Seth, who glanced back at me. Blushing, I faced front again. He probably thought I was such a dork. Rory's little sister, tagging along. Or maybe he didn't. I thought about how we both used to listen to Midnight Pete. And now there we were, both of us zoning out to the same sermon. I looked down at Seth's foot tapping along to a beat only he could hear. I almost laughed. The only thing in Seth's head was football stats and Guided by Voices songs, probably. I looked back at Rory, who sat ramrod-straight, watching Seth's dad. I nudged him gently in the ribs.

"Psst," I whispered. I was quickly formulating a good joke. "Wh—"

"Shh," Rory replied. *Shh?* He shushed me? Theodore Callahan, my former best friend, just shushed me in church. Well, I never. Seth looked over at me and smiled.

"Gum?" he asked quietly, offering me the pack. I took a piece. It tasted strange, like licorice and grass.

"What kind of gum is this?" I whispered again.

"It's all-natural," he explained.

"Seth. Twigs and bark are natural, but it doesn't mean they taste good."

At that, Seth snorted a big laugh that he covered with a cough. Rory and Seth's mom both leaned over and shushed us.

Seth's dad cracked a few jokes of his own, then wrapped it up with another prayer. He reminded us to sign up for the Habitat for Humanity build and that the ladies' yoga class in the Free Room had been changed to Thursday nights. One more song from the choir, and we were free to go.

"What'd you think?" Seth asked me when it was all said and done. I decided I better not tell him all my weird rambling thoughts about Agent Scully and God.

"You were right. It still smells like books."

He smiled. "We've got Krispy Kremes and coffee in the rec room, if you wanna hang out, do the whole meet-n-greet thing."

"That's okay. I told Janet I'd be home for lunch."

"Oh. Well, good to see you, anyway." Seth hugged me again. I was starting to get the drift. He's a hugger. "Come back sometime. Anytime you like."

"Thanks. Maybe I will," I told him. They weren't so bad, the Unitarians. And if I came back, next time, I'd wear jeans. Seth drifted off to say hello to his church friends, leaving me and Rory standing there, tugging at the sleeves of our mutually ill-fitting costumes.

"Looked like you're getting the hang of it," I remarked.

"The hang of what?"

"Y'know. The whole church thing. Praise the Lord, et cetera."

"It's not like that," Rory squinted. The rainclouds had blown away while we were inside, and the sun had broken out, all brilliant. "Things got pretty bad there, for a while. They really helped me out."

"Rory! How are you today?" A bearded guy in a corduroy blazer came by and squeezed Rory's shoulder, as if on cue.

"Doing well, thanks. How are you, Mr. Dunn?"

"Never better, kiddo! Hey, don't forget to give me a call when you're ready to bring the Buick over. It's an easy fix—we can work on it this afternoon if you like."

"Will do, sir. I'll give you a call when I get home."

"Excellent! I'll have Margie thaw some chicken, too, unless the Brocks have big plans for dinner."

"We usually just order Chinese on Sunday nights."

"All right, then! Dinner at our place."

"Sounds good."

"Terrific! Good to see you!" Mr. Dunn gave us the thumbs-up and went off to work the rest of the parking lot crowd.

"You know, you could've gone to Janet and Leo's," I told him. "Even if I wasn't there. Janet would've taken care of you. When you left your mom's."

"Yeah, well," Rory shrugged inside of his giant coat. "I guess I thought if you could make it on your own, I could, too."

"I wouldn't say I 'made it,' exactly," I said.

"Either way," Rory said. "We survived, didn't we?"

"I guess we did."

"Rory, honey," a gray-haired lady in a sweatshirt that said IF YOU CAN READ THIS, THANK A TEACHER put her arm around Rory. "I hope you're coming back to the rec room—I made your favorite banana bread!"

"Yes, ma'am, I'm on my way."

"We've got to feed this growing boy!" The woman patted Rory's back, laughing. "And you're invited, too, dear," she said to me.

"Thank you, ma'am, but I have to run." I told her, feeling like I did want to run. I could feel myself on the verge of tears again, but I didn't feel like crying because I was upset. On the contrary, I was suddenly overjoyed. While I'd been off looking for my mother, Rory had somehow managed to find an entire *family*.

It was a relief. Whatever happened to me, my former best friend was going to be okay.

LATER THAT NIGHT, I WAS ONLINE, watching Guided by Voices videos on YouTube, when my IM screen popped up.

SpookyKid: Are you listening to Midnight Steve?

Rory!

BloomOrphan: no. should I be?

SpookyKid: quick turn it on!

I OPENED THE COLLEGE WEBSITE AND turned on the radio stream. Put on my headphones and listened.

"Lula, huh? I hear that name a lot." It was Midnight Steve! Was he talking about me?! "Lula, honey, whoever you are, you must be breaking hearts all over town. So, what can I play for you, Seth?"

Seth! Seth was requesting a song for me on Midnight Steve?

"Um, I'd like to hear 'Learning to Hunt,' by Guided by Voices. Going out to Lula, if she's listening."

"Uhh . . . pick again, kiddo. Midnight Steve doesn't have that tune in the ol' library."

Ugh, Midnight Steve. He always did this. Got callers on the request line and then couldn't play their request. So lame.

"How about 'Hold On Hope,' also by Guided by Voices?" Seth asked. "Or 'Acorns & Orioles'? It's on an album Midnight Pete used to have, it's called *Under the Bushes Under the—*"

"How 'bout we give Lula some Coldplay, Seth?"

"I . . . don't think she likes Coldplay."

"Everybody likes Coldplay! Lula, wherever you are, here's a little Coldplay action comin' atcha from your buddy Seth and me, Midnight Steve, here on 88.2 FM."

I took my headphones off as the song started and typed a new message to Rory.

BloomOrphan: for the record, i do not like coldplay.

SpookyKid: lol.

BloomOrphan: srsly. what's he up to?

SpookyKid: I think he likes you.

BloomOrphan: pfft! sexy seth? no way. besides isn't he dating lori whatserface?

SpookyKid: She dumped him last spring for some college guy. He's making you a mixtape. Seth, I mean, not college guy.

BloomOrphan: yeah, he said he wanted to turn me on to guided by voices.

SpookyKid: His fave band. He couldn't believe you knew who they were.

BloomOrphan: blame midnight pete. anyway, I only knew like one song. and it was from the buffy soundtrack.

SpookyKid: Don't worry. Hang around Seth long enough, you'll never be able to get Echos Myron out of your head.

BloomOrphan: who?

SpookyKid: GBV song. From Bee Thousand. (I can't believe I know that.)

BloomOrphan: lol! did he make you a mixtape, too?

SpookyKid: No, but he's always playing it. Guess I caught the bug. BTW, he was really impressed you showed up at church today.

BloomOrphan: I was impressed with myself. I never have to get up that early anymore. afternoon classes.

SpookyKid: Lucky you. Are you coming to homecoming next week?

BloomOrphan: not sure. I don't go to school there anymore.

SpookyKid: jst wondering

BloomOrphan: are you going?

SpookyKid: Yes, if you can believe it.

BloomOrphan: do you have a date?

SpookyKid: Yeah, sort of. Seth doesn't.

A-ha! I get it now. He's trying to fix me up with his Insta-Brother.

BloomOrphan: maybe I'll put in a cameo appearance.

SpookyKid: Swell. I'll get you a ticket. It'll be fun. Pirate theme.

BloomOrphan: Arr, matey! I always wanted a peg leg . . .

SpookyKid: :)

sixteen

I PULLED LEO'S CADILLAC UP TO the curb outside the school gym. Kids I knew passed by outside, some of them looking in at me. This was turning into a Thing. I already wanted to go home.

"Don't forget the emergency brake," Leo reminded me. Even though we weren't staying. Well, he wasn't. Maybe I wasn't, either. I pushed the e-brake pedal in.

"What time should I come back for you?" Leo asked.

"I dunno," I murmured. "Maybe this is a bad idea."

"Nonsense. All your old friends will be there. Rory invited you, didn't he?"

"Yeah." All my old friends. All one of them. I couldn't believe Leo was supporting this silliness. This stupid dance.

"You want me to walk in with you? Anybody looks sideways at you, I'll kick their damn butts."

I laughed. "I think I can manage." I curled my fingers around the door handle, unable to pull the trigger. "Hey, uh, Leo?"

"Yeah?"

"I know probably now's not the time, but Janet and I were talking at lunch the other day." I took a deep breath. The rest of what I had to say tumbled out in a rush. "And, um, I wanted to say that. Well, I was thinking that even though you and my mom didn't get along too well beforehand, and it was wrong of her to have just up and left, it kind of sucks that you never would talk about her or let me know anything about her like she didn't even exist."

Now I really wanted to get out of the car. Leo sat there, visibly contemplating.

"I've been thinking a lot about your mom, too," he finally said, not yelling. "And I think you're right. Our . . . inability to get along made it hard for Christine to have a decent relationship with her own mother. And when it came to you . . . I always saw Chris as a careless person leading a reckless life, and I thought I was protecting you from that carelessness. But maybe all I was doing was just . . . making it worse for everybody." Leo shifted in his seat. I could barely breathe.

"I've been talking to Jan, myself," he went on, his voice quieter than I'd ever heard it. "And there are some things I need to work on. Not just with your mother, but with you, too. Because if my trying to protect you just ends up making you want to leave us and never come back, well, then . . ." Leo's voice hitched. He looked down at his hands. "I know I let my temper get the best of me sometimes. There are some . . . pretty big regrets I have, about the way I handled things with your mom when she was your age. I always thought if I had it to do over again, I wouldn't screw it up the second time around." He looked at me. "Did I screw it up? Irreparably?"

"No," I assured him. "Not irreparably."

"You sure about that?"

"Sir, yes, sir," I said softly.

Leo reached out and put his hand on my shoulder. Outside, other parents were dropping off their kids, rolling by us in their big SUVs, honking horns as they pulled away. Leo patted my shoulder. "Why don't you run on in there and have some fun?"

"Fun, huh?" I looked out at the gym and grimaced. "What do you say we forget this whole thing and go hit a bucket of balls down at the driving range?"

"Nope," Leo protested. "You're dancing tonight, kiddo. Go on, get."

I got out of the car. Leo did, too. He walked around the front, cutting the headlights' beam with his long strides. He got in the driver's side and slid the seat back. He closed the door and rolled the window down.

"Thanks for bringing me," I said. Even though it was Janet's idea.

"You're the driver," he said. "Thanks for letting me ride shotgun." It was his idea to let me drive.

"I'll call you when it's over. Or I'll get Rory to drive me home."

"Don't worry about it. Just have a good time." He looked up at me. "I love you, honey."

Whoa, super weird. Leo never used the l-word.

"Me too. I mean, uh." I was too weirded out to say the right thing. "Don't forget to take off the parking brake."

Oof, that was lame. Leo just smiled and released the brake with a pop. He cruised off in the Caddy, giving a big wave out the window as he drove away. I finally took a breath. That was actually less exhausting than I thought it would be. Now, to stare down my old nemesis—*Hawthorne High, we meet again.*

I strolled up to the gym, pretending like it was no big deal that I was wearing this stupid dress and that I was walking into this gym that I hadn't walked into since last spring. *Be Scully,* I thought, which was what I always thought when I felt like a total loser. *You're secretly carrying a gun and you can kick everybody's ass in here. And, if the need arises, you can also perform an autopsy.* It wasn't really working like it usually did, though. I was just lame old me. Walking into the darkened gym alone, beneath the arch of balloons in Fighting Eagles green and white. Inside, there was a fake ocean made out of gauzy blue-and-green fabric, a pair of inflatable palm trees and a display set up with two Styrofoam coolers painted to look like treasure chests, both full of cheap plastic beads. A banner tacked to the wall read HOME-COMING CASTAWAYS! Which seemed a little depressing, if you asked me.

"Lula. Happy Homecoming!"

I didn't even see her there, in the darkened entryway. Mrs. Lidell. Who was, evidently, tonight's faculty chaperone. Really, Hawthorne High? You couldn't have gotten Mr. Miller or Mrs. Dalrymple? Or how about Mrs. Havens? Everybody knows she's got no life outside of algebra.

"Oh. Hi," was all I said. "Rory invited me."

"He told me you might show up. Here," she reached

into one of the treasure chests and came up with a couple of strands of beads. "Everybody gets some pirate treasure."

"Gee, thanks." I put on the beads. Totally cheesy. "These really bring the outfit together."

She smiled. This was good, right? She didn't seem totally pissed off at me or horrified that I'd shown up.

"I, uh—"

"Sam!" We both turned around. A goofy-looking guy in a pirate hat and a puffy shirt stood by the ticket table, holding two cups of punch.

"That's Mark," she said.

"Your husband?" I asked. She nodded. *That* was the infamous Mark Lidell? This guy with the big teeth and the pirate hat was the dweeb she left Paris for?

"I want you to meet him. Mark!" I followed her to the ticket table. "This is Lula. One of my star students." It was nice that she didn't say *former* star student.

"Nice to meet you, Lola," Mark Lidell grinned broadly at me. Wait a minute, didn't he know who I was? Wasn't he going to grab me by the lapels and tell me to keep my grubby paws off his wife?

"*Lula*, honey," Sam nudged him, taking one of the cups of punch out of his hands.

"I hope Sam's not too hard on you. I know she likes to assign a lot of homework," he said. Still grinning. What a tremendous goofball.

"Not at all," I said. "She's taught me a lot."

"I bet! She's one smart lady." He winked at her. He actually winked. Oh, wow, this guy was unbelievable.

"Yeah. So . . . I'm gonna . . . grab some punch. Nice to meet you, Mr. Lidell."

"Likewise, Lola!"

Run away! I made for the punchbowl, double time. Watered-down pineapple juice and Sprite never tasted so good. Talk about an awkward situa—

"I forgot to give you your ticket." Sam Lidell found me by the punchbowl.

"Oh. Thanks." I slid the ticket into the tiny white purse Janet let me borrow. "Your, ah. Your husband seems nice."

"He is. He's got a good heart," she said. "You know, Lula—"

"Yeah. I know." I scanned the darkened gym, looking for Rory or Seth, but it was hard to see. Colored lights swung around in time to the Kanye song thumping out of the DJ's speakers. Maybe I didn't need anyone to swoop in and save me. Maybe I needed to talk to Samantha Lidell. Clear the air, just like I'd done with Leo. Maybe we needed to put the Humiliating Incident behind us once and for all.

"Mrs. Lidell, do you think—" I hesitated. "Could we talk?" I asked her.

"Sure," she replied. "Let's talk."

"Hi, Mrs. Lidell! Hey, Lula!" one of my ex-classmates, Bethany somethingorother, was standing there by the punch-bowl. "Are you coming back to class next semester?"

"Uh. I don't think so."

Bethany was still standing there, smiling politely at me.

"Say, I don't suppose you girls know where they keep the extra trash bags around here?" Mrs. Lidell interjected. "These are getting kind of full, and they didn't give me a key for the janitor's closet."

"Trash bags?" I repeated.

"Oh, I bet there's some in the locker room!" Bethany said. "They always keep a bunch of supplies and stuff in there."

"Thanks, Bethany. I'll try the girls' locker room, then." Mrs. Lidell kind of stared at me. "Well, good to see you, Lula. You girls have fun catching up!" She stared at me again. Ohh, now I get it—the girls' locker room! Nice covert ops, Sam.

I chatted politely with Bethany for a few minutes, finding out that the cafeteria food really sucked this year and that she had no idea that Rory was such a football superstar. I started to reply that I didn't either, when, thankfully, Tyrone Bosley came up and asked Bethany to dance.

The girls' locker room was empty and dark except for the lights over the row of showers. Hard shadows crossed the benches. Sacks of basketballs and soccer gear sat in lumps along the painted cinderblock wall. Samantha Lidell leaned against a row of lockers, her arms folded against her chest. My stomach quietly tied itself into a knot. *Oh, Lord, let this be over quick.*

"So . . . no trash bags?" I asked.

"You wanted to talk." Mrs. Lidell cut to the chase.

"Yeah. I did. I do. I um." Well, it was going splendidly so far. *Get it together, Lula.* "I wanted to apologize. Officially. For coming to your house and . . . behaving the way I did. It was pretty over the top, and I get that now. And I'm sorry."

"I think I'm the one who should apologize," she replied. "Do you have any idea how horrible I felt? How horrible I still feel? Every day, Lula. I feel fucking awful."

Wait a minute, Sam Lidell felt horrible? What on earth for?

"I know I shouldn't have been so hard on you at the game the other night, for starters," she went on. "But, Lula, you scared us all half to death. If something had happened to you—if you'd gotten hurt or worse . . ." she shook her head. "I could never have forgiven myself."

"But you didn't . . . do anything." I was totally confused, and still reeling from hearing Mrs. Lidell say the f-word. Sam was, like, wracked with guilt. Over me?

"I sent you out into the night and didn't see you again for four months! And that whole time I kept thinking, what if I'd given you a ride home? What if I'd made you stay until you calmed down? What if I had just been a little more understanding, somehow? What if I hadn't laughed at you? Maybe you wouldn't have left town."

I felt a sudden sting at the corners of my eyes, remembering her laugh.

"It wasn't just you. I got sort of . . . overwhelmed with everything." I tried to explain. "I mean, I know I humiliated myself in front of you and all, but that wasn't your fault."

"And I didn't mean for you to leave that night feeling humiliated. Or feeling like there was something wrong with you. With being who you are. It's all right for you to be gay, Lula. Or bisexual, or just still trying to figure it out. And I understand why you might have thought—why you thought of me that way. Kids have crushes on their teachers all the time. Especially teaching English—I stand there and fill your heads with poetry all day long. Trust me, if I was forcing you to solve quadratic equations, you wouldn't think I was so great."

"I think I'd still think you're great," I said. "Regardless of your syllabus. Your coolness transcends quadratic equations."

"My coolness," she sighed. "Kiddo, my coolness is in permanent storage."

"The thing is, when I came to your house that night . . . I really . . . I wasn't thinking," I confessed. "I wasn't thinking about, you know. That I was putting you in an awkward position, or whatever. My friend Jay thinks I was just acting out, but it was more like . . . I dunno, it was like suddenly my best friend in the world was on this whole other planet, like a total parallel universe, and you were the only other person I ever . . ." I caught myself. *Parallel universe?* "Sorry. I'm not explaining this right. Sometimes I'm so bad at just . . . being a normal person around other people. Jay thinks it's because I watch too much TV."

"Your friend Jay may be right about the TV," Mrs. Lidell said. "But if you haven't figured it out by now, then let me assure you, Lula—nobody's normal. And pretty much everybody you meet in life is trying to figure out how to be a so-called "normal person." As if it's some fixed point that you reach, like zero degrees Celsius. But everybody's just who they are. Weird, flawed, good at some things, bad at others. There's no one single person who's doing everything right all the time. Trust me on that. There is no such thing as *normal*."

"So, what you're telling me is, not only are there no normal people on this planet, but nobody's even figured out how to pretend? Not even you?"

"Least of all me."

"Well, shit," I said, and Mrs. Lidell laughed. "I'm never gonna figure this out, am I?"

"Listen, Lula, you're, what, seventeen? Eighteen, now? This isn't the final version. You've got years to figure out who you are and what you want out of life. Heck, I'm still trying to figure out what *I* want out of life. When I was your age, all I wanted was to run away and marry Paul Westerberg."

"Who's Paul Westerberg?"

"Look it up," she sighed. "God, I'm getting old. Look, my point is, you can be whatever you want. And whatever you want to be is just fine, as long as you're true to yourself. You can even change, if you realize that what you thought you wanted doesn't make you happy. There are no boundaries. Except that you can't be my girlfriend. Okay?"

"Okay." After everything that had happened, I realized that I didn't want to be Mrs. Lidell's girlfriend. I wished we could sit in her office and talk about Paris, though. Like we used to. "Can we just be regular friends? I mean, can we not be all awkward if we see each other again?"

"*When* we see each other again," she corrected. "And, yes, we can definitely not be awkward.

I COULD NOT BELIEVE MY EYES. Rory's Homecoming date was Speed Briggs. And, instead of being a scandal, everybody loved them. They were both attempting to breakdance to Biz Markie, and everybody was gathered around them in a big circle, shouting, "Go Rory! Go Rory!" and then, "Go Speed! Go Speed!" Some of the girls from our class would take turns dancing with them, and then they would all dance, shouting the lyrics along with the chorus: *Oh baby you! you got what I need! but you say he's just a friend! yeah you say he's just a friend!* I leaned against the wall, one of the Homecoming Castaways, watching from afar. I guess if I'd had more courage, I could've gone and joined in with them. But I didn't want to ruin it for him. I'd never seen him like that before. Just being silly. Having so much fun.

"Pretty crazy, huh?" Seth walked up from out of the crowd. Wearing sneakers with his suit. And a pirate eyepatch. "There's a movement afoot to crown them Homecoming Kings."

"They should be," I shouted over the music. Seth took off his eye patch and we stood and watched them for a minute.

"Speed just told me he gave up drinking for him," Seth said, nodding toward Rory.

"Wow. That sounds serious."

"Could be. You having fun?" Seth asked, rubbing his eye.

"Fun? Yeah, it's, uh . . ." I looked around at the Castaway Corner where I'd been hiding most of the night, with its fake ocean and volleyball net decorated with plastic starfish. "It's like gym class meets *Lost*."

Seth laughed and said something I couldn't hear over everyone cheering for Speed's attempt at the moonwalk.

"What did you say?" I shouted.

"Pretty loud in here. You wanna go outside?" He leaned in.

"Outside? Sure." He brushed his knuckles against my wrist, by accident, I thought. Then he threaded his fingers through mine. Suddenly I was holding hands with Sexy Seth Brock. It seemed like every girl in the gym was watching us leave. I didn't blame them. *Why am I holding hands with Sexy Seth?* Even Mrs. Lidell, smoking a cigarette under the dogwood, hiked an eyebrow at me. I shrugged my shoulders in response.

"My truck's parked over here," Seth pointed to the senior lot. "I, uh. Brought something for you. Rory said you might show up."

"He invited me," I tried to explain. "What about your, um—your date?"

"I'm flying solo on this one." He smiled back at me over his shoulder. My head was sort of mildly exploding as we wove through the cars until we got to the darkened corner of the lot where Seth's banged-up blue Chevy pickup was parked. He reached in his pocket for his keys and unlocked the doors. He let the tailgate down. There were thick wool blankets spread across the bed.

"Wait right there," he said, running around to the driver's side door. My heart was going a mile a minute. What was this? I was standing there with this guy I barely knew in a dark parking lot, and his truck bed was lined with blankets. Janet always told me, if some boy tried to get me into a compromising position, I should just leave. But he dedicated those songs to me. He tried to, anyway. Was I being compromised yet?

The window in the back of the cab slid open, and I jumped. I heard music—Seth had turned the radio on. I heard the unmistakable hollow *click-chunk* of a cassette sliding into a cassette deck. There was a hiss, and then the sound of wiry guitars drifted out to meet the night.

"Can you hear it all right back there?"

"Yeah," I said.

"Perfect." Seth got out and hopped up into the back of the truck. He stood at the end of the truck bed, offering me his hand.

"Come on up," he said. I stopped being nervous and climbed up into the truck bed, careful to keep my skirt from flying up. I sat down on the raised hump of the wheel well. Seth sat on the one opposite me.

"You like the music?"

"Yeah. It's good." I was pretty sure I'd heard the song before, on Midnight Pete.

"This is the mixtape I made for you. Here, this is the case for it." Seth reached into his shirt pocket and handed me an empty cassette box. I read the tiny ink letters crammed onto the spine. *Underground Initiations to Awful Bliss: Seth's Bad & Rare GBV Greatest Hits Vol. 001.* The first song was "Hardcore UFOs."

"It's an actual tape, too." I was impressed. It was a lot harder to make an actual mixtape than just burn a CD. "I'm glad I kept my old Walkman."

"I told you I was gonna bombard you with Guided by Voices," he said. Was he blushing?

"This is—thanks. This is cool." I didn't know what else to say. I wished we were somewhere else. Somewhere with people. I wished Rory was there. I wished I knew what to say. I wished this was easy.

"You wanna, um . . . you wanna look at the stars while we listen to it?" Seth knelt down in the truck bed, stretching out. "I parked away from all the lights and stuff so we could see better."

"Seth—" I laughed. I couldn't help it. This whole thing felt strange and silly.

"What?" he sat up.

"Look at the stars? I mean, seriously! What are you up to?"

"I just . . . I thought it'd be cool. We could listen to the tape together and look up at the stars. It's a nice night. And I made this tape kind of . . . specifically for the purpose of looking up at the stars. With you."

"With me?"

"Well," Seth hesitated. "I mean—yeah. Of course. With you."

"But—this doesn't strike you as odd? You're not weirded out by this in the least?"

"Weirded out? By what?"

"You and me! Out here like some kind of . . . I don't even know what. What is this? I don't get why you're being so nice to me. Don't you get it? I'm Weird Girl. You're Sexy Seth. You're the quarterback of the undefeated varsity football team. I'm a high school dropout. I mean, pardon my French, but what the fuck?"

"Geez, Lula." Seth raked his hair back. "I reckon I don't get it. I thought you were different from these girls that just expect me to be Mr. Perfect Quarterback. But you make it sound like we're in some . . . teenage high school movie or something. You know, I used to be this spacey little kid, always listening to my headphones. People used to call me weird, too, before they figured out I can throw a football. You think I don't get how people act? You think you're really just some loser I'm not supposed to be friends with because I'm this big jock with my head too far up my ass to know who you really are?"

"I—" I had no snappy comeback at the ready. "But you don't know. You don't know who I really am. For crying out loud, *I* don't even know."

"I know we were probably both lying awake in our beds

at night, listening to Midnight Pete on the radio when we were kids, hearing the same songs and not even realizing it. I know you're Rory's best friend. I've read everything you wrote. I know you left school to go live with your mom. I know they thought you were missing for a while. I don't know—" He looked away. "The only thing I don't get about you is why you left town like you did. But I guess you figured you had to. You're smart, and you're brave, Lula—"

"No, I'm not. It wasn't so smart of me to leave. It was stupid and selfish."

"Maybe it *was* selfish, but it was still brave. And you are smart. Hey, you're in college already. Even if it is *just* community college. I dunno, maybe you're right that I'm this dumb high school jock. Or whatever. Maybe compared to you, I am."

"Seth, you're not a dumb jock." I sat down beside him in the truck bed. Crossed my legs and tucked my skirt around me. "And I'm not that smart. I'm not that great. My own mother could care less about me. In the past six months, I've managed to piss off everybody that ever loved me, I ran away from home, and I've kissed two girls on the mouth. I also did some heavy canvassing for *The Campaign to Arrest Dick Cheney for War Crimes*. Now, are you sure you don't wanna go back up to the gym and find yourself a nice nubile cheerleader to make out with?"

At that, Seth threw his head back and cackled. "That's what I dig about you, Lula. You say the craziest stuff."

"But it's not crazy! It's true!" And I told him the story of going up to DC with Trey, working for Tracy's dad until I had enough money for the train ticket out west. I told him about my mother and Walter. Riding horses. Learning how to drive. And he just sat there and listened to it all.

"Now, where did kissing the girls figure into all that adventure?"

I sighed. How could I begin to explain myself when I still didn't understand?

"I'm not sure I—I'm not sure I know how it figures in."

"Are you dating anybody right now?"

"No." Dating. That word sounded so nice and normal. Dating was such a wholesome activity, so many light years away from showing up at somebody's house in the middle of the night and laying one on them in the desperate hope that they'll save you from your own edgeless lonesome.

"The truth, Seth, is . . ." What was the truth? I wished the truth was some fixed, solid little box I could explain and describe and understand. But the truth was this wobbly, gelled thing. I had this idea of my heart as this separate being that just spilled over everywhere, consuming whatever fell in its path. Like the Blob in that old movie. "The truth is, I don't know what I'm doing. I always thought—I always just had it in the back of my mind that Rory and I would end up together. And then he realized he was gay, and it took me a long time to realize that we weren't going to be what I thought we were. Then I . . . met this girl—a girl I thought I understood. I thought she understood me. And I thought maybe that meant we should . . . be together somehow. But I misread it—she was just trying to be a friend. And then there was another girl, a friend of mine, but she was just . . . using me to get back at someone."

"So what do you want? Deep down, do you really want to be with a girl? Or a boy?"

"Deep down, I want . . . I want somebody who sees me. I mean, really sees me. Sees everything I am, even all the horrible things I am. My dirty mouth and my stupid *X-Files* action figures and my total failure at graduating from high school and my messed-up mom and my crazy grandparents. I just want somebody who sees all that but . . . loves me anyway."

"What if somebody looked at you and couldn't see anything horrible?" Seth asked.

"Then I'd say they weren't looking hard enough."

"I'm looking right now." And he was. His eyes were burning right into mine. And then he kissed me. Wow. We kissed.

"Seth—" I whispered. There were still all these things I wanted to say to him. I wanted to protest; he was a good person, a preacher's son, a sweet guy with a dead brother who made mixtapes for girls he barely knew. And I was just some jerk who couldn't even pull off being a proper teenage runaway. But what happened was that neither of us said anything. We kissed again, and then he took my face in his hands and held my forehead to his, like we were trying to mind-meld. I touched his cheekbone and felt his tears against my thumb. I don't know why, but I was crying, too.

We sat there like that for a while. My foot fell asleep. Then we stretched out in the truck bed and watched the stars while his Guided by Voices mixtape played and flipped itself over and played again and we heard the dance start to empty out, the other cars revving their engines and pulling away, and Seth told me not to worry about calling Leo because he would take me home.

seventeen

THE BOYS DIDN'T STAY UNDEFEATED. THEY were knocked out in the first round of the regional playoffs. Still, we had a lot to celebrate. I had finally passed the driver's test. And Seth and I were—cue the normal—dating. It was my idea to have everyone over on Friday night for my big Peace Dinner. I was going to right all the wrongs of the past year with jalapeño cornbread, enchiladas, and tortilla soup. Of course, there would be a few notable absences. Rory was having a dinner of his own, celebrating his one-month anniversary with Speed. Jay was spending the weekend with a girl she'd met from Appalachian State; it was getting serious pretty quickly, because Jay was already talking about transferring her credits. And my mother was still halfway across the country, conveniently ignoring my existence. Still, I had made up little Tupperware containers full of Walter's legendary jalapeño cornbread for each of the absentees—Janet was even helping me mail a care package to Tracy and her dad up in DC.

So it was just Janet, Leo, Seth, and me. Which was actually kind of perfect. Leo wanted a chance to give Seth a proper grilling. Seth started off with bonus points for showing up in a sport coat and bringing his new iPhone.

"I've been curious about these things." Leo got out his reading glasses. "Mind if I take it for a spin?"

"Spin away, sir." Seth handed him the phone. Leo tapped away at the touch screen while Janet helped me set the food out on the table.

"Leo's already in hog heaven," she whispered. "You know he goes crazy for a new gadget."

"That's why I told Seth to bring it," I whispered. "He's actually kind of embarrassed about it. His dad got it for him to celebrate the end of the football season, and he doesn't really know how to work it yet."

"Janet!" Leo called out from the living room. "Come look at this doodad! It does everything. I'm gonna get us a couple of 'em."

"You boys put away your toys and come eat while it's hot," Janet called back. Leo and Seth walked into the dining room, Leo so engrossed in the iPhone that he bumped into his chair.

"This is quite a spread, Mrs. Monroe," Seth said.

"Thank you, honey, but the credit should go to Lula," Janet said. "She's been cooking all afternoon."

"Lula, you cooked all this food?" Seth looked across the table at me, surprised. "You didn't even tell me. It's amazing."

"You might wanna reserve judgment until after you've tasted it," I warned. "Up until now, the only thing I ever cooked was Jell-O."

"It looks great," Seth spread his napkin in his lap. "Mr. Monroe, would you mind if I said a few words before we eat? A blessing?"

Leo and Janet exchanged a look. We never said a blessing.

"Ah, sure, son. Go right ahead."

"This is one my dad likes to say." Seth dropped his head. We all followed his lead. "'As our bodies are sustained with food, may our hearts be nourished with love and friendship, in fellowship under God. Amen.'"

"Amen," Janet said. "Let's eat."

"I can get the PGA scores on this thing," I heard Leo mutter.

The food was barely on our plates before Leo started the full interrogation. He kept it mostly about football, at first.

"So, what are your plans, son?" Leo asked. "College? The Military? Military's a fine career for an athletic young man like yourself."

"I've been offered a few football scholarships already— nothing big, but I'm still deciding," Seth said. "I'm holding out for a school with a good nursing program. That's the field I'd ultimately like to be in."

"Nursing, you said?" Leo furrowed his brow.

"Yes, sir. I know, it sounds like a punch line. But when my older brother was sick, I saw how much help it could be, especially for a young guy like that, to have a male nurse. Some stuff's kind of embarrassing to have to tell a woman, you know? And there was this one hospital where, whenever he had to be moved, they'd have to go get the janitor to help them, because the nurses were all so small. He's a big guy. *Was* a big guy."

"Oh, honey," Janet reached out and patted Seth's hand.

"And you'd rather be a nurse than a doctor?" Leo asked. I felt myself cringe.

"I'd love to be a doctor," Seth told him. "But with my grades, trust me, you wouldn't want me to be the guy holding the scalpel."

"You're doing a lot better," I reminded him. "You just pulled your Chemistry grade up to a B plus."

"Because I've got all your notes from last year," Seth said.

"Now that you mention it, I'd rather have a male nurse, if I had to be laid up in the hospital," Leo mused.

"If you have to be laid up in the hospital, God help us all." Janet rolled her eyes. "Seth, honey, where are you thinking about going to school? State-wise, I mean."

"The scholarships I've been offered so far are close to home. But my dad's from Boston, and my mom's from Texas. I have family in both places, so I've been looking at schools there, too. Wherever I end up, I'm hoping that, uh. That Lula will transfer her credits and come with me."

I nearly choked on a tortilla. Way to put me on the spot, Seth. I didn't know what to say. We hadn't talked about any of this. We spent most of our dates in his room or mine, either watching *X-Files* DVDs or playing GBV records. Seth schooled me on the different Guided by Voices lineups and side projects, and I explained the finer points of the myth arc. I'll be honest, though: these debriefings were frequently interrupted by a lot of inappropriate giggling and kissing. Seth was turning me into a big mushy *girl*.

Anyway, I knew that what Seth wasn't telling Janet and Leo was that, grades aside, he wasn't sure if he had the stomach to be a nurse. He already had a back-up plan, if he couldn't take the blood and guts and bodily fluids. Seth wanted to open up a music store, right here in Hawthorne.

Sell records, CDs. Books about music. Maybe even have in-store performances. Without a record store in town, the only place for kids to hear music, let alone buy it, was on the computer, which Seth found, as he put it, "unbearably lonely."

"What about you, Tallulah?" Leo asked. "You, ah. You given any thought to Boston or Texas?"

"I haven't really . . . decided anything yet," I admitted.

"Have you thought about it, though?" Leo pressed.

"Actually, I've been thinking about . . . applying to the FBI," I blurted out. I'd never told anyone that. Not even Rory.

"The FBI!" Janet exclaimed. "Oh, honey, don't do that. You'll get yourself killed by terrorists."

"Yeah, Lula, come on," Seth laughed. "It's not all Scully and Mulder in real life."

"I know that. I know." I looked down at my plate, suddenly embarrassed. "I thought I'd be a good investigator. I always thought it would be cool to be in charge of finding missing persons. I just think . . . people shouldn't be lost, you know?"

"You can have a fine career in the Bureau, if that's what you want," Leo said. He narrowed his eyes at me. "You're a bright young woman. Every time you put your back into it, you've accomplished what you set out to do. I haven't always been pleased with the results," he cleared his throat.

"Leo," Janet whispered.

"I haven't always said it," he went on. "Especially lately. But I'm proud of you, Lula. I'm proud of the woman you're growing up to be. And I think that, if you choose to join the FBI, you'll be an asset to their institution."

"Thanks, Leo," I said. *Thanks*. It didn't seem like enough. I still needed to say *I love you, too*, but this didn't seem like the time or place.

"Whatever you decide," he swiped at his mouth with his napkin. "You've got this cooking down pat. This is the best damn cornbread I ever ate. Your mother taught you well."

"Actually it was Walter. My mother doesn't—she never cooks," I explained, suddenly feeling nervous. I couldn't believe Leo voluntarily mentioned my mom.

"Good man, Walter." Leo nodded. "We should have him come out for a visit. You reckon he golfs?"

"Golf? I, uh . . . I'm not sure." I swallowed. Have Walter over for the weekend? Walter, my mother's husband? The same mother we were pretending didn't exist, right? I looked up at Leo. He frowned and cleared his throat again. Something he did when he was uncomfortable and would rather be smoking.

"Son, let me have another look at that doodad of yours," he said to Seth. "And explain these 'apps' to me one more time."

KidKilowatt: r u serious about the fbi?

It was like Seth was reading my mind. I was online researching FBI recruiting when he IMed me.

> *BloomOrphan: I dunno. maybe. maybe another dumb idea.*

> *KidKilowatt: no, good idea! it just surprised me. I didn't know u were serious. I should've backed u up tonite.*

> *BloomOrphan: prob crazy anyway. you have to pass a physical fitness test!*

> *KidKilowatt: u could do it! u ride ur bike everywhere.*

BloomOrphan: . . . not to mention having to shoot ppl and stuff.

KidKilowatt: they have ppl who work in labs n stuff tho, right? u could be like the ppl mulder & skully go to for fingerprints & ballistics. ur so good at chemistry, u could do it, np.

*KidKilowatt: *scully, oops*

BloomOrphan: . . . maybe . . .

KidKilowatt: just don't fall 4 ur sexy partner. :(

BloomOrphan: never!!!

"Lula!" Janet knocked on my door. I jumped.

"Yeah?" I turned around. She poked her head in.

"You've got a visitor! Come downstairs." She was grinning this big dumb grin. I figured it was probably Seth, outside on the porch, and he'd been IMing me from his iPhone this whole time. Janet was a sucker for romance.

BloomOrphan: brb. janet calling.

I left the computer on and followed Janet down the stairs. Well, knock me right over with a feather.

"Rory Callahan, as I live and breathe."

"Hi," he said. "Sorry I missed the big dinner. Is it too late to hang out?"

"Not at all, honey," Janet answered for me. "You two want some popcorn?"

Popcorn. Janet used to make it for us on *X-Files* nights.

"Sure," Rory said, answering for me.

"Howdy, Rory," Leo called from his recliner. "You ever see *What's Up, Doc*? It's just about to start on TCM."

"I'll take a rain check," Rory said.

"Suit yourself. It's pretty darn funny."

"I'll bring the popcorn up. You two go watch your show." Janet shooed us upstairs. I walked back to my room in a daze, Rory following. He looked good. His khakis were pressed, and he had a new blue button-up shirt that made his eyes look extra-intense. He'd finally shaved his chin scruff, so he looked like himself again. But I didn't feel like I used to. Like I was secretly pining away. I just felt happy. Glad to see him. Glad it was just the two of us, back in my room.

"So . . . how was dinner with Speed?"

"Great. We went to that new Korean fire-grill place. Man, that guy can eat." Rory chuckled softly to himself. "How was dinner with Seth?"

"I think it went well. Leo didn't kill him."

"That's good."

"Actually, this is him on IM. Hang on just a sec, let me say goodnight." I bent over the computer keyboard.

BloomOrphan: gtg. tty 2moro am. xo.

"Since when are you reading *House of Mirth*?" Rory held up the book from my nightstand.

"It's for one of my classes. We had to pick a book for an extended essay project. You always told me I should read it."

"It's one of my favorites," he said.

"I know. We watched the movie together." I put the computer in sleep mode.

"The book's better."

"The book's more depressing. I keep waiting for Lily Bart to get it together and kick Bertha Dorset's ass, but it's totally not going to happen, is it?"

"Sadly, no," Rory confirmed. "Edith Wharton's novels are curiously devoid of ass-kicking. Who's Walter?" He was looking at the shelf above the bed, to the place where I used to keep my mother's things in a makeshift shrine. Her books were still there, behind a propped-up Dick Cheney pamphlet and the postcard Walter sent me.

"My mom's husband."

"Oh. Your stepdad."

"Something like that." It was weird to think of him as anything other than just Walter. But I guess that's what he was. "My stepdad. Yeah."

"He was a cool guy?"

"Very cool. He kept World War Three from breaking out between me and her."

"That bad, huh?"

"She wasn't cut out to be a mom. Her words. Hey, you wanna see something truly weird?"

"Okay, but I'm warning you," Rory said solemnly, "if it's monkey pee, you're on your own." He broke into a grin, and so did I. Rory quoting Agent Scully lines at me? It was almost like old times. I slid my desk drawer open and fished out the family portrait.

"It's not monkey pee, but it is too weird to leave on public display." I showed him the picture.

"Is this your mom?"

"And my dad. My real dad. And, technically, me. In utero."

"Wow. Look at you. Look at him. I mean, look at how you kind of look like him."

"I know. His name's Peter Hubbell."

"Like the telescope?"

"Yeah, but spelled differently. Still, pretty badass, right? I've got his phone number, but I haven't called him yet. I've totally stalked him on Facebook, though."

"Why don't you send him a message?" Rory studied the picture. "He looks like a nice guy."

"I dunno. Maybe someday. I'm not sure I'm really prepared to deal if he turns out to be a major jerk. Or if he just doesn't care. I mean, he wasn't exactly fighting for custody of me when my mom bailed."

"True," Rory agreed. "But maybe he's got a different side of the story."

"Yeah, maybe. Still, the whole mom thing was kind of a bust. I'm kinda maxed out on disinterested parents right now. Honestly, sometimes . . . sometimes I kind of wish I hadn't gone out there to meet her."

"But if you hadn't, you always would've wondered," Rory said softly. He handed the picture back to me. I put it back in its drawer.

"Yeah. Guess I had to burst the bubble sometime."

Rory nodded up at my wall. "What happened to your posters?"

"Oh, yeah. I, um. Redecorated." I shrugged. "Needed a change. You know."

"You threw them all away?"

"Nah, they're in the closet. In case I change my mind."

"Hey, if you ever decide to get rid of that *I Want to Believe* teaser poster, I call dibs."

"The one with Mulder and Scully walking away from each other, but their shadows cross and form an X?"

"That's the one."

"Hmm . . . hold that thought." I opened my closet door and took out the cardboard mailing tube that held all my rolled-up posters. I shook them out and unrolled them. When I found the teaser poster with the shadow X, I handed it to Rory. "Here. Take it."

"Seriously?" He seemed genuinely surprised. "You were so psyched when it came in the mail. Are you sure you don't want to put it back up?"

"I'm sure. That poster makes me sad, to be honest." I picked around in the pen jar on my desk for a rubber band. "The thought of Scully and Mulder walking away from each other kind of bums me out."

"Me too," Rory agreed. "But their shadows are still crossed. It's like, even when they're apart, they're still together. It's a cool, uh . . . visual metaphor."

"Consider that visual metaphor yours to keep." I handed him a rubber band, and he rolled the poster back up. From downstairs, we could hear muffled voices. Barbra Streisand. Leo laughing. I sat at my desk. Hesitating.

"Now, Theodore," I started to speak to him in my pretend-mom voice, like I used to. But it didn't seem to fit anymore. "Rory." I reached into the top drawer of my desk. "I have something else . . . I wanted to give this to you."

"What is it?"

"It's a letter." I handed him the envelope. "I wrote it after I got back, but I haven't been—I haven't had the courage to give it to you. It's an apology."

"You already apologized."

"It wasn't enough. I tried to think about how it must have been for you. Not knowing where I was, or what happened. I pretty much did the same thing to you that my mom did to me. And it sucks. It sucks to not know why somebody left you. Or to think that it's your fault. When it wasn't your fault at all."

"It was kind of my fault," Rory said. "I should have trusted you. We were best friends and I shouldn't have let anybody come between us. But I was afraid. I didn't even realize how afraid I was until now. I was so afraid of losing this, like, ghost of a relationship that I almost lost my best friend." His voice had gotten quiet. He went on. "Being with Tommy—Speed—makes me realize how much better it is, being with somebody who really cares about me and wants the same things I want. Somebody who isn't afraid to be seen with me. I mean, we still have to be careful where we hold hands around town, but, like, Tommy actually really wanted to go to that stupid Homecoming dance with me. I think even if the legal thing hadn't been an issue, Andy still would've wanted to keep me a secret. He still wasn't even out to most of his friends and his family. He never wanted to introduce me to his kids, or—" Rory's voice halted. "It's just way better now. I don't have to lie anymore. I should never have lied to you. And I really never, ever should have said all those hurtful things to you, and I apologize. I was such a jerk to you and I'm sorry. I love you. Lula. I never said that before. But it's true. Maybe I can't . . . love you like you want me to. Like a boyfriend. But you're my best friend, and I love you."

"Rory." I didn't know what to say. So I just said it. "I love you, too."

"Knock knock!" Janet opened the door, carrying a big white ceramic bowl in the crook of her arm. "Popcorn's ready!"

"Thanks, Janet," Rory took the popcorn. I turned away from them, wiping my eyes on my shirtsleeve.

"So bright in here! You guys can't watch your show in this." She flipped off the light. "Have fun! Don't stay up too late!"

I got up and turned on the lamp by my bed. Rory set the popcorn bowl down on my desk.

"Where were we?" he asked.

"Um. I was apologizing."

"No, I mean, where were we in the series?" He examined the DVD shelf. "Season Three, right? 'Pusher'? Or were we already up to 'Jose Chung' and the lava men?"

"I can't remember," I admitted. "It's been a while."

"Maybe we should start over," Rory suggested.

"From the very beginning?"

"Why not? Pilot episode. Boy meets girl. Boy loses girl to possible alien abduction . . ." He waved the first-season DVD box at me. "Tell me I'm crazy," he deadpanned.

"Mulder, you're crazy," I couldn't help smiling as I finished the quote. "But are you sure you want to do this?"

"Watch *The X-File*s? Do you even have to ask?" Rory cracked open the DVD case. He dropped the disc into the player. The machine hummed, warming up.

"Seriously, you really want to re-watch a nine-season-long television series, one episode a week, starting from the pilot episode? I mean, don't you have a life now? Aren't you gonna get bored?"

Rory yanked the pillows off my bed and propped himself up in his usual place on the rug. I sat down on the edge of the bed. Not quite able to settle in yet.

"Bored? Lula, come on." He grabbed the remote. "It's the beginning of a great adventure."

Rory turned on the television. The copyright warnings faded to black and the old, familiar theme song started up. Without missing a beat, we both joined in, whistling in unison.

It wasn't long before both of us were laughing again.

ACKNOWLEDGMENTS

Thank you to Jeff Bens for reading this back when it was a too-long short story and encouraging me to keep it in motion.

Thank you to Kat Georges, Peter Carlaftes, and Constance Renfrow at Three Rooms Press for your hard work, tireless dedication to getting it right, and unflagging enthusiasm. Thank you, Victoria Bellavia, for making it look beautiful.

Thank you to Emily Sylvan Kim, Manhattanville College, and the practitioners and staff of Sports Medicine at Chelsea for your continued support through the years.

Thank you to Jackie Sheeler, force of nature. Thank you to Jenn Northington for getting behind this book early on, and to Jesse Orona for schooling me on Dana Scully as Gay Icon.

I have the best friends in all of explored space—eternal gratitude to all of you!

Heather, Hannah, Liz, Flip. Ryan and Tracy. John P. Dang, y'all.

Thanks and apologies to my family—maybe someday I'll write something without so many damn cuss words in it. Sincerest thanks to my grandparents and my great-grandmother for being the village.

Thank you to the fandom and the fans.

Thank you to Chris Carter, Robert Pollard, and my parents.

ABOUT THE AUTHOR

MEAGAN BROTHERS IS THE AUTHOR OF two previous novels for young adults, *Debbie Harry Sings in French* and *Supergirl Mixtapes*. She has also been, variously, a musician, a performing poet, a record store clerk, and an adjunct professor of creative writing at Manhattanville College in Purchase, NY. A native Carolinian, she currently lives and works in New York City.

RECENT AND FORTHCOMING BOOKS FROM THREE ROOMS PRESS

FICTION

Meagan Brothers
Weird Girl and What's His Name

Ron Dakron
Hello Devilfish!

Michael T. Fournier
Hidden Wheel
Swing State

Janet Hamill
Tales from the Eternal Café
(Introduction by Patti Smith)

Eamon Loingsigh
Light of the Diddicoy
Exile on Bridge Street

Aram Saroyan
Still Night in L.A.

Richard Vetere
The Writers Afterlife
Champagne and Cocaine

MEMOIR & BIOGRAPHY

Nassrine Azimi and
Michel Wasserman
Last Boat to Yokohama:
The Life and Legacy of
Beate Sirota Gordon

James Carr
BAD: The Autobiography of
James Carr

Richard Katrovas
Raising Girls in Bohemia:
Meditations of an American Father;
A Memoir in Essays

Judith Malina
Full Moon Stages: Personal
Notes from 50 Years of The Living
Theatre

Stephen Spotte
My Watery Self:
Memoirs of a Marine Scientist

HUMOR

Peter Carlaftes
A Year on Facebook

PHOTOGRAPHY-MEMOIR

Mike Watt
On & Off Bass

SHORT STORY ANTHOLOGY

Dark City Lights: New York Stories
edited by Lawrence Block

Have a NYC I, II & III:
New York Short Stories;
edited by Peter Carlaftes
& Kat Georges

Quarter-Life Crisis:
An Anthology of Millennial Writers
edited by Constance Renfrow

This Way to End Times:
Classic and New Stories of
the Apocalypse
edited by Robert Silverberg

MIXED MEDIA

John S. Paul
Sign Language: A Painter's
Notebook (photography, poetry
and prose)

TRANSLATIONS

Thomas Bernhard
On Earth and in Hell
(poems of Thomas Bernhard
with English translations by
Peter Waugh)

Patrizia Gattaceca
Isula d'Anima / Soul Island
(poems by the author
in Corsican with English
translations)

César Vallejo | Gerard Malanga
Malanga Chasing Vallejo
(selected poems of César Vallejo
with English translations
and additional notes by
Gerard Malanga)

George Wallace
EOS: Abductor of Men
(selected poems of George
Wallace with Greek translations)

DADA

Maintenant: A Journal of
Contemporary Dada Writing & Art
(Annual, since 2008)

FILM & PLAYS

Israel Horovitz
My Old Lady: Complete Stage Play
and Screenplay with an Essay on
Adaptation

Peter Carlaftes
Triumph For Rent (3 Plays)
Teatrophy (3 More Plays)

POETRY COLLECTIONS

Hala Alyan
Atrium

Peter Carlaftes
DrunkYard Dog
I Fold with the Hand I Was Dealt

Thomas Fucaloro
It Starts from the Belly and Blooms
Inheriting Craziness is Like
a Soft Halo of Light

Kat Georges
Our Lady of the Hunger

Robert Gibbons
Close to the Tree

Israel Horovitz
Heaven and Other Poems

David Lawton
Sharp Blue Stream

Jane LeCroy
Signature Play

Philip Meersman
This is Belgian Chocolate

Jane Ormerod
Recreational Vehicles on Fire
Welcome to the Museum of Cattle

Lisa Panepinto
On This Borrowed Bike

George Wallace
Poppin' Johnny

Three Rooms Press | New York, NY | Current Catalog: www.threeroomspress.com
Three Rooms Press books are distributed by PGW/Perseus: www.pgw.com